RESTLESS WIND

RESTLESS WIND

WILD WIND SERIES
BOOK 3

NANCY MORSE

ISBN: 978-1543202199
      1543202195

CHAPTER 1
TWO WORLDS COME CALLING

Powder River Country, September, 1866

Deep in the heart of *Canapegi Wi*, the Moon When Leaves Turn Brown, the air was dry, and the restless wind swirled from several directions.

Katie McCabe sat astride her spotted Indian pony at the top of a pine-studded ridge, gazing down at the beaten trail. To the Indians it was known as the Powder River Road. To the whites it was called the Bozeman Trail, named for the man who, three years earlier, had staked out a wagon road following buffalo, Indian and trapper trails from Deer Creek, northward through the Powder River country that lay east of the craggy peaks of the Shining Mountains, and into Crow lands to the booming mining fields of western Montana.

This was Lakota territory. Yet every day more emigrants traveled the road in their wooden wagons, braving dangerous rivers and Indian attacks for the opportunity that lay westward. Miners leading pack mules followed the ruts in the road, hoping to stake their fortunes in the gold fields. Soldiers fresh from the battlefields at Antietam and Bull Run came seeking adventure. Soon, the Powder River Road was dotted with new forts to protect the intruders. First, Fort Reno on the Dry Fork of the Powder had been built. On Buffalo Creek the pine walls of Fort Phil Kearny had gone up seemingly overnight, and messengers had recently come to the Oglala camp on the Tongue to report that another fort was being built at the mouth of the Bighorn near Crow lands.

Everything around her was changing. But as her father, the trader Tom McCabe, used to say in his lusty Irish brogue, "Katie m'darlin', nothin' stays the same."

Like an eagle feather tossed this way and that on the wind, Katie's thoughts carried her far and wide, back to the little cabin along the Laramie that she had shared with her father and brother. With a pang, she recalled the times she had accompanied her father to Fort Laramie so that he could do a little trading, how she was awed by the pretty dresses worn by the officers' wives and loved the music coming from the barracks. He used to talk about Ireland, where he'd been born, and she had dared to dream that she might one day go there. But pretty dresses and gay music and notions of far-off lands were not meant to be.

The restless wind sighed through the grasses like a ghostly whisper out of the past as images from that fateful summer of 1851 sprang up suddenly in her mind.

The berries were turning red on the bushes when her father had donned his deerskin shirt and hand-stitched leggings trimmed with fringe and otter fur and rode to Fort Laramie on the North Platt, the flat-water river to the Sioux, to witness what everyone was calling a historic meeting. The whites called it the Fort Laramie Treaty Council. To the Sioux, it was known as the Council at Horse Creek. Even now, so many years later, and after so much had happened, she recalled vividly how her father had described the events when he returned home.

The Oglala had been the first to arrive. The prairies around the fort blossomed with more lodges than could be counted—Sicangu, Blackfeet, Crow, Mandan, Hidatsa, Arikara, and Cheyenne. Age-old enemies had put aside their warring to pitch their lodges on Sioux land. The Long Knives—the Sioux name for the soldiers—had erected a big tent. The headmen from the tribes, decked out in their finest feather bonnets and decorated shirts of elk and bighorn sheep hides, were invited inside to parley.

The whites wanted three things.

First, there was to be no more fighting among the tribes. The Lakota were to live in peace with their enemies, the Crow and Pawnee.

"Might as well tell the wind to stop blowin'," Tom McCabe had mocked.

Second, the whites wanted land and drew lines in the dirt to show where Lakota land ended, with everything else open for white settlement.

"How do they expect anyone to find a line in the dirt?" scoffed McCabe.

And third, travelers on the Oregon Trail were under the protection of the great father in the east and were not to be attacked, and if they were harmed, the great father would know it. The Indians wondered if that meant the trail was somehow holy, and that was how the Oregon Trail became known to the Lakota as *Canku Wakan Ske Kin*, or the Holy Road.

Each of the headmen had touched the pen to the paper holding the words of peace that were to be forever binding. McCabe told how the soldiers fired one of their big guns mounted on a wagon to show their power. The shell ripped through trees and tore up the ground with a deafening boom. "The fools," he spat. "In the time it takes for 'em to clean the barrel and reload, a group of warriors on fast horses can wipe 'em all out."

For agreeing to the treaty terms, the whites promised the Indians beef cattle, flour, beans, plows, and hoes. McCabe shook his head and asked sardonically, "What the hell are those Indians gonna do with farm tools 'cept melt 'em down for lance points and knives? Mark my words. They'll be raidin' each other in no time."

Sure enough, McCabe's prediction came true, and the first condition of the Horse Creek Council was broken shortly thereafter when the Crow began raiding the Blackfeet, and the Lakota sent raiding parties into Pawnee territory.

Wagons pulled by oxen and mules rolled into the Powder River country. The ruts in the Holy Road soon spread to several wagons wide, lining the hills and gullies, and the second condition of the Horse Creek Council was broken, this time by the whites who ignored the imaginary line in the dirt and slowly began to steal Lakota land.

The third condition of the treaty was broken when Red Cloud led his warriors on raids against the whites, burning wagon trains and killing emigrants up and down the Holy Road.

Four years after the Horse Creek Council the peaceful existence Katie knew in that cabin along the Laramie came to a screeching halt when she and her father traveled to Little Thunder's village on Blue Water Creek where her brother Richard was living with his Brulè wife. While there, a combined column of infantry and cavalry troops under the command of Colonel William Harney attacked, killing eighty-six Lakota men, women and children, as well as Tom and Richard McCabe.

In the aftermath of the carnage she'd been taken hostage and led at the end of a rope to Fort Laramie while the soldiers sang a tune that haunted her to this day.

We did not make a blunder.

We rubbed out Little Thunder.

And we sent him to the other side of Jordan.

On the march two bluecoats dragged her into a grove of pines and would have raped her had she not been rescued by Black Moon and brought to live among his people.

Alone and adrift in a hostile world, she found a home among the Lakota, and fell so deeply in love with Black Moon that she gave up the remnants of her white heritage to become his woman.

Years later, she would mistakenly think that he had been unfaithful to her with a Cheyenne girl, and she nearly died in the snow because of it.

But for everything she'd been through, it was the death of their newborn one cold, cruel winter that created a hole inside of her so deep it spawned a restlessness which, like the wind on this day in *Canapegi Wi*, would not go away.

Katie took a deep breath, filling her lungs with the crisp autumn air. She longed for springtime, when everything awakened from its winter sleep. The Lakota people said that buffalo hooves thundering against the earth awakened the plants in springtime, alerting the roots that it was time to send their shoots upwards to infuse the land with color and perfume. Springtime would bring the year's first rains, new buffalo calves, rivers and streams bursting with melting snow, and a rebirth of color and life to the land, but would it breathe hope into a heart dulled by the loss of hope?

Closing her eyes to the gust of wind that fanned her cheek, Katie whispered a prayer that her heart would awaken from the dark slumber into which it had fallen, for more and more these days she questioned where her rightful place was in the world.

She had never felt entirely at home in the camp circle. It was not that the people were unkind. On the contrary, they had been warm and welcoming since the first day Black Moon brought her to live among them. But she had never felt completely satisfied there. Something was missing. She could not put from her mind her childhood among a loving family. But that time was like a dream long vanished, beginning with the death of her mother to cholera and ending harshly on Blue Water Creek. At times, it seemed like something that had happened to someone else. At other times, like now, with the wind swirling restlessly all about her, it was as if it had happened only yesterday.

She did not know exactly when the thought first popped into her mind that she did not belong here, but once it did, it refused to relinquish its hold. There was much about this life that bothered her. The village was always moving, with long strings of travois and pack horses raising dust on the plains, fostering dreams of staying put in one place long enough to call it home. And everyone in the Oglala camp was a relative of marriage. These were Black Moon's people, not hers. She thought she had found a relative of birth when she'd been summoned to St. Louis by an aunt she hadn't known she had. For a while, the charged atmosphere of the city had distracted her, until her aunt died and she returned to the wild country around the Platte, and to Black Moon. But he had an extended family of aunts, uncles and cousins. *Tiyospaye*, the Lakota called it. She longed for a *tiyospaye* of her own, an extended family with whom she could be outspoken and impudent and even a little silly without receiving stares from dark, admonishing eyes.

Yet, every time she dared to think about leaving and returning to the world she left behind, she had merely to watch Black Moon gallop his pony to the top of a rise and sit there astride its bare back with the wind tossing his long black hair about his face, his proud, unflinching profile etched against the panorama. Each night spent in his arms beneath the buffalo robes aroused a passion in her as strong and powerful as if it were the first time, when he had taken her beneath the shaggy leaf trees and made her his own. Night after night when he spilled his hot seed into her, she prayed for a new life to grow within to help ease the pain of the little one they lost.

He was like no man she had ever met. He was neither the tallest nor the strongest of the Lakota fighting men, but his courage and bravery were unmatched. While others boasted of their victories, he barely talked about his exploits, even to her. He did not adorn himself with feathers or paint. No scalp locks hung from his hide shirt. In battle he rode his favorite bay gelding, not because it was beautiful and powerful like some war horses, but because it was fast and had endurance.

He was volatile and warlike, focusing his vengeance against the white men who stole Lakota land. And yet, for all his hatred of the *wasichus,* it had been his destiny to love a white trader's daughter. As it was her destiny to fall in love with the Lakota warrior who became her savior, her friend, her lover, her husband…her world.

What would Tom McCabe think if he could see her now, dressed in tanned elk skin, her long red hair braided and bound in rawhide, her skin almost as brown as the people she lived among, sitting astride her spotted Indian pony, watching from afar the white world she had forsaken for the man she loved?

She wished her father was there to give her advice on how to live as a white woman among the Indians and about the hard times ahead, with the army making increasing demands on the Sioux and the Sioux not willing to give up an inch of land without a fight.

Ever since the Sand Creek atrocity two years ago when the Colorado Territory militia had fired upon a peaceful Cheyenne village, the Sioux were fighting hard to protect their land and people.

And now, Black Moon was riding with Crazy Horse, and Katie's fears mounted—for him, for herself, and for the uncertain future.

She had ridden today much further than she had intended, having joined the other women to gather wild prairie turnips and then left them digging on the hillside to gallop her pony across the land in the futile hope that an exhilarating ride would chase away the uncertainty. Grappling with the doubts that plagued her, she gazed at the quaking aspen and scrub oak ablaze in color, with red, yellow, green and orange blanketing the hills in the distance.

The old ones told a story about why the leaves fall. Many moons ago, they said, when the world was still young, all the plants and the animals were enjoying the beautiful summer weather. But as the days went by, the weather turned colder. This made the grass and flower people very sad, for they had no protection against the sharp cold of winter. Just when it seemed there was no hope for them to go on living, the Great Spirit came to their aid. He told the leaves on the trees to fall to the ground and spread a soft, warm blanket over them. To repay the trees for the loss of their leaves, He allowed them one last bright array of beauty. This, they said, was why the trees take on beautiful farewell colors before turning to their appointed task of covering the earth with a thick blanket of warmth to protect the grass and flower people against the chill of winter.

Katie heaved a sigh. Soon, the branches would be bare, snow would cover the ground, and ice would clog the rivers and streams. She thought again of the Lakota legend and wondered who would protect her against the chill that had found its way into her heart.

A movement in the far-off distance caught her attention. A line of riders bound for the Montana diggings moved slowly along the Powder River Road through the heart of Lakota hunting grounds. Her muscles tensed at the sight of several mounted Indians fanned out across the top of a rise.

Throughout the spring and summer the Lakota had orchestrated a well-disciplined cycle of raiding. Without waiting for the warriors to swoop down upon the riders, she turned her pony's head away. With the restless breath of the wind blowing across the land she headed back to the Oglala camp in a valley of the Tongue River, her father's words echoing in her mind.

"Katie, m'darlin', nothin' stays the same."

CHAPTER 2
COLD ANGER RISING

The line of riders moved slowly north along the Powder River Road, each rider leading a pack mule laden with a canvas-covered load.

Hidden in a grove of short oak trees on a windswept rise, Black Moon watched them move along the dry, dusty trail that led to the Elk River and toward the thing that drew the white men like a hungry grizzly bear is drawn to an elk carcass. Gold. A cold anger rose within him. Even from this distance he could see that the riders had rifles. It was the first thing he looked for whenever white men were spotted. His fingers twitched against the elk hide case hanging from the neck rope of his bay gelding that held his muzzle-loading rifle.

Turning his unrelenting stare from the riders on the road, Black Moon looked at the man beside him and said, "They ride north to dig for the yellow metal in the mountains of Crow lands."

A stiff breeze tugged at Crazy Horse's braids. "I have enough lead balls, but only enough powder for five shots."

Black Moon nodded. "Only three of our men carry rifles, and our bows and arrows are no match for the white men who have more powder and shot. It would not be an even fight."

"White men always have more guns and bullets," Crazy Horse said bitterly.

"That is why we will let them pass."

"They do not know the country," Crazy Horse said. "That is our advantage. There are places farther north where we can ambush them."

Black Moon reached into a rawhide bag and came up with a strip of *wasna*. Katie had made a batch yesterday morning by parching some dry jerked meat, dampening it, and pounding it with a wooden mallet until it was light and fluffy. Tearing off a piece of the pemmican with his teeth, he gazed out across the land. The shining streak of water in the distance disappeared through clusters of trees as it went. Beyond it, rose the sharp rim of a butte, with the buttes to the east looking like purple mussel shells the farther away they were. "Maybe," he muttered as he munched. "But not today."

Looking askance at Black Moon, his face wearing a boy-like smile, Crazy Horse ventured, "You are eager to return home to your woman?"

Although Black Moon was older than Crazy Horse by nine winters, the two men shared a common goal—to rid the Long Knives from Lakota country. They were alike in many other ways, as well. Both were reticent, unassuming man who refused to participate in the *waktoglakapi*, the ritualistic telling of one's victories. They were leaders of their people who understood the responsibility and honor of leading their warriors into battle. They were not fearless, yet they acted in spite of fear. For these reasons, and others that were too subtle to define, Black Moon thought of Crazy Horse as his brother.

Black Moon's true brother had been killed many winters ago by a jealous rival, a man from their own village to whom Black Moon had shown no mercy when he avenged the killing. There had been so much misunderstanding between Black Moon and his peace-loving brother that it was not until Fire Cloud lay atop the burial scaffold that Black Moon realized just how much he had lost.

Black Moon liked Crazy Horse. Despite his formidable reputation as a fighting man, there was no pretense about the younger Oglala. Just last year he had been chosen as a Shirt Wearer. It was an honor Black Moon himself had once received, only to be stripped of the honor when he went to war against the advice and wishes of the council. But Black Moon held no hard feelings over it. If anyone deserved the honor, surely it was Crazy Horse.

In Crazy Horse, Black Moon saw much of himself. It was like looking into a pool of still water in which his own image was reflected. Not physically, for Crazy Horse was slender and his hair was brown, whereas Black Moon was sturdily built, well-muscled, and the braids that hung over his shoulders were as black as coal. But he sensed in the younger man emotions as turbulent as his own. The only thing in the two men's hearts that was different was that as much as they hated the whites, Black Moon loved a white woman.

She had left the lodge early that morning to dig for the wild prairie turnips that grew plentifully on the hillsides. He had watched her hike her elk skin dress above her knees and mount her pony, and it was with a predictable longing in the pit of his belly that he watched her ride off. It was always like that. Ever since the time she had left Lakota country and gone east and been away for a whole year, whenever he watched her leave, even if it was only to dig for prairie turnips, an insidious little thought lodged in his mind with the same discomfort as a pebble in his moccasin. Would she return to him?

He cast a sidelong glance at Crazy Horse and said, "She will never be quiet and demure like a proper Lakota woman. She is willful and has a sharp tongue, but she stirs me like no other. She left early to dig for *tinpsila*. She will be back by now, and I am eager to return to her."

But Crazy Horse did not fail to notice the shadow that moved across his friend's face. There was an air of strength and competence about Black Moon. He was a physically powerful man in the prime of his life, a veteran fighting man who held the white people, and especially the Long Knives, in disdain. Yet something was bothering him, and Crazy Horse suspected it had less to do with bluecoats or the white riders on the Powder River Road and more to do with Black Moon's white woman.

A cool breeze blew, rustling the manes and tails of their ponies. Black Moon turned away from the miners moving along the road. "Come, *misun*," he said, addressing Crazy Horse affectionately as a younger brother. "They will live to die another day."

CHAPTER 3
A PAINTED WING

Katie stood by the fire, stirring a pot of simmering prairie turnips when Black Moon entered the lodge. For a moment, he just watched her. She was wearing a dress of elk hide adorned with two rows of tin cones around the yoke and calf-high leggings covered with fine quillwork. As she moved, the tin cones made a soft tinkling sound and the flames lit little fires throughout her hair that was long and loose and as red as the setting sun.

The fire's glow upon her face reminded him of the first time he had observed her by the light of a fire. It had been just after the woman-killer Harney had attacked Little Thunder's band on the Blue Water eleven winters ago. He had moved through the decimated village with a hollowness in the pit of his stomach at the devastation brought upon those Lakota by the Long Knives. On the ride back to his village he had spotted a column of bluecoats leading their captives back to the soldier town on the flat-water. Two of the men had slipped away, dragging a red-haired woman with them. Something, Black Moon knew not what, had prompted him to intervene. He had drawn two arrows from his quiver, delivered two swift, silent shots, pulled the woman onto his pony, and found refuge in a cave from a gathering storm.

It was there that he had looked across the fire into the most beautiful face he had ever seen. She was white and he should have hated her, but he had found it impossible to turn his gaze away from all that red hair encircling an oval face with its flawless cheeks, slender upturned nose, and those eyes as green as the hills in springtime. It was an image he carried with him to this day, a vision time could not erase. But it was not just her beauty that thrilled him. Unlike proper Lakota women, she dared to speak her mind, telling him what she thought whether he wanted to hear it or not. Her laugh moved over him like the murmur from a rock-filled creek. Her woman's body aroused a need in him that went beyond any words he could say. Her wild, reckless courage was more like a man's, and her spirit was so much like his own.

Clearing his throat, he shook himself loose from the vision of her and came forward. "Your husband is hungry."

Katie looked up and gave him a smile that was deceivingly sweet. "Does my husband have two hands?"

"He does."

"Then he can fill his own meat bowl while I finish here."

She turned back to the simmering kettle and watched from the corners of her eyes as he laid his bow and quiver of arrows aside, hung the elk-hide case containing his rifle from the tripod that held his other things of war, and spooned some meat into a bighorn bowl. Taking the bowl to the man's place, he dropped down into a cross-legged position, and with a disgruntled look on his face, began to eat.

The left side of the lodge as one entered was where the man sat and ate. The right side was where she belonged. The place at the back, behind the fire, was the honor-place where special guests were seated. Callers who dropped in for a little while were seated at the first space to the right of the entrance. A place for this and a place for that, Katie huffed to herself as she stirred the kettle. The contrast between the freedom of a ride across the flat, open prairie and the rigidity of the social rules within the tribe were sometimes difficult for her to reconcile.

She thought back again to the cabin along the Laramie. Her mother had set certain rules for her and her brother to follow. But then the cholera swept through in forty-nine, claiming her mother's life, and her father, perhaps to lighten her grief, had placed little restraint on her. The only thing he would not allow her to do was go riding by herself. He had claimed the times were too dangerous with the whites pushing harder every day and the Sioux becoming increasingly hostile. She hadn't understood then just how ominous a warning it was, or how bad things would become and how she would wind up smack dab in the middle of it all.

The fire glistened in her eyes as she recalled the major events that had changed the course of her life. The battle on Blue Water that took the lives of her father and brother brought a fiery Lakota warrior into her life. The battle on Box Elder Creek that sealed her fate as a renegade when she had fired into the ranks of attacking soldiers. The winter when the snows came early and her newborn died in her arms. The Sand Creek massacre of Cheyenne women and children two years ago when Black Moon was wounded by a soldier's bullet and she thought she lost him to a Cheyenne girl. With a tremble, she wondered what would come next.

She was unaware that her movements had ground to a halt and that she was staring motionless into the flames until a gentle hand touched her cheek.

She looked up from the fire at a face that was burned a deep brown by the sun and bore the stamp of strength, and into the dark eyes that had the power to turn her to liquid with a single glance.

"There is something nipping at your heels. You are not happy."

He said it as more of a pronouncement than a question, causing her to shudder with how well he knew what was in her heart.

"There has been much sorrow in my life," she said softly. "But not any more than what your people have borne, so I should not complain."

"*My* people? I thought after all this time that they are your people, too."

Katie put the stirring spoon aside, leaving the turnips to boil and bubble, and turned away from the kettle. "I was welcome among them. Turning Hawk and Kettle took me into their lodge as a daughter, and the others were kind. But I know they all questioned your wisdom in bringing me here. And I also know how hard it has been for you to see past the color of my skin."

"Do you doubt my love for you?" Black Moon questioned.

"No." She lowered her lashes. "It is myself I doubt."

"Your love for me?"

"That has never been in question. I love you more than I can say. It is just that…" Her words trailed off into uncertainty.

"You will always wonder what your life would be if you had stayed with the whites."

She gave a little nod in reply.

"To wonder is a good thing," Black Moon said. "It is how we learn. Each day when I take Little Storm out to hunt, he wonders if that will be the day his arrow brings down a long-ears. One day his arrow will find its mark and he will no longer wonder. Our nephew has seen only seven winters, but already he shows the promise of being a strong hunter." He paused to draw in a deep breath and asked, "Do you wish to go back to the whites?"

"No! That is not what I wish. I want only…I thought…I would like to go to the new fort on Buffalo Creek. Just to do a little trading," she hastened to add when she saw him stiffen. "I could use a new kettle. It would not be like before when I was gone for so long," she said of the year she had spent in St. Louis away from him. "I will not stay there. I will return to you."

Pte Wakpa. Buffalo Creek. The words resounded in his brain. He nodded toward the sputtering kettle. "Your turnips will spill out. We will speak of this later." He turned from her and went back to his place, but he had lost his appetite. It was only the scratching at the hide entrance telling of a visitor that forced him to curb his impulse to fling the bighorn bowl across the lodge.

Claw entered. Skirting the fire, as well as Katie who kept her eyes respectfully lowered, he went to the honor-place and sat down. He withdrew his pipe from its beaded bag and held a bundle of sage over the fire, waiting for the gray smoke to rise before smudging a pinch of tobacco and placing it in the bowl.

After offering the pipe to the powers of the Earth, the Sky, the Four Directions, and finally to *Wakan Tanka*, he uttered a brief prayer and drew the first puff. When the sweet, pungent scent of red willow bark and bearberry leaves was wafting upward and out into the night through the smoke hole at the top of the lodge where the poles were gathered, he asked his son, "What did you see on your journey to the Shining Mountains?"

"White men traveling north to dig for the yellow metal."

"What did you do about it?"

"Nothing. Crazy Horse wanted to go after them, but they had more guns."

"Crazy Horse. Hmm. That one reminds me of you. He will not stop until all the whites are driven out."

"We cannot stop," Black Moon said. "We are better fighters, and we know the land. That is our strength."

The flames glowed over Claw's face, showing the passage of many years carved into his brown skin. "But as you say, they have more guns. That is their strength."

"I may not have as many bullets as the Long Knives, but my will to keep our land is stronger than any bullet. Still, if I could arm my warriors with the guns they call breechloaders, we would have a better chance of defeating them. But since we do not have them, we will have to come up with something new."

"The white man is slowly causing us to change our ways," Claw said. "Look around you. Our women use cooking pots like white women use. And blankets made of trade cloth. The white man does not tell us we must use these things. We do it because it makes our lives easier. One day your warriors will have guns, but I wonder if we will forget how to make bows and arrows. Sometimes, the new way is not always the better way." He drew in a long breath of kinnikinnik and let it slowly spiral out of his mouth. "I want Little Storm to grow up in a Lakota world where the old ways are honored."

"My nephew is not causing too much trouble at your lodge, is he?"

"No. I like having my grandson with me. It makes me feel closer to the son I lost."

They did not speak often about Fire Cloud. What more was there to say other than that he was a good and honest man who devoted his life to peace? Black Moon's heart had hardened against his older brother because Fire Cloud had married Katie, and it was only when Fire Cloud was gone that Black Moon learned the two had not lived as husband and wife, but merely as friends. Even now, so many winters later, the guilt he felt for misjudging his brother hung over him like a heavy robe. The only thing that helped ease the burden of his guilt was having taken Fire Cloud's son as his own to raise.

"Perhaps it is better that my brother is not here to see how things are going," Black Moon said. "His heart was too kind for the things we must now do. Only Turning Hawk still calls for making peace with the whites." He shook his head. "That one will never understand why peace is not possible."

"Turning Hawk is an old man," Claw said. "Sometimes, it is hard to change an old man's mind about things."

"Are you talking about Turning Hawk or about yourself?" Black Moon asked.

"Maybe both," his father replied.

"And what is hard to change your mind about?"

Claw cast a quick glance at Katie who had retreated to a corner with an awl and sinew and Black Moon's hide shirt in her lap, and lowered his voice. "Grandchildren. When you lost your little one, I prayed there would be another to take her place. I have tried to tell myself that one grandchild is enough, but this old man would like to have more. Have you been trying to make another one?"

Black Moon smiled slyly. "We try very hard."

"*Wakan Tanka* will decide if it is to be."

Father and son fell silent as they smoked by the light of the crackling fire. At length, Claw said, "I will return to the earth one day, but I want it to be somewhere along our own trails. I hope it will be before this land is spoiled by the whites." He tapped the ashes from the pipe bowl into his palm and tossed them into the fire. Returning the long-stem to its beaded bag, he rose and walked to the entrance. "We must not forget the old ways, for they are what makes us who we are. If we cast them aside, it will be the same as throwing ourselves away, and if we do that, we will not have to worry about the Long Knives defeating us. We will defeat ourselves." Sweeping aside the hide at the entrance, he bent, and left.

From where she sat in the corner mending Black Moon's shirt, Katie had listened to their hushed conversation. At Claw's mention of grandchildren, her hand went to her belly that once had swelled with an unborn life and was now barren. Claw was not the only one who wished that a new little one's cry would fill this lodge. Her heart was heavy with the disappointment of it. But that was not all that had her questioning things these days. When Black Moon and Claw had spoken about fighting the whites, she had lifted her gaze and looked into her husband's eyes and seen his grim determination, and she knew that he could not help being what he was, a warrior. She struggled to push the worst possibility from her mind. Several Lakota men had been killed in recent skirmishes with the soldiers. She did not want him to die. He was her world. She wanted to grow old with him, and if God or *Wakan Tanka* willed it, to have many children with the man she loved.

There was just one thing standing in the way of that dream, and that was the seed of doubt that had been planted in her long before this night and which continued to grow with each passing season until it sprouted through her entire being. What if she had stayed in the white world? What if she had married Josh McIntyre, the handsome cavalry lieutenant who'd been in love with her? What if she had remained in St. Louis and claimed the vast inheritance left to her by her aunt? What if? What if?

It was cool in the lodge. Katie put her sewing and her misgivings aside and got up. As she was adding some wood to the coals in the fire pit, she felt his hand in her hair, his long, slender fingers burying deep and drawing her head back.

She quickened like lightning at his touch.

With a practiced hand, he stroked her neck and throat and bent her backwards, supporting her with a sinewy brown arm as he placed a lingering kiss on her lips.

"Come," Black Moon whispered thickly. He took her hand and led her toward their sleeping robes.

She held back a little. "I thought you wanted to talk."

His mouth curved in a gentle smile. "There will be time later for talking."

Katie shuddered with yearning. Her fingers ached to touch the brown skin beneath his hide shirt. His strong musky scent rose to meet her, and she could bear it no longer. She came into his arms quivering with desire. It had been this way from the start. Whenever she'd been consumed by rage and grief, he had used the power of his body to teach her that nothing mattered except the savage bliss of his possession.

He guided her to the robes. So great was his desire for her that he felt an animal power surging through his loins, and he pushed her down with more force than he intended. If she was going to leave him, it would be with his memory to haunt her. And if his love for her was not enough to bring her back to him, then maybe this would be.

In spite of the urgency racing through him, he did not want to hurry. He wanted the fire between them to burn strong and steady and long. Yet it was all he could do to hold himself in check as he tugged the elk skin dress up past her hips. She raised her arms, holding them languorously over her head as he slipped the tanned hide up and off.

Her long red hair slid off her shoulders, unveiling her breasts to his hungry eyes. Settling himself beside her, for those first few moments all he did was look at her, his gaze sweeping along her smooth torso, her softly rounded belly, up and down the length of each slender leg, and the dark crown of curls at the top of her thighs. Without taking his eyes from her, he rose. Towering over her, he drew his buckskin shirt up over his head, kicked off his moccasins, shed his leggings and let the breech clout slide from his hips.

Katie's chest rose and fell in rapid motions as she gazed up at him. The firelight played across his naked chest, dancing along his slim hips, and glistening in the drop of moisture that clung to the tip of his potent erection. He was all stealth and muscle, power and vitality, a dizzying combination of hardness and softness that drew a faint breath of awe from her.

Dropping back down beside her, he pulled her on top of him. He lay back on the buffalo robe, kissing her throat, burying his face in the valley of her breasts, her hair falling all around as his hands traced the swells and hollows of her body.

Raising his knees, he closed them around her hips. With a low groan, he cupped her buttocks, raised her slightly, and brought her down upon his hardened shaft. His hands went to her waist, guiding her in a steady rocking motion as he slid deeper into her. In a rush of words, he breathed, "Not to hurry."

She obliged, moving up and down in a slow rhythm, lifting her hips so that his tip toyed at her entrance, and then coming down hard to swallow him up within her warm, wet heat.

He pushed his hand between her legs and caressed her, teasing her until her whole body trembled.

Katie gazed down at him through desire-narrowed eyes. The fire's glow traced his high cheekbones and the strong line of his jaw and lingered on the lashes of his closed eyes. There was an intensity about him, a severity she had never seen before in their lovemaking.

The fingers of one hand bit into her flesh, forcing her to move faster and harder, while the thumb of his other hand circled and stroked the source of all sensation and pleasure.

He made it last and last until his restraint deserted him. Lifting her off himself, he pushed her back against the robe and covered her body with his, moving into the space she created between her spreading thighs. Closing his teeth on her shoulder, he pushed against her, the hard grip of his fingers hurting her. But it was a sweet pain, one she would have endured a thousand times and more. The sound of his breathing was like an animal pant, the rush of his heated breath against her flesh like a hot iron branding her every place it touched.

She met his invasion with a sharp upward arch of her body. Squeezing her hand into the space between their bodies, she wrapped her fingers around his seed, kneading the soft flesh, then molded her hand to his arousal, fingers pulsing around him each time he withdrew for another hard thrust. She felt the wet hot dew as it spilled from him, and drawing her hand away, she wrapped her legs around him and drew him in as deeply as it was possible for him to be. Her own climax washed over her on a wave of unbridled pleasure, wrenching a cry from her throat, and in a small, detached corner of her mind came the hope that from this coupling his potent seed would create a new life.

The night sun climbed high in the sky and peered down at them through the smoke hole at the top of the lodge. Black Moon lay on his back, one arm bent behind his head, the other wound around Katie's shoulders, holding her close, tying to steady his emotions. His body was hot despite the cool night air. She stoked a fire inside of him that he had no wish to control. He tilted his head toward her. She was so beautiful it took his breath away. The light of the dying fire cast a rosy glow on her smooth white skin, and the hair that spilled over his arm caught the flames along each strand. She was his now, but it had not always been so. And the road to claiming her had been long and hard-fought.

When she married his brother out of obligation to Turning Hawk, he had stood by in bitter silence, crushed. When a Crow thief had stolen her from their village, it was he who traveled deep into Crow country to bring her back. When she went to that place in the east, it was his heart that broke with longing for her. It was only when his brother was killed that he was able to make her his wife in the Lakota way, and in fulfilling his duty by taking his brother's wife as his own, he had finally won the prize he had long sought. After all that, he was not about to lose her, not to another man, nor to a thief, nor to all the wondering in the world.

And yet, to keep her here against her will was not a good thing. He remembered the time when, as a small boy, he had opened his palm to reveal to his mother the painted-wing he had captured. Pretty Shield had looked at the creature and told him that if he held onto it tightly, it would surely die, but if he held it loosely, it would remain in his hand until it decided to flutter away. Like that painted-wing, Katie was a beautiful creature that could never really be captured. To force her to stay with him would be as sure as losing her.

He glanced down at their intertwined fingers. Her hand was small and white, his large and permanently burnished by the sun. Turning his gaze on the face of the moon overhead, he said, "With the new sun I will ride to Crazy Horse's village to sit in council with the others to decide what should be done about the whites coming to Lakota country. When I return, we will talk more about this."

"I would like to go before the snows come."

Black Moon knew that she was apprehensive about the snow, stemming from the time two winters past when she thought he had been unfaithful to her and she had ridden off in distress, only to get caught in a blizzard that nearly killed her.

"I will take you to the new soldier town when I return from the council."

Katie shifted in his arms and looked at him. "You must not." Her voice brimmed with apprehension. "If they were to put you in their jail like they did once before, this time I would not be able to help you."

Black Moon's neck still bore a scar from the time he'd been imprisoned in the white man's cage at Fort Laramie. When all had seemed lost, Katie had appeared as if out of a dream and handed him a length of rope, telling him he was to tie one end around his neck and loop the other end around the wooden beam in the cell. It was a crazy plan. If it worked, he would be free. If it did not, he would be dangling from the end of a rope. But it had worked, and thanks to her cleverness and her courage, he'd been able to return to his people.

"I cannot let you go alone."

"I will ask the trader to go with me," she said.

"The trader is here?"

"He came while you were riding with Crazy Horse. His wagon is at the edge of the circle." She felt his resistance. "He has been a good friend to me. And to you," she added, knowing it was not something he wanted to hear. "Two times he helped me find you. The first time when you were a prisoner at Fort Laramie, and again when you were wounded in battle and brought to the Cheyenne camp."

She made no mention of Pine Leaf, the Cheyenne girl who had nursed Black Moon back to health and who foolishly thought she could take Katie's place as his wife. It was only Katie's clever matchmaking that turned Pine Leaf's head in the direction of Red Thunder, the handsome Cheyenne warrior she eventually married. The last Katie heard, Pine Leaf's belly was swollen with her second child.

"Why must you go to the white man's town?" Black Moon asked. "If you want a new kettle, you can get it from the trader."

"I cannot explain," she replied. "I know only that I have to go."

Drawing in a frustrated breath, he let it out with slow resignation.

"Then you will go."

Katie sat up. "I cannot go like this."

"Without clothes?" Black Moon teased, running a hand along her arm and cupping her breast in his palm.

"I meant dressed in elk skin."

"Perhaps the trader has a white woman's dress. I will give you a good knife to trade for it."

"You do understand."

He rubbed his thumb over the back of her hand. "I understand that I must let you go for you to return to me."

Katie pressed the softness of her cheek against Black Moon's face, and whispered, "I will always return to you."

But even as she spoke the words, Katie felt the rumblings of something deeper and more urgent tugging at her heart, and she knew it would take more than mere words for her to keep that promise.

Chapter 4
Keeping Secrets

The next morning, there came a scratching at the hide entrance to the lodge. Looking up from the pot of chokecherries she was stirring, Katie saw her mother-in-law enter.

She was called Running-water Woman, named for the Niobrara, the smooth-flowing river upon whose shore she'd been born. After Pretty Shield, Black Moon's birth mother, had been gone for many winters, Claw had taken Running-water Woman as his wife. Pretty Shield had never approved of Katie's marriage to Fire Cloud and then to Black Moon, but Running-water Woman was more accepting of her white daughter-in-law. There was a quiet strength in her that Katie admired. Perhaps it was because the Oglala woman had seen her share of tragedy, having lost her husband to a soldier's bayonet in the battle on Box Elder Creek and her only son and daughter-in-law to the cholera.

Glancing past her, Katie asked, "Little Storm is not with you?"

"He went out very early to gallop his new pony up and down the flats."

Turning back to the chokecherries, Katie said, "Black Moon captured the iron gray when he raided the soldiers. The white men's horses are so much bigger than our own, and I thought it would be too much for Little Storm to handle. My nephew has seen only seven winters, but Black Moon said the boy is special so he should have a special horse." She gave a hapless little shrug. "I just hope he does not fall off and break any bones. Then we will have to use the horse to pay the medicine man to fix him."

"Every day the boy becomes more like his uncle."

"Touch The Clouds would not be pleased," Katie said, mindful of Lakota custom not to speak the names of the dead, using Fire Cloud's spirit name instead.

She remembered Fire Cloud fondly as a kind-hearted, soft-spoken man who had struggled to reconcile his duty to Turning Hawk by taking her as his wife and his love for Good Deeds, a sweet Oglala girl. She knew how difficult it had been for him, for she was in love with Black Moon, yet her own sense of obligation to Turning Hawk had made it impossible to refuse. All that was behind them now. Fire Cloud was gone, Good Deeds was killed by a soldier's bullet at Box Elder Creek, and their son was now Katie's and Black Moon's to raise. No, Fire Cloud would not be pleased that his son was becoming more like Black Moon every day. Yet warriors were necessary to keep the Lakota way of life strong. The old ones said it was better to lay naked in death as a warrior with a strong heart than to be wrapped up well with a weak heart.

While the chokecherries simmered in a small metal pot hung from a tripod above the flames, Katie scooped a handful of dried chokecherries from a painted parfleche and mixed them together with dried and pounded elk meat, adding some rendered fat to hold the mixture together.

"Will you keep Little Storm with you until Black Moon returns?" Katie asked as she worked the mixture with her hands.

Running-water Woman gave her a questioning look.

"I will speak with the trader today and ask him to take me to the fort on Buffalo Creek," Katie explained.

"Claw will be happy to have his grandson with him."

Katie was thankful that her mother-in-law did not press the issue. It had been hard enough explaining to Black Moon why she felt the need to go to the fort.

"Your husband is not happy with your decision?"

Katie gave her a wry look. "My husband is not happy with many things I do, but that has never stopped me."

Running-water Woman sighed and said, "Husbands are not always understanding. My husband would not be happy if he knew I can speak the white man's language."

"I have never heard you speak it. How did you learn?" Katie asked.

"When I was a young girl, a speaks-white trader stayed at our village during the winter moons. At night I pretended to be sleeping when he taught my father the words. But Claw would not like it, so I do not speak it. I am not as brave as you."

"Sometimes it is best to keep our secrets close," Katie said. Like the secret longing she had to find out if there was any place for her in the white world.

"It is no secret that our men have been invited to a big council at the village of Crazy Horse," Running-water Woman said, drawing Katie away from her thoughts. "He says there can be only one outcome. The Long Knives must be defeated. They do not belong here. This is our land. They are not like Lakota warriors. They think the only way to win is by killing. That is what they did to the Cheyenne at Sand Creek, and before that at Box Elder Creek, and before that on Blue Water. The only way to get rid of them is to kill them."

At the mention of Blue Water, Katie's fingers stiffened as she worked the chokecherry mixture. What lay behind her was terrible and had changed the course of her life, but the thought of what lay ahead sent a shiver coursing through her body.

Katie knew the white men better than anyone. They were relentless in their pursuit, whether it was for land or gold. But killing them was not the answer. For every one killed, ten more would come, then a hundred, then a thousand. There was no stopping the future, and right now, Black Moon was on his way to the council that would determine that future.

Chapter 5
Council Fires

Black Moon, Swift Bear, Turning Hawk, and several other men from the village started out early while the sun still slept. With the others riding on ahead, Swift Bear and Black Moon followed at a leisurely pace behind them.

Although smaller in stature than Black Moon, Swift Bear was nevertheless a great warrior. Armed with his medicine, the stuffed skin of the long-legged owl, tied to his head, he rode against their Crow and Pawnee enemies, counting many coups and earning the thin scar that slashed across his face. On this morning, the hardened warrior noticed that his friend was unusually reticent. Reining his pony close to Black Moon's, he ventured, "Has she said anything to you about her unhappiness?'

Black Moon was not surprised by Swift Bear's perception and answered truthfully, "No. But she has been quiet lately, and that is not like her."

"Perhaps she still mourns for the little one you lost."

"It is more than that."

"Have you asked her what troubles her?"

"I have resisted the urge to ask too many questions."

"Are you afraid of the answers?"

Black Moon shot him an icy look. "I have never been afraid to look truth in the face."

"That is what I am counting on," said Swift Bear. "For there will be much truth floating around the council lodge."

"If you mean Turning Hawk's truth, that one has spent too much time looking back to the way things were to see ahead and how things will be."

"He is not a bad man," Swift Bear remarked.

"I never said he was. He took my woman into his lodge when I brought to live among us. And he was my brother's mentor."

"That is where your brother got all those peace notions in his head."

"My brother owned a kind, peaceful heart long before Turning Hawk took him under his wing." What Black Moon did not say was that Fire Cloud could have refused Turning Hawk's advice to take Katie for his wife and avoided the heartache it caused so many, including Good Deeds, the young woman who loved Fire Cloud and bore his son. Hiding his bitterness behind a brittle smile, Black Moon said, "Let us not delay. There are important men waiting in the council lodge who will have much to say."

"As will you, I am sure. You have always had a strong voice in the council lodge."

"I have always spoken the words that need to be spoken," Black Moon said. "Today will be no different."

They found the village of Crazy Horse situated in a thin grove of rustling cottonwoods northwest of the Tongue River. Gray plumes of smoke were rising from the cook fires as they rode in. The skins of the council lodge were lifted and propped from the ground so that the autumn breeze could pass under them. Inside, a fire crackled and burned brightly, throwing its glow across the faces around it.

Turning Hawk went to the north side where the old men sat, for north was the home of the cold moons, and the old men seated by the fire had earned the deep creases on their faces over many hard winters.

Black Moon and Swift Bear took their places across from the old men alongside the other warrior leaders Hump, the Minniconjou, and White Elk from the Northern Cheyenne. Having earned the right to lead men into battle, no one questioned the experience and reputation of these men.

Among the youngest of the warrior leaders was Crazy Horse, but as strong as his reputation was, his experience was like a snowflake against a blizzard, and so he would not speak today.

A medicine man called Red Eagle lit his pipe and offered a prayer. "Great Spirit, We thank you for the courage you have given to these warriors. Help them keep our people strong." The pipe was then passed from man to man, east to west.

After each man in turn had smoked, White Elk, the Cheyenne leader, spoke. "The Long Knives are not honorable enemies, but we can learn from them. They fight to kill, and so must we."

"We cannot let them rest," said Hump. "We must make their fear of us grow stronger every day."

Approving grunts filled the lodge.

"Why is the leader of the Bad Faces not here?" Black Moon asked. "Did Red Cloud not think it was important enough to come?"

"Maybe it is for the best," said Swift Bear. "That one took it upon himself to speak for all the Oglala at the treaty meeting on Horse Creek when he told the Long Knives we will not sell our land."

"And when the whites looked to him as the leader of all the Oglala, he did not bother to tell them that he is not," Black Moon said. "No one among us has the power to decide something for all the people. I do not tell my warriors that they must follow me into battle. I do what my own voice tells me I must do. The decision is theirs to make. One person telling others what to do is a dangerous thing. It is the same as saying that we must work for peace when we know that peace is not possible." He shot a pointed look at Turning Hawk. "This is a different kind of enemy. To them, war is for killing. They did it on the Blue Water. They did it at Box Elder Creek. They did it at Sand Creek. We must not let them do it here. To defeat this kind of enemy it is necessary to know as much about them as we can."

Turning Hawk shifted in his cross-legged position. His gray hair hung in two thin braids over his shoulders, and the lines on his face crisscrossed like well-traveled trails. He knew that Black Moon had not forgiven him for pressuring Fire Cloud into marrying Katie and that there would be never be any agreement between them. "It may be hard to believe that this frail old man was once a formidable fighting man," he said, "but back then, the enemy was the Crow and the Pawnee. The weapons we used were bows and arrows and war clubs, and warriors fought for the honor of striking first coup, not to kill for the sake of killing. Perhaps in learning about this new enemy, we can find the way to live in peace with them."

"Peace?" Black Moon echoed. "You have been crying for peace for a long time, but does it look to you like the white man wants peace? Every time we thought it was possible, we were proven wrong. We watched the man called Bozeman pounding stakes into the Powder River Road and we thought nothing of it until we realized he was marking a trail for more whites to follow. Now the Holy Road stinks from the dead animals they leave along the way. They have ruined the land so badly the buffalo will not go there anymore. Is that what you want to happen to us up here?" The firelight glanced off the contours of his face as he shook his head vehemently. "We all know that peace is not the way to solve this problem."

All heads around the fire nodded in silent assent, except for Turning Hawk's. Black Moon rose and stood there for a moment looking down at the faces around the fire. "I will ride against the Long Knives. Any who wish to join me can do so." He gave Turning Hawk a swift, penetrating stare. "I will have no trouble finding men to follow me." With that, he left them to their talking and went outside.

Sunshine bounced off his black hair as he made his way to the pony herd. Finding his pony, he knelt down and untied the hobbles on its front legs.

"I will ride with you."

Black Moon looked up to see a familiar figure approach.

"The *washicus* are hard to understand," Crazy Horse said as he stroked the neck of Black Moon's pony, his soft-spoken voice contrasting his reputation as a fearless warrior.

"Now that their war has ended, they have again set their sights on Lakota land," Black Moon said with disgust. "We are like the herds of buffalos, few and scattered. They are like locusts that fly so thick the whole sky is darkened. You can count on your fingers from sun-up until sun-set and they will keep coming faster than you can count."

A dark shadow passed across Crazy Horse's face as if a cloud had blotted out the sun. "It is too easy to hate them."

"I have learned something about the Long Knives from watching them," Black Moon said. "There is always one who leads into battle and the others follow. If we can get the leader to chase us, the others will follow. We have only to cut off the head of the snake."

"And I have been watching the soldier town on *Pte Wakpa*," Crazy Horse said. "With each new sun the bluecoats ride out to get the wood for their fires. That is when we can lead them into a trap."

Black Moon nodded. "I will call my warriors together."

CHAPTER 6
BETWEEN TWO CREEKS

"Are you expecting trouble?" Katie asked, when she noticed that the trader's eyes kept straying to the surrounding hills.

"Red Cloud's been raiding wagon trains up and down the trail," Jasper Gillette said as he steered his wagon along the beaten path that was littered with oxen bones and burned-out pieces of wagons, evidence of Sioux hostility. "This road ain't safe to travel on. They don't call this the bloody Bozeman for nothing."

Seated beside him, wearing the calico dress she traded Black Moon's good throwing knife for, Katie gave him a wry look. "That doesn't stop you from trading at the camps."

"My wife is Oglala and lives with my kids among Red Cloud's Bad Faces. They all know me."

"I remember something my father said shortly before we rode to the Brulè village on the Blue Water," Katie said, her voice taking on a sad, reflective note. "He said the Indians were under pressure from the westward-moving whites, and men under pressure sometimes forget who their friends are."

"Ain't that the truth," Gillette said. "Times sure have changed from when your pap was trading with the tribes. Back then, they mostly wanted beads and blankets and cooking pots. These days, they want guns."

But that was not all that had changed, Gillette thought, recalling the first time he'd seen Katie. It was when she returned from St. Louis and showed up at his trading post near the Deer Creek mail station. She'd been wearing a fancy dress that looked like it was right out of a catalog with its flounced skirt and frilly sleeves. To his surprise, she had traded that fine dress for an Arapaho one of deer skin. He couldn't remember when he'd seen anything prettier than her, in silk or buckskin, then or now. She surprised him further that day by asking him to take her to Fort Laramie where Black Moon was imprisoned. She had a knack for getting him to go against his better judgment, like the time some years later when she asked again for his help in finding Black Moon who had disappeared, and they found him at a Cheyenne winter camp recovering from a bullet wound.

"I don't know why I let you talk me into making these trips with you," Gillette complained.

"You have been a good friend to me and my husband," she said.

"With the way Black Moon hates the whites, I doubt he'd count me as one of his friends."

"It's not all whites he hates," Katie said. "It's the soldiers. He's aware of the difference between the soldiers and plain old white men. And contrary to what you might think, he does not kill indiscriminately. He knows who his enemies are, and he is trying to keep his people safe from them."

"It's different now from the old days when the Sioux raided mostly for honor," Gillette brooded. "Now the raids are done mostly by small bands of warriors who strike hard and fast, inflicting as much damage as possible. It ain't pretty, but it's effective. There's only two men capable of rallying their warriors for that kind of fighting. One of them is Crazy Horse. That one's relentless. The other one is your husband. I ain't never seen a more brilliant leader than Black Moon. They're a lot alike, both reckless and not afraid to make bold decisions. Some men dream of becoming leaders. Those two come by it naturally. But all the leadership in the world won't make a bit of different without firearms. Although the Sioux outnumber the soldiers at the fort, they're not as well equipped." He cast a sidelong look at Katie. "I heard you got yourself a heap of money waiting for you back east. There's no telling what all that money could buy."

"Are you suggesting—?"

"I ain't suggesting anything," Gillette interrupted, feigning innocence. "Look! There she is." He pointed toward the outpost in the foothills of the brooding Bighorn Mountains. "Fort Phil Kearny, built to protect freighters, gold prospectors, and emigrants along the Bozeman, and to keep the Sioux away from the railroad."

"What railroad?" Katie asked.

"The Union Pacific. It's still hundreds of miles south of here, but it's coming closer every day."

So far removed was she from the white world that she hadn't even known about the railroad. "How much else is going on in the world that I'm not aware of?" Katie wondered aloud.

"Sure enough, things are changing."

Katie looked at this man who was her only white friend. He was dressed much the same as he'd been when she first met him, in a buckskin tunic over a plaid woolen shirt, deerskin pants with long fringes along the outer seams, and beaded moccasins on his feet. His hair, beard and mustache were snow-white. He was still a fine-looking man, but the lines etched into the corners of his eyes were deeper than they'd been that day, and the furrow of his brow was more pronounced, proof that the years had taken their toll. Perhaps it was the rigors of traveling from Indian village to Indian village, or the burning of his store by a Cheyenne war party in retaliation for the attack on a Cheyenne village at Sand Creek by the Colorado Territory militia two years ago. Or maybe it was just that the way of life he knew, from his early fur-trapping days to his trade with the Indians, was drawing to a close.

"You never told me what brought you west," she ventured.

His face took on a reflective expression. "I guess you could say I was born with a wandering nature. My father was a schooner captain in Maine. My mother taught piano. They both tried admirably to get me to stay home, but at the age of seventeen I set out to see the world. I got as far as Dakota Territory. An old buffalo hunter told me to go home as fast as I could. I didn't take his advice. In those days hardly any Indians had ever seen a white man. We're talking eighteen twenty-eight or thereabouts. Back then, I was a curiosity to them. They let me come and go as I pleased. It wasn't until later, when the fur trading companies began moving westward along Indian trading routes that things began to change. Then the government bought Fort Laramie from the American Fur Trading Company, and things ain't been the same since. Can't say I want to be around to see what this place turns into."

"Do you ever think about going back?" she asked.

"There ain't nothing for me back there. This place has been my home nigh on to forty years. I've got me a wife and a family, and so far I've kept my scalp. I'd say I'm a pretty lucky fella."

As they neared the fort, Katie's attention was drawn to a detachment of soldiers escorting a group of wagons laden with timber.

"The nearest stands of timber are several miles away, so the wood trains go out every morning to cut the wood they need for heating and cooking," Gillette explained. "The Sioux just naturally prey on them. I guess that's been keeping your husband busy."

Falling in line behind them, Gillette steered his wooden wagon through the western gate of the fort in a jingle of metal.

At the sight of soldiers being drilled on the parade ground, Katie's guard went up around her, for she knew first-hand how dangerous men in regimental blue could be.

"What will we tell them about me?" she whispered as they passed the civilian guards.

"The truth," Gillette slyly replied. "You were captured by the Sioux and traded back to me for some trinkets."

Katie chuckled under her breath. "You have a strange way with the truth. We both know I wasn't captured."

"But they don't know it. The post commander here is Colonel Henry Carrington. The Indians call him Little White Chief. His men don't particularly like him. With Red Cloud, Crazy Horse, and Black Moon attacking along the bloody Bozeman, he has more to worry about than some white woman. Chances are, he's never even heard of you and won't much care what you're doing here. Come to think of it, you never did say why you wanted to come here."

"Except for you, the only time I hear my own language spoken is when I talk to myself. I wanted to see pretty dresses and hear gay music." Katie looked around at the emigrants milling about, the men with skin burned red by the sun and the women with pale faces and haunted eyes beneath their bonnets, at the contingent of soldiers in blue uniforms, at the sawmill, and the regimented life inside the walls of the fort, and a shadow of uncertainty swept over her face. "Now, I'm not so sure."

She cast a longing look back over her shoulder just as the big wooden gate was closing behind them. The sun in this Moon When Leaves Turn Brown shone brightly over the wide expanse of land beyond the fort, and white wisps of cloud rode in a clear blue sky. Back at the Oglala village the meat racks were bent under the weight of meat drying in the sun from the autumn hunt. The old grandmothers would be busy keeping hungry dogs and playful boys from making off with too much, and the women would be pounding pemmican and filling the parfleches for the winter moons ahead. At night, the air would fill with smoke from the evening fires outside the lodges, and the earth would reverberate with the beat of the drums.

"Do you want to go back?"

Gillette's voice wound its way through Katie's scattered thoughts.

Yes, an inner voice screamed. *I want to go back to Black Moon, to the man I love with every fiber of my being.* But going back to him now would be like giving only part of herself to him.

She didn't know if coming here was the right thing to do, or if returning to St. Louis was the answer to the questions she had about herself and her place in the world, that part of herself she had lost somewhere between Blue Water Creek and Buffalo Creek, but she had to find out.

The scent of sage came drifting down the wind. With a pang, it brought the image of Black Moon braiding and burning sage, how the white smoke billowed and swirled around his head as his lashes closed over his midnight eyes and he uttered a prayer, and how the aroma lingered in his long, black hair after the braided sage had burned out.

There was a deep pause. Then, her face dark with distress, heaving an involuntary sigh, she found her voice. "Not yet," she answered. There's something I have to do first."

CHAPTER 7
WOOD TRAINS AND WAGON TRAINS

The warriors were fanned out across the top of a ridge, waiting for the wood detail of one or two wagons and a small escort of soldiers to leave the fort. The plan was to lure the Long Knives into an ambush by leading them across the creek, through the gully, and over the ridges and slopes, with Crazy Horse and Black Moon acting as decoys. But as the morning wore on, and the sun reached middle sky, the big wooden gate of the fort remained shut.

Crazy Horse fidgeted in his hide saddle, and complained, "They told us there would be no soldier towns built in Lakota territory without our permission."

"When did you ever know the Long Knives to keep their word?" The bitter question was voiced by Gall, a tall, imposing Hunkpapa, one of Sitting Bull's most loyal followers who had joined the Oglala in their raids along the Holy Road and the Powder River Road. "The Long Knives are only men and can be defeated," he asserted.

"Why are they not coming out?" Crazy Horse asked.

Sitting stoically astride his bay gelding, Black Moon looked down upon the fort with contempt and apprehension. "They will come," he said. "When they do, we will ride out as decoys. To them, we will look disorganized and uncertain. When they are certain of a quick victory over us, that is when we will strike."

No one dared contradict the *blotahunka*, the war leader. He had proven himself a fearless adversary with actions that set him apart from the others. Any who rode with him could attest to his bravery, and they also knew that true victory could not be achieved without him.

A movement from below caught the attention of the warriors. Black Moon's fingers tensed around his pony's jaw rope, and he came erect in his saddle as the big wooden gate of the fort swung open.

Holding the farseeing glass to his eye, Swift Bear grunted. "It is only one man driving a wagon." He passed the glass over to Black Moon.

Black Moon put the glass to his eye and moved it back and forth across the panorama until the moving wagon below came into view. It was the trader, the one Katie called her friend. When Black Moon returned to his village after several days in council with Crazy Horse and the others, he found his lodge empty. His father told him that Katie had left with the trader. Why was the trader now traveling alone? Where was Katie? Was she still inside?

"Wait here," he told the others. "I will ride there and speak with him."

With a kick of his moccasins, he urged his pony down the steep hillside and into a gallop to catch up with the wagon.

Jasper Gillette heard the thunder of hooves behind him. Turning, he saw a mounted Indian riding hard in his direction. His hand went to the Sharps carbine laying across his lap. He had obtained the rifle in a trade with a Union soldier who served with the Michigan volunteers and came west after the war looking for a different kind of action than what he'd seen on the battlefields of Fredericksburg and Chancellorsville. The fast, breech-loading rifle had been used to kill Confederate soldiers, and Gillette would not hesitate to use it to kill an Indian. But he stopped short of taking aim and firing when, even at the distance of an arrow's flight, he recognized the rider.

The big bay gelding drew up alongside the wagon and then ahead of it. With a sudden jerk on its jaw rope, it came to a stop with dirt and dust rising from its unshod hooves in front of the wagon, blocking its path.

Gillette brought the wagon to a sharp halt and stared at the figure before him. Strapped to the Lakota's arm was an unpainted rawhide shield covered with tanned rawhide from the buffalo's hump, the strongest part. He'd seen shields like that before. Originally twice the size it was now, it had been heated slowly in the ground beneath a fire for many days, shrinking and becoming so thick that arrows and lances could not penetrate it. A rifle rested across this Indian's saddle pommel. Slashed diagonally across his chest was the strap that held his bow and otter skin quiver at his back. Despite the autumn nip in the air, he was naked except for deerskin leggings and breech clout, and the sun bounced off his brown skin and shone like fire in his dark eyes. There was nothing friendly about him, and Gillette caught himself hoping that Katie was right when she said her husband knew the difference between the soldiers and an old white man like himself.

With a subtle tensing of his knees, Black Moon urged his pony forward.

Gillette forced a calmness into his demeanor that he did not truly feel, but he could not stop the flinch that came with the sound of that deep voice asking…no, demanding…in Lakota "Where is she?"

Answering in Lakota, Gillette said, "She is not here."

Black Moon jerked his head toward the fort and said, "She is inside?"

Gillette shook his head.

"You will tell me all you know."

It was obvious to the trader that Black Moon was here to attack the wood train and that his warriors were not far away. With the prospect of battle firing Black Moon's blood, Gillette knew he had to choose his words carefully, lest he bring the Lakota's wrath down upon himself. He steadied his voice and said, "She stayed only one day and left with a wagon train."

"Where did she go?"

"To the fort on the flat-water near Cottonwood Springs."

"The wagons all move toward the setting sun," Black Moon said. "Why would this one go the other way?"

"Those emigrants decided to turn back when the trail became too dangerous."

At the confusion he saw swirling in Black Moon's eyes, he said, "The talking wires are there. Katie said she wanted to send a message." He had tried to talk her out of it, what with the territory between Fort Phil Kearny and Fort McPherson on the North Platte teeming with hostile Indians, but she'd been adamant.

"What message?"

"I do not know," he answered truthfully.

Black Moon's dark eyes narrowed with suspicion. "There is more that you are not telling."

Licking his lips nervously, Gillette said, "The fort on the flat-water is near the iron road."

Maza canku. The iron road, with its houses being pulled one after another by the great iron beast. Was Katie on her way to the iron road that would take her far, far away from him and the life they knew as husband and wife? A bitterness welled up from the pit of Black Moon's belly, filling his throat with bile. She was going back to that place in the east. She was leaving him.

For many moments Black Moon was silent, giving Gillette the opportunity to watch him carefully from beneath lowered lids. Unlike the other warriors, this one did not adorn himself with eagle feathers. There was no symbol painted on his buffalo hide shield, nor did his pony bear any decoration. Beneath his plain countenance and aura of quiet dignity, Gillette sensed an undercurrent of physical menace about him. Coupled with surprising grace, he was a compelling figure, a walking contradiction, a warrior who hated the whites and yet loved a white woman, and Gillette suspected it was that very thing dividing him down the middle that made him a man like no other, not even the infamous Red Cloud, or the Sicanju leader Spotted Tail, or relentless Crazy Horse.

"Where is the wagon that goes for the wood?"

Black Moon's deep voice startled Gillette out of his thoughts. "They gathered enough wood yesterday. They are not coming out today."

Nodding toward a ridge in the distance, Black Moon said, "My warriors wait. I must go."

"Will you attack the fort?" Gillette asked apprehensively.

Black Moon shook his head. "They have the gun that shoots twice."

Gillette nodded with understanding. Black Moon was referring to cannons loaded with canister rounds, turning an artillery piece into a giant shotgun, which prevented him and Crazy Horse from a direct attack on the fort. But the fort commander, Colonel Carrington, didn't know that, and undoubtedly expected a full-scale attack at any moment. While at the fort, Gillette observed that most of the soldiers still had Civil War muzzleloaders, and although the cavalry unit had seven-shot Spencer carbines, and the civilian teamsters, loggers and scouts in the field carried Henry 16-shot lever action rifles, he'd heard the men complaining that there was less than fifty rounds of ammunition on hand for each man. Under such conditions, an all-out attack on the fort would not have been impossible. An army of agile warriors could easily vault the palisades, especially from horseback, but that was something Black Moon didn't know, and Gillette wasn't about to tell him and risk the lives of the women, children and civilian workers at the fort.

Black Moon watched the trader closely. As if reading his thoughts, he said, "Killing is not something I enjoy, but if it is the only way to drive the Long Knives out of my country, then it is something I will do."

With that, he raised his rifle above his head and let out a piercing war cry that bounced off the surrounding hills. With a hard jerk on the jaw rope he wheeled his pony around, and laying on the lash, he galloped away.

Jasper Gillette drew a deep breath and let it out slowly, and it was only when the dust kicked up by the flying hooves of Black Moon's pony had settled that he relaxed his finger on the trigger of his rifle.

The autumn breeze swirled from several directions, rustling the mane and tale of Crazy Horse's pony that pranced nervously beneath him as he waited for Black Moon to return. As quickly as the bay gelding had disappeared down the slope, it reappeared.

Black Moon guided his pony to the place where Crazy Horse and the others waited. "The wood gatherers are not coming today." He glanced toward the sky. "We will wait until they do come out, maybe with the new sun, maybe the one after that. Let us find a place to make camp."

When a night sun strung as tight as a bow string hung high in the sky, Black Moon sat alone at a dying fire a distance away from the others. Surrounded by silence broken only by the breeze rustling the treetops and the howl of a true-dog in the distance, he struggled to gather his thoughts.

People came to him to talk, and the old ones wanted him in the council lodge, making it difficult for him to be alone with the thoughts he shared with no one. But on this night, not even the solitude offered any peace or comfort from the grim reality that Katie was gone. Again. She had come back to him last time, but would she come back this time?

He told himself it did not matter, that his sole purpose in life was to protect his people, not his own heart. And yet, the news that Katie was on her way to the iron road that would take her back east was like a war club to the stomach. The old ones said that heartache fell into every life as surely as the snow fell in winter. So much had been taken from him. Hail Storm, a beloved young cousin. His honored place as a Shirt Wearer, for going against the wishes of the council by leading his warriors in the battle that cost Hail Storm his life. His brother, who died when there was still much misunderstanding between them. Pretty Shield, his mother, when her body, weakened by the death of her son, could no longer sustain her. Lone Horn, his oldest and best friend, killed in the Box Elder fight. And the hardest of all to bear, the little one, the daughter who had not lived beyond her second day.

The words Katie whispered to him on their last night together lingered painfully in his mind. *I will always return to you.* But would she?

CHAPTER 8
THREE HUNDRED MILES

After a breakfast of coffee, bacon, and dry bread, the teams of oxen were hitched up. The oxen were slow and lumbering, but if the food ran out, at least they could eat prairie grass.

It was a mild day, and the mid-morning warmth, coming on the heels of the cold prairie night, caused the wood of some of the wagon wheels to shrink and the iron rims to roll off from the wheels not having been soaked overnight in a stream bed. After replacing the damaged wheels with spare ones slung under the wagons, the wagons were rolling.

Katie sat on the perch, staring listlessly at the flat, treeless prairie beyond the bobbing heads of the oxen. A light breeze blew across the short grass, carrying the smell of sagebrush, dust, and heat, mingling with the sweat of the oxen and the faint scent of the linseed oil used to waterproof the canvas bonnets of the wagons. All along the side of the trail the remains of oxen and mules lay strewn over the land, the bones whitened beneath the prairie sun, some crumbling to dust by the passage of time.

Walking beside the wagon was Ned Jeppsen, the emigrant who had offered her a ride to Fort McPherson. In early spring he had set out from his home in Little Falls, Minnesota with his wife and two children and met up in Independence, Missouri with the wagon train bound for Oregon. But the trail to his new home on the frontier was fraught with tragedy. His seven-year-old daughter had wandered off looking for flowers and disappeared, likely having fallen prey to wild animals, and his eleven-year-old son had succumbed to mountain fever. When his wife's long skirts got caught up on the wheels and dragged her under the wagon, he'd been unable to stop the heavy, slow-moving oxen fast enough to save her. At Fort Phil Kearny he decided to turn back to Minnesota, leaving behind his hope for the future and two holes in the ground, hastily scratched out, but deep enough so that they would not be clawed out by wolves. The only things left from Minnesota were the horse hitched to the back of the wagon, a few belongings inside, and his Kentucky percussion rifle.

The victim of tragedy herself, Katie knew the desolation of heart endured by people like Ned Jeppsen who'd been obliged to go on and leave their loved ones here in the wilderness. She was grateful for his offer of a ride to Fort McPherson, and since they'd left Fort Phil Kearny five days ago, she'd come to admire him for his steadfastness. She watched now as he dipped his hands into a bucket hanging from the rear axle and swabbed the mixture of animal fat and tar over the hubs of the wheels to keep them greased. Climbing down from the perch, she handed him a rag.

Wiping the grease from his hands, he tilted his hat back on his head. "Thank you, ma'am."

"I thought we agreed that you would call me Katie."

He offered a little smile. "Thank you, Katie."

Despite his attire of worn cotton calico shirt and wool homespun pants tucked into muddied boots, he was actually a nice-looking man when he smiled, which had not been very often at first, but happened more frequently as the days wore on. His eyes seemed to change color from brown to light green depending upon the time of day, and locks of sandy brown hair fell from beneath the broad brim of his straw hat.

Reaching into her pocket, Katie took out a length of buckskin and began to braid it as they walked beside the wagon.

"You're pretty good at that," Ned said as he watched her nimble fingers.

"I grew up along the Laramie," she said. "We always had need of buckskin for repairing things like harnesses, bridles, saddles, and the fringes on my father's pants." She didn't tell him that she had found many uses for buckskin living among the Oglala. There was no sense explaining something he was not likely to understand.

"Nooning!"

When the sun was overhead, the wagon master, a tough-minded man named Sam Bass, cantered up and down the line of wagons announcing that it was time to break.

One by one the wagons stopped. While the draft animals rested and the children played, the people gathered over a cold meal of coffee, beans and bacon that had been prepared that morning.

Two hours later, on the move again, Katie pointed to the four flat-topped mesas rising on the horizon. "Pumpkin Buttes. The Indians call them *wagamu paha*, or gourd hills. The Belle Fourche runs from there. My father used to say it was one of the prettiest little rivers he ever did see."

"Back in Little Falls we have the Mississippi," said Ned. "There's a place where the water tumbles over an outcropping of granite into a beautiful waterfall. The Ojibwa call it *kakabikans*, which translates to something like the little square cut-off rock."

"Do you miss it?" she asked.

"What I miss is having someone to sit with on the porch watching the sun sink behind the hills and the way it sparkles over the river." She saw a shadow pass across his face. "Having someone to share those little moments with, is what makes everything else bearable."

Katie could not stop the same thought from running through her mind. Was she foolish for thinking there was something more for her somewhere out there? Would her memories be enough to sustain her? McCabe used to say that memory was like riding a trail at night with a lighted torch that cast its light only so far and beyond it lay the darkness.

At six o'clock the wagon master called a halt. With the Black Hills looming in the distance, the wagons were moved into a circle for the night. The evening lay before them, cold and sweetly scented with sage. Dozens of fires glittered inside the circle of wagons. After a simple supper cooked in a shovel over a dung fire, some of the travelers sought the comfort of sleep wrapped in blankets on the ground, or beneath their wagons, or inside their wagons among skillets, coffee pots, and tin plates.

Katie gathered some oxen chips, tossed them into the fire, and sat down to the feel of the orange flames warming her face. She glanced around at the emigrants shivering in their blankets. They seemed surprised at how cold it became at night on the prairie and were fooled by distances, thinking the hills were much closer than they actually were. They scrawled messages on boards and rocks and animal bones for those who followed. Just that morning she saw a buffalo skull bearing the ominous message *For God's sake, turn back now*. Beside it, standing crookedly in the earth, was a plank of wood in the shape of a crude cross. Etched into it with a red-hot piece of iron were words that tore at her heart. *Jane Ellis, Died May 8, 1865, Aged Two Months.*

These homesteaders had sold off their land back home, many saving for months and years to afford the trip west. They filled up their wagons with household goods and furnishings, much of which had to be discarded along the way when the load proved too heavy for the draft animals. She admired their tenacity and their determination to provide a better life for their children. But what about the Lakota children whose futures were uncertain because of it? More than ever, she felt herself torn between two worlds, a part of each, yet belonging to neither.

After placing a feedbag on his horse, Ned joined Katie by the fire. Squatting on his heels, he mused, "I wonder how much further we have to go."

"Three hundred miles, from what the wagon master said," she replied as she tossed another oxen chip onto the fire, causing the flames to flare.

"They burn admirably," Ned remarked.

"I grew up using buffalo chips for our fires. They didn't throw sparks onto our bedding or clothes," she said, adding with a chuckle, "and with them in our cooking fire we didn't need pepper." But her soft laughter died to a regretful tone. "Of course, most of the buffalo are gone now."

The strains of a fiddle and the accompanying twang of a banjo overrode the sudden silence that descended over them. Katie watched as the weary emigrants found the energy to rise from their fires and dance to the tune of *Buffalo Gals*.

"How wonderfully they dance," Ned remarked.

"The wonderful thing," she said, "is that after all they've been through they dance at all."

The tune summoned a memory. The place and time were different, but the dancing in the midst of despair was all too familiar.

It was the year before Blue Water. The buffalo had been moving southward in long, dark rows. The scent of snow was on the wind, and the air filled with the sound of popping trees as frigid temperatures caused the branches to split.

In the cabin she shared with her father along the Laramie, a spiral of pewter smoke rose from the iron kettle hung from a tripod over the fire and traveled up the stone chimney to mingle with the pale daylight. Outside, the sound of a horse's hooves crunched against the hard-packed snow. The rustle of branches, and a lusty voice thick with an Irish brogue, brought her head up from the rabbit stew she was stirring in the kettle.

"Open the door, Katie!"

Rushing to the door, she stood aside as her father dragged a fresh-cut fir tree into the cabin. Snow fell from the shoulders of Tom McCabe's buckskin shirt, melting upon contact with the heated air of the cabin. "Fetch me a bucket."

She pulled the milk bucket off its peg on the wall and gave it a shake to dislodge any tiny creature that might have taken refuge inside.

McCabe placed the rough-hewn trunk of the tree into the bucket and held it in place while she threw in handfuls of pine bark to keep the tree standing straight.

Later, as shadows of night were stretching across the hills, McCabe sat in his old pine rocker, the smoke from his pipe filling the cabin with the sweet fragrance of sumac leaves and the bark of the dogwood, a mixture the Sioux called kinnikinnik, while she decorated the tree with scraps of calico cloth and colorful ribbons he'd brought back from Fort Laramie.

Suddenly, the door flung open. A gust of wind blew snow into the cabin, followed by a tall, red-headed man and an Indian woman.

Dropping what she was doing, she had rushed to greet her brother and his Brulè wife.

The pair shed their heavy buffalo hide robes and warmed their hands by the fire. "We left the village two days ago," Richard McCabe said. "The snow's so deep in places I didn't think we'd make it in time for Christmas."

"Tis best to be careful on the trail," McCabe had said. "These're uncertain times. I heard at Laramie that all friendly Indians have been ordered to move to the agency."

"In this weather it'll take time to gather them all together," her brother had said.

"Aye," said McCabe. "Them soldiers at Laramie are carolin' now, but come spring they'll be on the march lookin' for hold-outs. When ye get back to yer village, tell Little Thunder to strike the lodges and go into the hills until this mess blows over."

"Enough of that talk, you two," she had complained. "It's Christmas and I've been cooking all day. Sit down and let's eat."

She spooned rabbit stew into burl bowls and set a tin dish of salt-rising bread on the table for dunking. For dessert there was a vinegar pie and preserved berries.

After McCabe had eaten his fill and the table was cleared, he sat back and said, "That was delicious, Katie, m'darlin'. Now I'm thinkin' there're some presents under that tree just beggin' to be opened."

The ominous military threat had been momentarily forgotten as the gifts, wrapped in brown paper and tied with string, were brought forth. There was a bone-handle knife for Richard, a beaded tobacco pouch for McCabe, a new calico dress for Katie, and for Bone Bracelet, Richard's Brulè wife who didn't understand the Christian holiday, a tin mirror.

Sounds of merriment streamed from the little cabin along the Laramie. Katie taught her sister-in-law the English words to Silent Night and Bone Bracelet sang along with her mis-pronounced words.

Afterwards, Richard played *Buffalo Gals* on the fiddle and

McCabe danced a lively Irish jig while singing along.

Buffalo Gals won't you come out tonight
Come out tonight, come out tonight
Buffalo Gals won't you come out tonight
To dance by the light of the moon

What they didn't know was that in that Moon of Popping Trees the soldiers had already started up the Platte with their big wagon guns in search of hold-outs, and life as they knew it was about to change forever.

"You never said where you're headed, or why."

Ned's voice drew Katie away from haunting memories of the past. "St. Louis," she answered.

"Do you have relatives there?"

"I did. Once. But no more."

The flames cast a reflective glow over her face as she looked away from the dancers and gazed out into the darkness beyond the circle of wagons, to the prairie at night and the way the sun sank low, sending shadows down from the rolling hills in the distance. With the wagon train covering a good ten miles a day, and three hundred miles to go, each mile and every day took her further away from Black Moon.

It hadn't been her intention to go back to St. Louis, but she reasoned that perhaps once there, she might find some solace from everything that was uncertain on the harsh and often cruel plains. She would stay just long enough for the soot and grime of the city, for the steamboat whistles and crowded streets, to remind her, as it had once before, where she really belonged.

CHAPTER 9
LITTLE NOISES

The deep pit Black Moon dug held the glowing embers of the fire long after the flames had burned down. He sat motionless on the cold ground below the crest of a ridge, beneath a thick robe, moving only to add wood to replenish the flames. In a place such as this, lonely and obscure, he could sit and think. His spirit was troubled, and his heart was weighed down by sadness and uncertainty.

Far below, the land he knew since birth was changing. New tracks were made on the old trails, not by moccasins or pony drags, but by iron horse shoes and wagon wheels. And more soldier towns like the one on the Laramie were being built to protect travelers on the Powder River Road and the Holy Road. What did his mother, the Earth, think of all these changes? Was she as saddened by them as he was?

As the western sky turned as dark as soot, Black Moon felt the burden of leadership heavy upon his shoulders. The buffalo herds were shrinking, the Long Knives were multiplying, and the emigrant trains were bringing diseases that swept through entire villages. The Long Knives would not stop until every single Lakota was either corralled on the agencies or dead. To die fighting was a good thing for a warrior like himself, but what about the ones left behind to face a life of confinement on the agencies? Yes, they would be alive, but being alive and living were not the same thing. Deep down inside he knew that the Lakota were but a flickering flame in a strong wind.

Each thrust by the Long Knives was like a lance to his heart. Yet another thrust had come, this one not from the hated Long Knives, but from one Black Moon loved despite everything, the one he called *Mitawa*, My Own.

For a man who followed his own inner voice, why did he find it hard to accept that Katie was following hers? Perhaps it was because he had always thought of their voices as one. He just never imagined that her voice would steer her away from him.

When he returned from the council at Crazy Horse's village and found her gone, he nearly went out of his mind with worry. He went about the village with a straight back and the sure step of a man who knew where he had been and where he was going, but those closest to him knew that with Katie's leaving, a part of him was crumbling inside. As the days passed, a darkness filled his heart, and instead of her warm, woman's body beside him each night, he took his anger to bed.

How many nights had he lain awake watching her breathing beside him? He loved listening to the little noises she made in sleep. He always thought they were sounds of contentment. When did it change? When did her happiness turn to discontent? He never thought of being anyone other than who he was. For him, it was enough just to be. But as much as he wanted to believe that she was Lakota, the truth was that she was not. She was white, and the white people always wanted more than what they had. They wanted to be more than what they were.

He had always just assumed he would take a Lakota woman for his wife. Who would have thought that a green-eyed white woman would steal his heart like a common thief, or that this fierce Oglala warrior would be driven to his knees over it? He told himself that his responsibility was to his people, not to his own desires. This was not the time for weakness. Too many things were happening to his land and his people for his mind and heart to be elsewhere. And yet, thoughts of her haunted him, and even as he told himself he should hate her for leaving, even now, he loved her.

The wound at his shoulder began to ache. It was a relentless reminder of the time two winters past when he'd been recovering in a Cheyenne camp from a bluecoat's bullet, and Katie found him there, and thinking he had left her for a Cheyenne girl, she had almost died in the snow. The warmth of his body had brought her back to him then. What, if anything, would bring her back to him now?

Finding no answers to the turmoil that drove him to seek this lonely, windswept place, he pulled his robe tighter around himself and sat before the dying fire, feeling lost and wondering if those little noises had been a sign of things to come.

CHAPTER 10
THE BLOODY BOZEMAN

The wind changed, and the clouds parted overhead. With the wagons circled for the night, Katie lifted her face toward the light of the moon, unaware that Ned was watching her intently.

His voice drifted into the air across the crackle of the fire. "The wagon and oxen cost me four hundred dollars, and the supplies a thousand. I figure if I sell everything, I can make some of my money back. And I still have about a hundred dollars left from the cash I brought along to pay for supplies, ferry tolls, wagon parts, and food for the first winter on the frontier." He paused to gather his courage. "I don't have much to offer, but I'm a hard worker. Katie, I'd be mighty honored if you'd come back to Little Falls with me. In time, we could build a good life for ourselves."

She looked at him. He had changed from his dusty daytime clothes into clean trousers and a linen shirt beneath a black vest held closed in front by little horn buttons. When he leaned forward to toss a stick onto the fire, she noticed that the back of the vest was of printed calico with a buckle. With a start, she realized that he was wearing these clothes for her. When had his feelings for her changed from friendly accommodation to something more?

In answer to the plaintive plea in his tone, she said, "Ned, you're a fine man, and one day you'll find a woman to fill the emptiness you're feeling now, but I'm not the one. If I were to be with any man, it would be my husband."

"You're married?" His surprise echoed in his disappointment.

"Yes," she softly replied.

"I can't imagine any man letting you go."

"He didn't. I chose to leave. There's something I have to do."

"I can tell something's weighing heavily on you."

"Is it that obvious?"

"Not to anyone who's not looking close. These past weeks on the trail I noticed that you sometimes get this far-away look in your eyes. It was there just now when you were looking out on the prairie. It's as if you're searching for something…or someone."

"I am," Katie said.

"And that someone's not me."

The firelight danced in her long red hair when she shook her head. "It's me," she confessed. "I seem to have lost sight of myself. It's like the wind that blows sure and steady on the plains, hot in the summer and bone-chilling cold in the winter, but there, always there. And just when you think you know it, it blows up in ways you never imagined, swirling this way and that, like it's restless and looking for a place to settle. I've become like that restless wind."

He knew from their talks around the nighttime fires that she was born and raised in this harsh, unforgiving place, and she had hinted to spending time back east, but that was all he really knew about her.

"I don't blame you for wanting to find your place in the world," he said. "Heck, that's what I did when I sold the farm, auctioned off my livestock, packed up my family, and headed west."

"How did your wife feel about that?" she asked.

"Would you believe she liked the idea?" He smiled as the memory flooded back. "Women dream a lot of dreams while they're bending over a washtub." But like everything else he had lost, the smile died. "We're a lot alike, you and me. I've seen my share of tragedy, and I suspect so have you. I don't know anything about your husband, but I'll tell you this. He must be a good man to have gotten himself someone like you. And you're lucky to have him. Sometimes, we don't know what we have until we don't have it anymore. There's folks here who can tell you that. Some of them lost loved ones to Indian attacks along the Bozeman. You can't blame anyone for turning back. I guess we're lucky we haven't had any Indian attacks since we left Fort Phil Kearny six days ago."

"Tell me, Ned, have you ever heard of Red Cloud?" Katie asked.

"Oh, sure. Who hasn't? They say he's been on the warpath since Carrington arrived to build more forts. At Phil Kearny I heard some of the soldiers talking. They said there's no certainty about the attacks, except that one is always due at any given moment."

"And Crazy Horse?"

"Wasn't he was one of the leaders in the battle of the Platte River Bridge last year?

"And Black Moon?"

Ned suppressed a shudder. "I hear that one's the worst of the lot."

"I'll make more coffee," she said, adroitly changing the subject. Tossing the old grounds into the fire, she got up and went to the wagon. That morning she had roasted some coffee beans in a skillet and then ground them in the grinder, one of the few necessities Ned had refused to discard along the trail.

So much for Black Moon being a good man, Katie thought grimly as she tossed fresh coffee into the pot. She knew the truth, that beneath the fierce exterior beat a kind and generous heart, and that the things he did which struck terror into the white men was so that his people might live. Men like Ned Jeppsen didn't know him the way she did, as a humble man, a loyal son, a good husband, and an unrelenting warrior. They didn't know about his humility, how he shunned attention and yet always went first into battle. Far from perfect, he was often given to self-doubt, and yes, even fear, and was as familiar with grief as any of them.

Her love for Black Moon was without question. The passion he aroused in her was as vital as the air she breathed. Each time she watched him lead his horse away through the circle of lodges to fight the Crow or the Pawnee or the soldiers, the fear in her heart was but a minor thing compared to the excitement of watching him come riding back in with an expression of victory on his handsome face and the thrill of battle firing up his lovemaking later that night. To these people, he was something to fear. To her, he was a man, no more, no less. And no matter where the restless wind took her, he would always be in her heart. And that was by far the safest place for him to be, for as Claw was fond of saying, the heart is stronger than stone.

She dipped the ladle into the water bucket strapped to the side of the wagon next to the brake lever and was about to fill the coffee pot when the muted cry of a screech owl froze her in mid-motion. She glanced quickly around the circle of wagons. No one seemed to notice it, not even Ned who appeared to be lost in thought. The plucky little owls hunted at night, waiting on perches to swoop down on small nocturnal creatures. But there were no trees on the prairie upon which to perch. Turning toward the darkened land beyond the circle of wagons, Katie's gaze swept back and forth in a wide arc. A shiver coursed up and down her spine. She knew an Indian signal when she heard one.

Dropping the coffee pot, she looked around and spotted the wagon master squatting before one of the cook fires, smoking his pipe, and rushed to him. "Mr. Bass, may I speak with you privately?"

He tapped the tobacco out of his pipe and tossed it into the fire. Reaching for his wide-brim felt hat, he got up and followed her behind one of the wagons.

Hooking his thumbs into the suspenders holding up his canvas-like pants, he asked, "What's on your mind, miss?"

Katie lowered her voice and said, "You need to get everyone under their wagons. There's going to be an attack."

"Don't worry, miss," he said in a placating tone. "Contrary to popular belief, Indians are among the least of our problems in transit. Oh, yes, there have been a few isolated incidents, but the majority of settlers make their cross-continent journeys without encountering trouble. Any Indians we see will likely come begging for sugar, flour or tobacco."

"Mr. Bass, I am telling you—" she began warningly.

"And as head of this wagon train, I am telling you that while Indian attacks have happened, they've mostly been by the Shoshone on trains moving west, and we're traveling east."

"These aren't Shoshone," Katie said urgently. "They're Sioux.

Probably Oglala. And most likely it's Red Cloud."

The wagon master gave a caustic laugh. "You've been reading too many dime-store novels, miss. Assuming you know how to read."

Katie bunched her fists with convulsive anger, not only from his insulting insinuation that she could not read, but by his pigheadedness that was going to cost these emigrants their lives.

"They don't call this trail the bloody Bozeman for nothing," she said, tersely echoing Jasper Gillette's graphic description.

"As I recall, you were given a place aboard this wagon train back at Fort Phil Kearny," he said. "If I were you, I wouldn't go stirring up trouble for these poor people. They've been through enough." With that, he turned and walked away.

Racing back to the wagon, Katie grabbed Ned's Kentucky percussion rifle from inside. Pulling the feed bag off his horse, she threw on the saddle and hastily untied its halter from the wagon and was about to lead it away when a flaming arrow shot past her and hit the wagon. The horse let out a frightened whinny as the canvas burst into flames.

Within moments, all hell broke loose as a swarm of mounted Indians converged on the circled wagons. Bullets splintered the wagon boxes. The canvas covers were shredded by arrows and burst into flames. Women ran screaming and crying. The oxen were bellowing. Katie watched horrified as one man took an arrow in his back. Another was wounded in the face. The wagon master was shot and killed where he stood. From beneath the wagons came the pop of returning gunfire as the panicked emigrants fired blindly into the darkness.

Ned looked about wildly. His wagon and many others were on fire. Above the roar of the flames and the pop-pop of gunfire he heard the wild whoops and hollers of Indians. From out of the mayhem he saw a horse bearing down on him. As it pulled alongside him, he heard Katie's frantic voice shout out to him.

"Get on!"

For one incalculable moment he stood rooted to the ground, unable to move. An arrow whizzed by his head, jolting him into action. Reaching for the hand she held out to him, he grasped it and jumped up behind her.

With a savage kick they were off. Galloping through the circle, dodging flying arrows and bullets, they sailed over the tongue of one of the wagons and tore across the dark prairie, not daring to look back.

CHAPTER 11
A PILE OF WOOD

Daylight found them following a trail thick with saltbush and dotted with prairie dog villages. Keeping to the small trails off the Bozeman they struggled through crooked gorges scarcely wide enough for a wagon to pass through. At one point, Ned lifted his weary gaze, and suddenly realizing the direction in which they were heading, exclaimed, "Hey, this isn't the way to Fort McPherson."

"We're going to Fort Reno," Katie said.

"But that'll take us right into the heart of the Indian trouble. You saw what they did to the wagon train."

"Your horse won't make it all the way to Fort McPherson. But don't worry. The Sioux don't regard Fort Reno as much of a threat, so they're not likely to attack."

They passed a hungry night in a sage-covered valley off the trail. As they sat quietly shivering against the cold, Ned asked, "How is it you know so much about what the Sioux will and won't do?"

"My father was a trader and my brother was married to a Brulè girl."

"How'd you know those Indians were going to attack the wagons?"

"I heard their signal."

"Did you learn that from your father?"

"No. I learned that from my husband."

"Is he a trader?"

"He is Oglala. His name is Black Moon."

"Black—" Ned nearly choked on the name. "Oh, Lord. I had a feeling there's more to you than meets the eye. All right, Katie, you might as well tell me the rest."

And so, she told him. All of it. From the tragedy on Blue Water Creek to this moment.

For several minutes he said nothing as her incredible story unfolded. Then, nodding toward her feet he said, "I was wondering about those. You don't see many white women wearing calico and moccasins."

"I thought elk skin might attract too much attention," Katie said with a laugh. "As for these…" She wiggled her feet. "It's been a long time since I wore shoes. Moccasins are much more comfortable and make a lot more sense since the hard leather soles of boots slip badly on smooth grass."

"Do you love him?" he asked suddenly.

If she was surprised by his question, she gave no indication of it, replying smoothly, "More than life itself."

A paralyzed silence fell over them. Feeling the weight of his eyes upon her, Katie lifted her gaze and said, "I wouldn't blame you if you got on that horse and rode as far and as fast away from me as you can."

"You didn't run out on me. You saved my life. Why would I run out on you? Because your husband is a dangerous Sioux warrior?"

Katie looked at him by the light of the moon. This naïve, hopeful pilgrim had come west to carve out a better life for himself and his family, not knowing what he would find. Yet despite the heartache and disappointment he encountered, he was as courageous in his way as the man she'd left behind. They were not so very different, the Lakota warrior and the Minnesota farmer. They were about the same age, and both men possessed generous hearts and a fierce determination to protect those they loved. She caught herself wondering if she could ever love a man like Ned Jeppsen. She supposed she could, but it would pale in comparison to the all-consuming love she felt for Black Moon.

If Ned was unconvinced of their safety, his first glimpse of Fort Reno the following morning gave him even more reason to fret. It sat on a small rise carpeted with thistle by the north bank of the Powder River, surrounded by arroyos and low washes whose cracked mud beds made good hiding places for Indian war parties. The outpost itself was a mass of weatherworn logs with a few crude buildings and a stockade. Standing guard over its section of the Bozeman Trail, it was a way station and forwarding supply depot for Fort Phil Kearny.

They rode past a lonely trading post and a ferry crossing, and as they approached the fort, they could see its two defensive bastions holding mountain howitzers, with rifle loopholes bored through the adobe walls, giving the place the look of a prison.

"They call this a fort?" Ned muttered under his breath of the unimpressive pile of wood when they passed through the gate.

"At least we can get some rest," Katie said.

"And then what?"

She shrugged. "You get the horse fed and watered and find the sutler's store where we can get some supplies, and I'll see about getting us an escort to Fort McPherson, or at least as far as Fort Laramie."

As Ned led the horse away, Katie brushed the dust from the skirt of her dress, smoothed down her hair, and made her way across the parade ground. Fighting down her disdain for men in regimental blue, she forced as much calmness as she could muster into her demeanor, and approached one of them. "Can you tell me who is in command here?"

"That would be Captain Proctor," the soldier replied.

"And where will I find him?"

"He's over yonder with Captain Fetterman."

Shielding her eyes from the glare of the sun, she looked in the direction in which he pointed at a building of cottonwood logs chinked with mud daub and a sod covered roof, and headed toward it.

Inside, two men were engaged in conversation.

"I heard it went pretty bad at the Laramie council," Captain Joseph Proctor said as he leaned back in his chair with his dusty boots propped up on the desk.

"It was a disgusting farce," spat the other, "with those damn Indians telling us how we drove away the buffalo and threatening that if we dare venture into Powder River Country, our command won't have a hoof left. I have no doubt of the ability of my regiment to whip the Sioux wherever we find them."

"Be careful William. I'm sure Red Cloud would have something to say about that."

Captain William Fetterman snorted with contempt. "You should have seen him. He stood there with his chin jutting out, saying how we stole the road and that he wouldn't talk to us anymore and that as long as he lived he would fight us. Colonel Carrington was furious, but he didn't let on."

"Well, Carrington's at Phil Kearny now, and with the hits they've been taking from the Sioux, he has his hands full. For all the filth and squalor of this place, I'd rather be here than anywhere between the north bank of the Powder and the gold camps of Montana. At least here we have a chance of staying alive."

"You can stay here at Reno if you want," Fetterman said, "but I'm leaving for Phil Kearny with orders installing me as second in command of the Eighteenth Infantry Regiment. I'm not one for sitting around. I can't wait to get into the field. Give me a good Indian fight."

Their conversation was interrupted by a knock on the door.

"Come in," Proctor called.

At the sight of the red-haired woman who entered, he hastily removed his boots from the desk. The legs of his chair thudded against the planked floor as he rose.

"Excuse me, gentlemen," Katie said as she entered, "but I am in need of your assistance."

"We are at your service, ma'am. I am Captain Proctor." He nodded toward his companion. "And this is Captain William Fetterman."

Her gaze went to the man with the wild, dark muttonchops and the smoldering glare who stood by the window.

So, he thinks he can whip the Sioux, she thought contemptuously, having overhead his arrogant claim through the open window. He was like so many of the others, a soldier who understood little about men like Red Cloud and Black Moon and less about Indian warfare, and she could not help but wonder where his hubris would lead him.

"What can we do for you, ma'am?"

Turning back to Captain Proctor, Katie said, "Our wagon train was attacked two days ago. We were fortunate enough to escape and make it here."

"We?"

"Mr. Jeppsen and I."

Fetterman came forward, his gaze moving pointedly to the moccasins on her feet. "It must have been Red Cloud making good on the threat he made at the Laramie council."

"I'll send Company B of the Second Battalion out to assess the situation," Proctor said.

"That's not advisable," Fetterman cut in. "All seven companies of the Second Battalion of the Eighteenth Infantry will be riding with me to Phil Kearny. Since July there have been casualties and loss of livestock. My sources tell me that in one raid alone, two hundred mules and some horses were stolen. If Red Cloud is on the warpath, you'll need the remainder of your regiments right here."

"Good God, man," Proctor objected. "Someone has to see to those poor souls."

Fetterman aimed a penetrating stare at Katie and asked, "Do you know if anyone survived the attack?"

Katie had never met Red Cloud, but the leader of the Bad Faces had earned a reputation as one of the most feared warriors on the plains, known for his bravery, stealth, and brutality. It wasn't likely that he and his warriors had left anyone from the wagon train alive. Swallowing hard, she said, "It didn't appear that way."

"You are welcome to stay here under our protection," Proctor said.

"We would rather continue on to our original destination, Fort McPherson," she said. "But you can appreciate our reluctance to make the journey alone. I was wondering if you could provide an escort for us."

"Sorry ma'am," Fetterman said, "but that's out of the question. And now, if you will excuse us, we have matters to discuss."

Katie stiffened at his brusque dismissal. "Thank you, gentlemen," she said, and turned quickly away.

She stepped out into the early-morning sunlight, feeling restive and uneasy and not knowing what her next move would be. She had planned to merely do a little trading at Fort Phil Kearny, but once there, her gaze had wandered idly about the garrison, taking in the sights and sounds of everything she had left behind, each memory stinging like the lash of a whip. So, she had joined a wagon train of disillusioned emigrants heading east, returning to the only place she knew where she could get away from it all. St. Louis. She told herself she needed distance from the growing hostilities between the Sioux and the Army, from the ever-constant wondering of what her life would have been had she married Josh McIntyre, the handsome cavalry lieutenant who'd been in love with her, from the relentless heartache of losing a child, from loving a Lakota warrior who, at any moment, might be killed in battle, and from the despair that came from feeling lost and alone.

She had hoped to get to Fort McPherson and send a telegraph to the lawyer in St. Louis who was handling her Aunt Virginia's estate, asking him to wire sufficient funds for her to purchase some suitable clothes and a train ticket for the trip back east and to arrange a hotel room for her there. It wasn't likely she would want to stay in the big house overlooking the river that Colonel Abner Beauregard had built for her aunt. Too many memories resided in that house, bittersweet memories of Josh McIntyre, and acrimonious memories of her aunt.

Virginia Devlin Beauregard had been a domineering woman who thought the wildness could be bred out of Katie with silks and satins and who, after suffering a debilitating stroke, had shrewdly extracted a promise from her niece to remain in St. Louis for a year while she recuperated. A whole year away from Black Moon had felt to Katie like an eternity, and in the end, she returned to the country around the North Platte, choosing her love for him over the vast inheritance left to her when her aunt succumbed.

As Katie stood gazing across the dusty parade ground, she thought about the inheritance. All that money was just sitting in a bank earning interest. Suddenly, something Jasper Gillette said came back to her. "There's no telling what all that money could buy." Like arms and ammunition for Black Moon to continue his fight against the bluecoats, she dared to think. Slowly, the idea took shape in her brain. She could discreetly purchase the arms and pay to have them transported west. It was risky, but not impossible. The inheritance, however, came with a stipulation. In order to claim it, she had to make St. Louis her permanent home. Could she do it? Could she give up the man she loved in order to help him save his people?

For several moments she weighed her options, the ends of her long red hair flicking about in a stiff autumn breeze, when she heard Captain Fetterman's voice stream through the open window.

"I am confident we can defeat Red Cloud, Sitting Bull, and Black Moon. We should follow General Connor's orders to his subordinate officers to find the hostile tribes and kill all the males over the age of twelve. Better yet, over the age of seven."

"You're talking about killing children," Captain Proctor exclaimed.

"Those children will one day be the warriors who will kill us," came the stony response.

A chill careened down Katie's spine when she realized the danger Little Storm and all the other innocent Lakota children were in. As she stood in the middle of the parade ground with the wind against her face, she resolved that St. Louis would have to wait.

Ned was emerging from the sutler's store with a package in his hands when he looked up and saw Katie hurrying toward him. "I got us a few things we'll need for the ride to Fort McPherson."

"We're not going to Fort McPherson," she said. "They can't spare any troops for an escort."

"Are they expecting trouble here?" he asked, trying to keep the alarm out of his tone. "I thought you said Indians don't attack Fort Reno."

"They don't. The regiment is riding to Fort Phil Kearny to join Colonel Carrington. And I'm going to find Black Moon."

"What!"

"They're planning something terrible, Ned. I have to warn him."

"What about St. Louis?"

"I have to do this first."

"Katie, be reasonable."

"I am being reasonable," she insisted, her mouth tightening. "And there's no use trying to talk me out of this."

He stared at her for a moment. The courage and strength in life demanded of men were rare to find in a woman, but this one possessed both in abundance. Her jaw was set, and in those fiery green eyes Ned saw the rigid determination that told him it was useless to argue. "Are you asking me to go with you?"

"No, of course not. That would be asking too much. But..." She paused. "There is something you can do for me. I know the money in your pocket is all you have left in the world, but could you buy me a horse?"

"What about my horse?"

"You'll need it to get to Laramie or McPherson, or wherever you decide to go from here."

"The only place I'm going from here is with you," he declared.

"Ned, I can't ask you to do that. It's dangerous out there."

"Well, I figure if we meet up with any Indians, if you tell them who your husband is, maybe they won't scalp us."

Katie suppressed the impulse to laugh at his naïve optimism.

"Besides," he added, "I don't much care for this little godforsaken post."

"We have days of travel ahead and miles of prairie to cross," she said. "Take a good look around. In a few days you'll look back fondly on this little godforsaken post."

He took her by the arm and turned her toward the sutler's store. "Come on. Let's see if we can trade these boots of mine for a pair of moccasins, and then let's buy you a horse and saddle."

"We'll need another gun, too," Katie said.

Ned smiled wryly. "And I'll bet you know how to use it."

It cost Ned a five-dollar gold piece from his savings to buy the .50 caliber Hawken muzzleloader from the blacksmith. Cupping his hands, he hoisted Katie into the saddle of the horse he bought, handed the Hawken up to her, and climbed aboard his own mount. Squinting up at the sun, he said, "We'd best be on our way if we want to cover enough ground before nightfall."

With a jingle of bridle bits and the squeak of saddle leather, they urged their horses to a trot and headed toward the big wooden gate, but just as they were about to depart Fort Reno, a voice called out behind them.

"Halt!"

Armed soldiers rushed toward them.

"What's the meaning of this?" Ned demanded when one of the soldiers grabbed his horse's reins and another grabbed Katie's.

"Captain Fetterman says you're not going anywhere."

As they were led away under armed escort, Katie sat stoically on her mount, green eyes fixed stonily ahead, her defenses going up to guard her like Black Moon's smoked buffalo hide shield. Her experiences at the hands of the bluecoats had never been good, and she sensed that this time would be no different.

CHAPTER 12
THE HEART OF ALL THINGS

After several weeks alone in the wilderness, Black Moon returned to the Oglala village nestled in a wide gully that opened onto the Tongue River valley. In the days that followed, he hunted alone, bringing down rabbits and pronghorns with his arrows. At night, with the rhythmic pounding of the drums sounding like the heartbeat of Mother Earth, he sat by himself under a thick robe, taking no part in the dancing. A chill breeze blew over the land, and in this *Waniyetu Wi,* Winter Moon, his heart felt as bare as the branches of the trees.

His friends tried in vain to lift his spirits. "Perhaps you should take another wife," Swift Bear suggested. "It will help settle your restlessness."

For his effort he received a scowling look.

"We have made some good hunts," said Crazy Horse, hoping to draw his friend out of his sullen mood. When that didn't work, he added, "Let us go against the wood wagons again. A good victory is what you need."

Shooting a heated look at Crazy Horse, Black Moon said, "You, of all men, should know what it is like to love a woman."

All around the fire knew he was referring to Black Buffalo Woman, the niece of Red Cloud, who Crazy Horse had been openly courting. The only problem was that she was another man's wife, and although it was a Lakota woman's right to divorce her husband, it was equally obvious that Black Buffalo Woman's husband was not about to let her go.

Black Moon spoke in a voice scarcely louder than the crackling fire. "The only one hurting over my woman leaving is me. But if you pursue the woman you desire, many others will be hurt. Black Buffalo Woman's husband should not be underestimated. Ever since he was passed over as a Shirt Wearer in favor of you, there has been bad blood between your people and his. I would watch out for that one. If he thinks you have been intimate with his wife, he would be within his right to cut off the tip of her nose before throwing her away. And there is no telling how he would avenge himself on you. You would also be stripped of the bighorn shirt. That is something I know about," he added, his tone reeking with bitterness. "And I can tell you, there is no honor in that." With that, he got up and stalked off, leaving his friends shaking their heads.

As the setting sun bathed the autumn clouds in shades of lavender, Claw found Black Moon sitting beneath an old cedar tree on a hillside overlooking the village, smoking his short-stemmed pipe, the sign that he had lost a place of high honor.

Dropping to the ground beside his son, Claw reached into the bag at his belt and took out his own pipe. The bowl was carved from the deep red stone that came from Pipestone Creek, and the accompanying stem was made of ash. He moistened the stem with his lips, inserted it into the barrel, and gave it a short twist. Holding a pinch of red willow tobacco between his thumb and forefinger, he offered it to the sky, the four directions, and the earth, placed it in the pipe, lit it, and took several puffs.

With the fragrant smoke swirling around his head, he said, "The days grow shorter. Soon, the snows will be deep and the winter winds will howl like wolves. Many of the summer camps have already moved to winter locations. We must strike the lodges, load everything onto the drag poles, and move to the heart of all things, to that little secluded cottonwood valley in the shadow of *Mato Paha* for better protection against the coming winter moons. It is time to return to the sacred hills."

Somewhere in the foothills a bull elk whistled as a contemplative silence fell upon Black Moon. Returning to the *paha sapa*, the heart of all things, always felt like coming home. The hills were the center of the Lakota world. It was where the Sun Dances were held and the strongest lodge poles were gathered. It was where, as a boy on the edge of manhood, he had hunted and played. It was where he had gone to discover his path and had the vision that told him he would be a leader of his people. As much as he loved the Powder River country and the shadowy pines of the Shining Mountains, no place gave his life meaning more than the sacred Black Hills.

Yet the hills of his youth were changing. Bearded, unkempt white men set up tents along the streams where they dipped flat pans into the water and swirled it around. They were trespassers and thieves, stealing the yellow metal from the streams the way the whites stole the land.

"The people are waiting for a sign from you to pack their things." Claw said, drawing Black Moon away from his thoughts.

"We cannot move," Black Moon objected. "What if she returns and does not find us here?"

"You are no longer a reckless boy," Claw responded. "You are a man who has seen more than thirty winters and you are responsible for more than yourself. You belong to the people."

The high, lonesome call of snow geese heading south for the winter drew Black Moon's gaze skyward. "I wish I could follow them," he muttered absently.

"Your place is not to follow," Claw said. "It is to lead."

"I no longer wear the bighorn shirt," Black Moon reminded his father. "They took that away from me a long time ago."

"Tomorrow is shaped by what we learn from yesterday."

Black Moon knew his father was referring to the incident that had cost him the bighorn shirt and compelled him to smoke the short-stem, when he had defied the wishes of the council and attacked a group of miners, resulting in the death of his young cousin. Even now, so many winters later, the memory still haunted him.

As if reading his son's thoughts, Claw admonished, "No amount of guilt can change the past. You do not have to be a Shirt Wearer to lead. Your power was given to you through your vision." His tone softened. "You are a man like all other men. You make mistakes and you suffer for them. But you are also a man like no other. You are not fearless, yet you act in spite of your fear. You understand the responsibility of leading men into battle. The day will come when the old ones will call their grandsons to their sides to tell them a hero story, and the story they tell will be of you."

"Hiyu wo, takoja wica wawoptetusni wan tawoecun ociciyakin ktelo." Come, grandsons, I want to tell you a hero story. Black Moon could still hear his grandfather's voice calling him and his brother to his side by the fire on cold winter nights to tell them stories about the men who had come before them, those who fought their Crow and Pawnee enemies, those who ran off the first white men, and those who advocated for peace. Even back then, before his brother had seen six winters, and he five, he recalled how the stories of the war heroes had always filled him with awe, while his brother's face would light up at the stories about the peace-talkers. It was a difference that divided them right up to the end, and Black Moon could not help but wonder whose hero story Claw was telling to Little Storm.

Tapping the ashes out of the bowl, Claw said, "For the first years of your life you belonged to your mother and grandmothers. After you learned courage from them, you learned the way of the warrior from the Miniconjou."

He was speaking of Lone Horn, a leader of fighting men, who had taken Black Moon under his wing. A man of his reputation could have chosen the son of any influential family to mentor, but he chose instead the reticent son of Claw, sensing in the young Oglala a self-confidence and a strength that would serve the people well in the hard times ahead. The lifelong friendship that had been forged between them ended in the battle on Box Elder Creek when Lone Horn had staked himself out and was mortally wounded by bluecoat bullets before Black Moon could get to him in time to pull the Miniconjou's lance out of the ground.

"You are the man you have become not because of your mother and grandmothers, or because of the Miniconjou's teachings," Claw went on, "but because of the fires inside you. When you were born, I sang a welcoming song for you. I felt the strength within the little bundle I held in my arms, but more important, I felt the promise of hope for the people. It is time for you to stop walking around as if you are dead and put the needs of the people ahead of your own."

As Black Moon looked out over the ridges and rolling hills, his father's words brought his fire flaring to life. Lakota culture and his own inner voice would not allow him to be any less than what he was—a warrior and a leader. As a warrior, he was prepared to give all that he was on behalf of the people. As a leader, it was his place to go first into battle and be the first to meet any challenge. His back straightened, his eyes flashed, and the old vehemence rifled his tone.

"Tomorrow is also shaped by what we do today. We will make a hunt. When the meat packs are full, we will strike the lodges and move to the heart of all things and make the winter camp at *Mato Paha*. Then I will gather my warriors and go against those who would steal Lakota land and Lakota lives. I will do this so that the people may live."

Satisfied, Claw cleaned the pipe bowl, detached the stem, blessed the pipe, and placed it back into its beaded pouch. "The trader is here. He comes from the camp of the Bad Faces with news. He is waiting in your lodge to speak with you." He got up and stretched his legs. Looking down at his son, he said, "A Lakota warrior defends the people. That does not mean that now and then something will not kick you hard. The woman will return to you if it is *Wakan Tanka's* wish."

CHAPTER 13
THE TRADER

In all the years since Jasper Gillette set out from Maine to make his fortune in the unchartered west, roaming the Upper Missouri trading blankets, beads, and guns for buffalo robes and beaver pelts, he'd had his share of violent run-ins with the tribes, but he never felt as close to dying as he did right now.

He remembered a time when Lakota land stretched from the Muddy River in the east, to the Running Water and the Shell in the south, to the Shining Mountains in the west, and around to the Elk River east to the Knife flowing back into the Muddy. The people moved with the change of seasons and the movement of the buffalo. But while the seasons continued their eternal flow from one to the next, the buffalo herds that once covered the prairies from horizon to horizon had dwindled. With the arrival of the Union Pacific Railroad to the south also came the buffalo hunters whose deadly accurate .50-caliber Sharps rifles would soon wipe out whatever buffalo were left. Gillette felt a kinship with these people. His wife, after all, was Oglala. But the connection went deeper than that. If the buffalo went, so would the tribes, and so would men like himself.

Whatever affinity he may have felt vanished, however, when the hide flap covering the entrance to the lodge was swept aside and Black Moon entered.

He was dressed in a plain buckskin shirt, leggings and breech clout. His hair hung in two long black braids over his shoulders. Unlike his brethren who were fond of eagle feathers and ribbons, the only discernible adornment he wore was a scowl on his face as he stomped to his place and dropped to the ground, as fluidly and silently as rainfall. Despite the grace with which he moved, he was like flint, hard and easily sparked, much like the strike-a-light Gillette kept in a beaded pouch at his belt.

Gillette thought back to the last time he had seen Black Moon. That Black Moon had let him ride off unharmed that day had more to do, he suspected, with Katie than with any benevolence on the Oglala's part. But Katie wasn't here, and despite her claim that her husband knew the difference between his enemies and other white men, Gillette wasn't so sure he'd be leaving this village alive. Not with the news he'd come bearing.

Clearing his throat nervously, Gillette said, "I have come from the sacred hills where the Bad Faces have moved for the winter."

From across the fire, Black Moon's dark eyes assessed the trader with the same suspicion he had for all white men, but when he spoke, his voice was surprisingly soft and tinged with awe.

"The old ones say that in the time before time began *Ite*, the mother of the four winds, and *Iktomi*, the trickster, created *Pte Oyate* and chose the Wind Cave of the *paha sapa* as the place where we would be delivered from beneath the earth to the surface that was plentiful with game."

Gillette had once stood before the entrance of the Wind Cave and felt its breath upon his face. He did not know how or why the cave seemed to inhale and exhale like a living thing, only that it did. And who knew? Perhaps the Wind Cave had indeed brought forth *Pte Oyate*, the Buffalo Nation.

Black Moon went on in the same respectful tone. "We go to that holy place to gather our lodge poles, do the Sun Dance, seek visions, and place our dead high on scaffolds so that over time their flesh and bones become one with that most sacred of places. We do not own those hills. The *paha sapa* owns us."

Gillette had not expected to hear Black Moon speak in such

reverential terms and with such quiet dignity despite the fierceness of his demeanor, but then, there was much about Black Moon that Jasper Gillette did not know. Like why, for instance, was the *blotahunka*, this band's head warrior and revered fighter, not also a member of the *akicita*, the select society of warriors. Yet beneath his apparent composure, Gillette had only to glance at the red willow tripod to the right of the front entrance of the lodge upon which hung Black Moon's warrior things to know that this fighting man was in a constant state of readiness and not to be underestimated.

While Gillette struggled to find the words he had come to say, Black Moon spoke again. This time bitterness rankled his tone.

"The buffalo herds are shrinking, while the Long Knives' presence on our land is growing, and the emigrant trains that follow the Holy Road and the miners who travel the Powder River Trail bring disease to my people."

"The whites are building more iron roads and soon the Powder River Trail will no longer be necessary as a route to the yellow metal," Gillette said.

"And the Holy Road?"

Hesitantly, Gillette replied, "The whites see opportunity in the west and to get there they must travel the Holy Road, what they call the Oregon Trail. I do not think they can be stopped."

"Is that what you have come to tell me?"

Gillette shifted uneasily in his cross-legged position before the fire. "There is more."

"I have endured the loss of my brother, my mother, a favorite cousin, a good friend, and my only child. I have survived a bluecoat's bullet and their iron cage. I am not afraid to hear whatever it is you have to say."

Proceeding cautiously, Gillette said, "You will remember I told you that Katie went with a wagon train to Fort McPherson."

"You have news of my wife?" Black Moon asked eagerly, his calm deserting him at the mention of Katie's name.

Drawing in a deep, supportive breath, Gillette said, "The wagon train was attacked before it reached Fort McPherson."

A tense stillness came over Black Moon. "How do you know

this?'

"Because it was Red Cloud who attacked it. My wife lives among the Bad Faces. I learned about it when I returned to her village."

"What else did you learn?"

There was no turning back. Gillette swallowed hard. "There were no survivors."

Black Moon winced as the news hit him with the impact of an arrow. No! It was not possible that *Wakan Tanka* would have taken her from him!

In the firelight that glanced off the planes of Black Moon's face Gillette saw his expression change from disbelief to raw anger, but never to acceptance. "Did anyone in Red Cloud's camp tell of a red-haired woman?"

"No, but—"

Without waiting to hear the rest, Black Moon leapt to his feet and sprang into action. Scooping up his hide saddle, he grabbed his rifle scabbard, bow, and otter skin quiver from the tripod and stormed to the entrance.

"Where are you going?" Gillette called out after him.

He paused to shoot a furious glance at the trader from over his shoulder. "She is not gone. If she was gone, I would know it in here." He pounded his chest with a clenched fist. Suddenly, nothing else mattered. Others could lead the hunt and the move to *Mato Paha*, but this was something only he could do.

Gillette followed Black Moon from the lodge and watched as he threw the hide saddle onto the bay gelding, untied the pony from its picket, and jumped astride its back.

With a savage kick, Black Moon galloped his pony past women hunched over cooking kettles, men sitting with their backs against trees sharpening arrows, and children playing games in the stiff November breeze.

The thunder of hooves drew Claw from his lodge in time to see his son sweep by with a look of vicious determination on his face. Spotting the trader, Claw rushed to him.

Upon hearing the trader's news, Claw shook his head. The woman. Always with his son it was about the woman. He recalled the time when Black Moon had brought the woman to live among them and had wanted her for his own, but Turning Hawk had refused. Even now, so many winters later, Claw shivered at Black Moon's words when admonished for wanting something that would never be his. *"Never?"* he had seethed. *"We will see about that."*

And when a Crow warrior abducted her, it was Black Moon who traveled alone and at great danger to himself deep into Crow territory to rescue her, even though she was his brother's wife.

Claw was troubled over his son's state of mind in the wake of losing the woman he loved. "Recklessness has always been my son's way," he told the trader. "While it serves to inspire his warriors to fight with him, I wonder if, now that his woman is gone, that recklessness might be the very thing that leads to his death." He placed a hand on the trader's buckskin-clad arm. "My friend, I would ask you to go with him. Take my pony. She is fast. You can catch up with him."

For several moments Gillette was silent as he contemplated the extent of what the old Oglala holy man was asking. "It is not likely he will want my company."

"That is true. My son does not welcome help from others. He prefers to do things his own way. But you have been a good friend to my people, and if what you say is true and my daughter-in-law did not survive the attack, he will need someone to remind him that to die in a reckless way is not what she would have wanted."

The trader looked down at the brown fingers encircling his arm and then up into the old man's dark, troubled eyes. They both knew that what Claw was asking was dangerous. Men swirling in grief were not always rational, particularly one for whom mistrust and belligerence were ingrained in his nature. There was a deep pause as thoughts darted through Gillette's mind. Finally, with a resolute sigh, he nodded.

Minutes later, the rawhide fringes on Jasper Gillette's shirt flicked about in the breeze as he galloped out of the Oglala camp astride Claw's fast pony.

CHAPTER 14
BLACK MOON'S WOMAN

"That's her. I'd recognize that face anywhere."

"Are you sure?"

"Yes sir, Captain Fetterman. I'm not likely to forget. It was when I was garrisoned at Fort Laramie some years back. They brought her in on orders from General Worth. She was to be escorted east by the Eleventh Ohio Cavalry to Fort Randall. You could hear her and the General yelling at each other in Old Bedlam. The General wanted to know where to find that renegade, Black Moon, and from what I heard, she refused to answer and gave him a real hard time."

"And why did he think she would know something like that?" Fetterman questioned.

"Because she's Black Moon's woman."

Captain William Fetterman's jaw tensed beneath his dark muttonchops. Turning a sulfurous glare on Katie, he asked, "Is this true?"

His stare unnerved her. "I—I— " she stammered.

Ned stepped forward and asserted, "She's my wife."

"How interesting," Fetterman remarked. "And did you know that your wife is or was living among the Sioux and that she is or was married to one of them?"

"I knew it," Ned tersely replied. "She was abducted and forced to live among them. From what I have heard, she wouldn't be the first white woman held captive."

"No, indeed. But if she was held against her will, why would she refuse to answer General Worth's question of where to find Black Moon?"

"She was fearful, of course."

"Of course," Fetterman repeated, his tone dripping with sarcasm. "And when did you two marry?"

Thinking quickly, and hoping Fetterman would not detect the nervous catch in his voice, Ned replied, "On the trail. A minister who was traveling with his wife on the wagon train performed the ceremony." It was partly true. There had been a minister traveling with them, but since he and his wife were killed with all the others when the Sioux attacked, there was no one left alive to refute Ned's story.

"Be that as it may," said Fetterman, sounding skeptical, "your wife will have some answering to do about that renegade Black Moon. She'll be coming with me to Fort Phil Kearny. We'll let Colonel Carrington decide what to do with her."

Ned started for the door. "I'll get the horses."

"You won't be coming with us. Until this matter is resolved you will have accommodations here. You are permitted free access to the compound, but you are not to leave the fort under any circumstance."

"You can't do that!" Ned exclaimed.

"I can, and I have." Turning to Katie, he said, "My regiment will be leaving shortly. We'll wait outside while you two say your goodbyes."

When Fetterman and his men had left the room, Katie turned a frightened gaze on Ned.

"Don't worry, Katie," he said soothingly. "I'll do whatever I can to help you."

"There's not much you can do here. But—" She hesitated.

"But what? Tell me what I can do."

She glanced quickly at the closed door and lowered her voice to a whisper. "If you can somehow get out of the fort, you could ride hard and fast to find Black Moon and—"

Ned's eyes grew wide.

"I know it's dangerous," she said urgently. "But he has to know what they're planning." She looked up at him, green eyes beseeching. "They're talking about killing children. *Children*, Ned." She saw him waver and knew she had struck a tender chord. "You were a father. They love their children as much as you loved yours."

"I wouldn't know where to find him," he said grimly.

"They most likely moved to Bear Butte on the northeastern edge of the Black Hills. There's a little cottonwood valley there where they make their winter camp."

"Good God, Katie, even if I could find the place, they'd kill me before I got the words out," he said with bleak certainty. He ran a hand through his hair, shaking his head. "Besides, I don't speak their language. If I could find them, and if they don't kill me on sight, how will they know what I'm telling them?"

"I'll teach you the words. *Cante waste nape ciyuzapo*. I greet you from my heart. Then ask for Claw. *Sake*. Claw. His wife speaks English. She'll translate the words for you."

Betraying Running-water Woman's secret might cause friction between Claw and his wife, but Katie trusted that Claw would place more importance on saving his people than on preserving marital harmony.

She also knew that all it would take for Ned to do what she was asking was to promise to return with him to Minnesota. It brought to mind the time she had promised to marry Lieutenant Josh McIntyre in return for his help in freeing Black Moon from the cell at Fort Laramie. Now, as then, she struggled with her conscience. How could she make a promise that she would not be able to keep? But more than that, how could she ask Ned to risk his life? She knew as well as anyone that an inexperienced white man alone in this wilderness was as good as dead.

She held his troubled gaze. Seeking to assuage his fear, she said, "On second thought, I have a better idea. I have a friend, the trader Jasper Gillette, who has helped me before. He goes to Fort Phil Kearny to trade. He'll know how to get word to Black Moon."

"Katie, I—" he began on a desperate note, and stopped, not knowing what to say.

At the apology she saw written in his eye, in a steadfast voice she told him, "Never apologize for wanting to stay alive." She took his hand in hers. "You're a good man, Ned Jeppsen. My only regret is that after today we won't see each other again. Go back to Little Falls and make a new life for yourself there."

He lifted her hands to his lips. "Katie, you are a brave and special woman. I would have been proud to call you my wife. Now I'll be honored to call you my friend."

She gave him a brief, heartrending smile before she broke free and left.

CHAPTER 15
COLD BUT ALIVE

"Mr. Peterson, I need your help."

The blacksmith turned his sweating face from the bellows when Ned entered the shed. "What can I do for you, Jeppsen? Don't tell me you need another horse."

"No. But I feel it's only right to tell you that the army won't like what I'm about to ask."

"I don't work for the army," the blacksmith replied.

Ned sat on a hard wooden bench and watched the blacksmith bring his hammer down on a red-hot iron, causing sparks to fly. "What's the best way to get out of here?"

"Yeah, I heard they took your wife away a couple days ago and they ain't letting you leave. She's mighty pretty, that woman of yours. I'd be going after her too if she was mine."

Ned let the remark pass without comment. All the wishing and hoping in the world wouldn't make Katie his, not when there was a Sioux warrior somewhere out there who she loved.

"I don't have much money left, but whatever I have is yours."

"Maybe just enough for a bottle of chain lightning. The sutler's gin ain't never seen juniper."

"So, you'll help me, then?"

The blacksmith rubbed his chin. "I can get you a uniform to wear and have your horse waiting at the lower corral at dawn. You can slip in with the detail when they go out to cut wood. Just keep your head down and your hat brim low and they won't know the difference. Once you're out there, you can slip away. From there, you're on your own. I'd suggest changing into your own clothes as soon as you can. You wouldn't want any Indians out there taking you for a soldier. Not that they wouldn't kill you anyway."

Ignoring the grim prophecy, Ned asked, "How do I get to Bear Butte?"

"Bear Butte?' the blacksmith echoed. "I heard they're taking your wife to Phil Kearny."

"I can't explain," Ned said. "And trust me, the less you know, the better."

"Whatever you say. If you head north along the Belle Fourche, you should see Bear Butte. Can't say I blame you for wanting to get away from this pile of wood. This place don't even deserve to be called a fort. Winter's coming, and I sure hope it's better than last year when the mice and rats got into the flour sacks, and the snows were so bad all the slabs of bacon stocked in the warehouse rotted. You shoulda seen all that green slime hanging off the lean meat."

"Why do you stay?" Ned asked.

"I make a decent enough living repairing wagon wheels that break along the Bozeman. The wooden wheels get so shrunk from the heat that the metal rims wobble and fall off. The axles and spokes are also in bad shape. There's just so much the wheelwrights can do to forge new rims on their charcoal bonfires, so they come to me. Besides, I ain't got nowhere else to go. You're lucky to be getting out of here."

"Lucky?" Ned repeated grimly. "I'd take my chances with mice-infested flour and rotting bacon compared to whatever's out there on the prairie."

"Are you sure you wanna do this?"

Ned thought back to the hushed conversation he'd had with Katie in Captain Proctor's office before they took her away. She had tried to sound confident that her trader friend would be at Fort Phil Kearny to help her, but the look of uncertainty in her beautiful green eyes betrayed her. "Sometimes you have to do the thing you think you can't do."

The blacksmith just shrugged. "The days are short this time of year. You don't want the darkness to catch you on the trail."

The next morning, Ned donned the scratchy blue jacket the blacksmith had gotten for him. Like most of the uniforms he saw worn by the men at the garrison, the jacket was of poor quality and looked as if it would fall apart at any given moment. Slapping a worn slouch hat onto his head, he found his horse saddled and waiting where the blacksmith said it would be.

When the wood-cutting detail left the fort, it was easy enough to fall in with them for the four mile ride to the pinery. When enough wood had been cut and the detail headed back to the fort, Ned dismounted and lagged behind on the pretext of removing a stone from his horse's hoof. Once they were out of sight, he mounted and took off.

The air was brisk and cold, eagles and hawks prowled the sky, and red sandstone cliffs rose up behind him as he rode on into the afternoon following the Belle Fourche northward.

The sun was straight up when he led his horse to the bank of the river. While the horse drank, Ned stripped off the regimental blue. Lying flat on his belly, he cupped his hands and splashed water over his face. He took his own shirt and pants out of his saddle pack and was about to put them on when he spotted movement on a nearby rise.

Indians! Convinced it was a war party, in his haste to get away, he jumped on his horse and hightailed it out of there dressed only in his long johns and the moccasins he'd traded his boots for.

That evening he secreted his horse in a grove of sandbar willow. A fire, even a small one, would throw light deep into the darkness, and he couldn't take the chance of being discovered. With stars twinkling in the cloudless sky, he sat on a fallen log shivering the night away, cold but alive, and asking himself for the thousandth time what the hell he was doing there.

***

As day surrendered to night, Black Moon and Gillette stopped in a shadowy gully and made a cold, fireless camp.

Through the darkness Gillette watched Black Moon reach into a bag made from the skin of a bighorn sheep and take out his short-stemmed pipe. Raising the pipe and murmuring words of supplication to *Wakan Tanka*, he offered it to the four winds—first to the west, then to the north, then to the east and the south—before offering it to the sky, and finally earthward. With the smoke rising thick and aromatic, he sat unmoving, smoking in ominous calm while staring out into the darkness.

There were many realities in life that could not be avoided, and as surely as life moved in a circle, Black Moon had seen his share of heartbreak. But mostly, it was the power of a woman that held him in her grip.

While Gillette lay snoring, Black Moon's thoughts carried him back to the time he had rescued Katie from the two bluecoats who would have raped her had he not intervened. Afterwards, as they sat alone in the cave, she had tried to act so brave in the wake of the tragedy on Blue Water that took the lives of her father and brother. She'd been shaking like a frightened long-ears, and when he called her that, she had glared back at him with those magnificent eyes and boldly declared, "I am no rabbit. My name is Katie, and I will answer to no other." When he had expressed his hatred of the whites, she had shoved back the sleeve of her dress and, holding her arm out to him, exclaimed, "Look! Do you see the color of this skin? It is white. If you hate all whites so much, why did you save this one?" To which he had responded. "Perhaps it was for the pleasure it gave me to kill those bluecoats."

But in the days and weeks that followed, bringing her to live among his people, he came to question the true reason he saved her. Never had he seen a woman more beautiful. Her eyes, as green as the sacred hills in springtime, her hair the color of the setting sun, and her boldness, so much like a man's, thrilled him. She should have been his enemy, yet try as he might to hate her, he wanted her more than he had ever wanted anything…then and now.

He had lost count of the times he sat against his willow backrest watching her crush buffalo berries and then pat them with her delicate fingers, making the little humming sounds to herself as she worked, every now and then turning to him with a smile. She would pretend to be angry with him when he dipped his fingers into the small metal pot hanging from a tripod over the flames, but when he brought his berry-laden fingers to her mouth, she would suck the flavor off them like a greedy child before bringing his mouth to hers and kissing him the way only she could do. He loved the taste of her mouth, especially when she had buffalo berries on her lips.

Tapping the spent ashes from the pipe, Black Moon placed it in its pouch and lay back against the ground. As he drifted off to sleep, her voice wound its way through his dream of her.

"I will always return to you."

CHAPTER 16
THE STRANGER

Days of relentless riding brought them to the Belle Fourche.

Swirling breezes collided at the top of a ridge from which they had a clear view of the panorama. Black Moon stretched out an arm and said in his deep voice, *"Mato Paha."*

Sitting back in his saddle, Gillette gazed at the formation rising in the distance. Bear Butte wasn't actually a butte, but a worn and ancient mountain. According to Lakota legend, long ago a giant bear and a water monster battled for many days and nights, the battle so fierce it filled the valley with blood. The giant bear was wounded by the monster's jagged teeth and crawled away to die. The ground erupted and darkness covered the earth. Fire and ash, water and mud went into the sky. The bear's body disappeared, leaving in its place a hill in the shape of the sleeping bear. Gillette told that story to his own children and was obliged to admit that whenever he visited the mountain with his wife's band of Bad Faces, he felt an unexplained welcome there, like the guest of a place that spoke to him without words.

Guiding their horses down out of the hills, they followed the Belle Fourche southward. When the sun was in middle sky, they spotted something in the distance. Gillette squinted into his farseeing glass at a spot on the riverbank. "What the—?"

He handed the glass to Black Moon who held it to his eye and sneered, "A bluecoat's clothes."

Nudging their mounts forward, they approached for a better look. Sure enough, in a crumpled heap on the ground was a soldier's clothes. A man's plain pants and shirt lay nearby. Hastily rolling up the clothes, Gillette tied them to the back of his saddle.

They had not gone far when Black Moon's pony's ears bent forward. Its nostrils flared as it tested the wind, but it gave no indication of danger. "There is something up ahead among the shaggy-leafs."

Gillette glanced at the grove of pine trees to which Black Moon gestured. "Grizzly?"

"I do not think it is a long-claws," Black Moon replied. "My pony is alert but not alarmed." Dismounting, he drew an arrow from the otter skin quiver at his back, just in case.

The two men crept silently forward, moving from tree to tree, careful to avoid scattering dead leaves or stepping on broken twigs to alert their presence.

They peered through the branches and saw a white man sitting on the ground dressed in his long johns, flapping his arms about himself in a vain attempt to ward off the November chill.

With his gaze locked icily on the stranger and an arrow nocked on a taut bowstring, Black Moon moved forward, ready for the kill, but Gillette put a hand up and shook his head emphatically.

Black Moon signed, "One less bluecoat is a good thing."

"We do not know if he is a bluecoat," Gillette signed back. "I will speak with him. If he is a bluecoat, then you can kill him."

Without taking his eyes off the white man, Black Moon nodded slowly and stepped aside, allowing the trader to pass.

Leading his horse by the reins, Gillette approached the stranger. "I sure hope you got more to protect yourself with than that thing."

Ned Jeppsen jumped to his feet and reached instinctively for his Kentucky percussion rifle. "Don't come any closer," he warned through chattering teeth.

"Hold on now," Gillette said. "I mean you no harm. If I was gonna kill you, you'd already be a dead man."

"What do you want? You can see I've got nothing to steal."

"You got a horse."

"Mister, the least you can do is leave me my horse. I already lost all my clothes."

"Well, ain't that the truth. How'd you come to be nearly naked out here in the middle of nowhere?"

"I was washing up by the river when I spotted a war party and didn't have time to put my clothes back on."

"More likely a Sioux hunting party," Gillette said. "You're near their winter camp." He eyed Ned up and down. "So, what are you, a deserter?'

"Heck no," Ned exclaimed. "I'm just a farmer from Minnesota."

"I reckon those were your clothes I found back there. What were you doing with a soldier's jacket?"

"The blacksmith at Fort Reno got it for me. It was the only way I knew to get out of there. But I didn't expect to be out here half-naked like this."

"This land sure does bleed the dignity out of you," Gillette said. "At least you had the sense to get in among the pines that block the wind. Where are you headed?"

"To find an Indian named Black Moon?"

Gillette's gaze narrowed. "What do you want with Black Moon?"

"I need to get a message to him."

"What kinda message?"

Ned hesitated, unsure of whether he could take this man into his confidence.

Guessing his uncertainty, Gillette said, "We ain't been properly introduced. I'm Jasper Gillette. I trade with the Sioux."

Expelling a sigh of relief, Ned lowered his rifle and rushed forward, extending his hand. "I sure am glad to make your acquaintance. My name's Jeppsen. Ned Jeppsen. Katie told me about you. She said you're a friend of hers."

"How do you know Katie?"

"We were traveling together on the wagon train bound for Fort McPherson when we were attacked." He ran a hand over his eyes in a vain attempt to wipe away the image that would remain forever burned upon his memory. "The way those Indians killed innocent men and women, I've never seen anything like it."

"Over the years I've seen some raw and ugly things done by Indians and whites," said Gillette. "The Indians scold their children by saying 'Be good or the white man will get you', and the whites scare their children by saying, 'Be good or the Indians will get you. Suspicion and mistrust run deep on both sides. How'd you manage to get away?"

"It happened so fast. Katie got my horse and we just tore out of there like the devil was after us and made it to Fort Reno. We were leaving the fort to bring Black Moon the message, but one of the soldiers recognized her from some years ago at Fort Laramie and told everyone she's Black Moon's wife. They took her to Fort Phil Kearny. I was under orders not to leave Fort Reno."

"This ain't good," Gillette muttered to himself. Turning away, he gave out with a whistle that sounded like the song of a whippoorwill.

From out of the trees appeared a tall, broad-shouldered Indian with serious features leading a bay gelding by its jaw rope.

Ned took a cautious step back. "Who's that?"

"You said you have a message for Black Moon. Well, there he is."

"Th—that's him?"

"In the flesh."

"Where's the war paint and feathers? Don't warriors wear feathers in their hair?"

"Some do. This one doesn't."

"Does he understand English?'

"It ain't likely. I'll translate for you."

The man who approached was not at all what Ned expected. Like others of his tribesmen, his skin was burned brown by the sun. But there was something different about him that made the hairs at the back of Ned's neck stand on end. Tall and well knit, he walked with a straight, proud bearing, black eyes flashing with hostility. Within the muscles encased in his plain hide shirt Ned sensed a strength that went beyond anything physical. This man was not just any Sioux warrior.

He was a leader of warriors, a man in the prime of his life, whose taut, sinewy body exuded competence and determination. He was a man who understood what was at stake and would act upon his courage. He was the incarnation of war, and along with the fragrance of pine in the cold air came the scent of danger.

"*Toka,*" Black Moon said with a growl.

"Wh—what's that?" Ned asked nervously.

"It's the Sioux word for enemy," Gillette explained.

"Tell him I'm not his enemy. I bring a message from Katie."

At the mention of Katie's name, Black Moon surged forward like a bobcat, ready to pounce on the stranger. Gillette stepped between them and spoke something quickly to Black Moon in Lakota.

"I told him you're not a soldier," Gillette said. "That saved your life...for now."

"What do you mean for now?"

"Only that it depends on what your message is."

Ned swallowed hard, not knowing if the next moment would be his last. Clearing his throat nervously, he began, "Tell him—"

"Don't talk to him like he ain't here," Gillette interrupted. "Tell him yourself."

Screwing up his courage, Ned turned to Black Moon and spoke while Gillette translated. "At Fort Reno Katie overheard one of the officers say he wanted to kill all Indian children over the age of seven. She said she had to warn you."

Gillette felt his anger rising. His own children were over the age of seven. "What's the name of the officer," he demanded.

"Fetterman. Captain Fetterman. We were getting ready to leave when they stopped us."

There commenced a conversation between Gillette and Black Moon, and judging from the way Black Moon's body tensed and his dark eyes flashed, Ned guessed the trader was repeating what he'd told him about Katie being recognized and taken to Fort Phil Kearny.

Turning back to Ned, Gillette said, "He wants to know why they didn't take you, too."

"I don't know, especially since I told them I'm her husband."

"Oh, Lord," Gillette groaned. "He ain't gonna like that."

"I only said it so they wouldn't know who her real husband is," Ned hurriedly explained as Gillette translated.

Black Moon took a menacing step toward Ned, an angry scowl flashing across his face. "Did you touch her?"

"No!" Ned exclaimed. "We never…I never…No! She saved my life when she got me away from the attack on the wagon train. I owed her my life." With Gillette rapidly translating, Ned bore up bravely under Black Moon's relentless glare. "If you must know, I asked her to come back to Minnesota with me as my wife, but she refused. She said if she was to be with any man, it would be her husband."

Black Moon listened in tightlipped silence. He wondered bitterly how many more men would want Katie for their wife. First, it was the bluecoat she had promised to marry in return for the bluecoat's help freeing him from the house of iron doors at Fort Laramie. What, if anything, did she promise this ragged-looking white man who did not have the sense to keep his clothes on? Tearing his gaze away, he stared coldly out among the sage, soap weeds and rocks, a stiff breeze blowing against his back from the north as he mulled over the disturbing news the white man carried.

Turning back to Gillette, he said, "You ride to my camp and give the warning." Pivoting sharply, he stalked off.

Gillette called out to him. "Where are you going?"

"To get my woman."

Muttering an expletive, Gillette hurried to his horse. Untying the roll from the back of his saddle, he tossed the pants and shirt to Ned. "Get dressed."

Ned hastily pulled the pants of wool homespun fabric up over his legs, his fingers fumbling with the buttons on either side of the fly.

"Take this, too," Gillette said, tossing the army jacket to him. "Now mount up. There's only one place you'll be safe out here."

Ned buttoned the front placket of the shirt with the narrow band collar. Stuffing the blue jacket into his saddle pack, he questioned, "Where's that?"

Gillette nodded toward Black Moon and answered stoically, "With him."

"Why can't I go with you?"

"Because I got a hard message to deliver, and I don't need your death on my conscience."

"You mean they'd kill me even if I was with you?'

"Hell son, they might even kill me."

Ned grimly weighed his options. He could follow the trader and risk the wrath of a band of angry Sioux, or he could go with Black Moon. Something told him that either way he was a dead man.

Leaving Ned to ponder the dire circumstances, Gillette caught up with Black Moon.

"You must bring the stranger with you."

"I will not ride with a white man," Black Moon shot back.

"I am a white man. You rode here with me."

"You are a friend of Katie's."

"So is he," Gillette reminded him.

Jumping onto his pony's back, Black Moon cast a disdainful look back at Ned. "Why should I care what happens to him?"

"Because Katie would care."

"He will slow me down."

"Have you thought about what will happen when you get to the fort on Buffalo Creek? You cannot get inside," he said, shrewdly adding, "but he can."

Black Moon sat tense and erect in his hide saddle. No matter how hard he tried to convince himself otherwise, he knew the trader was right. Jerking on the jaw rope, he turned his pony's head toward the northwest, and said grudgingly, "Tell him to follow." With a savage kick, he lashed his pony into a gallop.

CHAPTER 17
LOG WALLS

Planted squarely in the heart of prime Lakota hunting land, and commanding a view over a good section of the Bozeman Trail, Fort Phil Kearny was an imposing symbol of American military power.

Having selected a site at the forks of the Big and Little Piney Creeks near a source of water, the post commander, Colonel Henry Carrington, had set up a timbering operation and brought in a steam-powered sawmill to supply the thousands of logs needed for construction. Within its log walls were thirty buildings, including barracks, mess halls, the commanding officer's quarters, a hospital, a bakery, the quartermaster's corral, and a stage for the regimental band. But the fortification had one major flaw. With the nearest stands of timber several miles away, detachments were forced to leave the confines of the fort to obtain the wood essential for heating and cooking, an occurrence that Sioux raiding parties took full advantage of with increasing regularity.

Over the summer and into the fall, the Sioux drove off more than two hundred mules and horses belonging to the sutler, killed a trader and seven of his men, attacked a civilian train, and ambushed an Army train at the Clear Fork of the Powder River. By the time the regiment under the command of Captain William Fetterman turned off the Bozeman Trail and rode into the garrison, the road between the North

Platte and the Powder was strewn with new graves, oxen bones, and burned wagons.

As the men of the regiment rode past the sentry stands and parade grounds toward the newly constructed barracks with its shingle roof, Fetterman reined his mount in the direction of the plank and batten structure that was the office of the commander of the Mountain District. Leaving Katie to shiver in the stiff November wind, he dismounted and went inside. A short time later an enlisted man emerged and took her horse by the reins.

As she was being led away, Katie's gaze swept the scene, noticing things she hadn't paid attention to on her brief visit to the fort weeks ago. She judged the logs of the palisade to be at least eight feet high. A firing ramp was built high along the inside of the wall, with apertures for cannons and blockhouses on the corners for additional fields of fire. Sentries manned the walls. Only a massive and determined Indian attack would be capable of taking the fort.

She spotted a group of emigrants milling about looking uncertain and apprehensive as an officer inspected their wagon train. The women were dressed in dusty calico and linsey-woolsey and wore fearful expressions beneath their poke bonnets. The faces of the men were wind-burned.

"What's the hold up?" the wagon master demanded.

"I'm sorry," the officer said, "but ever since a small train bound for the Montana gold fields was massacred, Colonel Carrington has ordered all trains to be halted and allowed to proceed only if there are thirty or more armed men in each party." Upon his examination, he concluded, "It looks like everything's good here. You can proceed."

Katie watched as the women and children climbed aboard the wagons, and she cringed at the crack of the whips as the oxen lumbered forward. With a shudder she recalled all the grave markers she'd seen along the trail and sadly wondered how many of these emigrants would reach their destinations alive.

She was escorted to a house made of pine logs, recently felled and not quite dry judging from the smell, with small pine poles closely set for protection and a clay roof. Inside, pieces of sheeting served as window shades, and the floor was covered in gunny sacks that had been sewn together by the company tailor. The room into which she was shown was not crowded with furniture, yet surprisingly, was pleasantly decorated. A carved walnut settee hugged one wall. Two walnut cane arm chairs flanked a wood stove that kept the small parlor warm. Between them sat a delicately carved rosewood tea table.

When the door closed behind her, Katie let out a frustrated breath and walked to the window. Holding the sheeting aside with one finger, she peered out. Laramie, Reno, Phil Kearny. A fort was a fort, she thought with dismay. This one was not so very different from the others. Nor were the men.

It was not surprising that given only one shabby uniform that was useless in the cold weather, many enlisted men discarded their blue woolens in favor of buckskin and Spanish spurs. Since Indian Territory was outside of the United States, civil law didn't apply here. Men convicted of crimes in the U.S. weren't criminals on the plains, so men on the run from the law were an excellent source of recruits, although not many of them stayed. McCabe used to say that the main problem the cavalry faced was not the Sioux, but desertion. He called them snowbirds, men who joined the Army to see themselves through the winter and then deserted come summer.

The horses they rode lacked the speed and stamina of Indian ponies, which hardly mattered since, from what she had observed, many of the men lacked skill in the saddle. For the most part, these were men who could not adjust to life after the War Between the States and had drifted into the army where they were mustered into the worst job of all—cavalry deployed on the plains.

As she gazed outside, Katie had no idea what her next move would be. No doubt, she would be brought before the commanding officer. Unbidden thoughts plummeted her back in time to the verbal battle she had waged with Brigadier General Marcus Worth at Fort Laramie.

McCabe had complained that the commander of the troops along the Overland Road on the Platte knew nothing about Indians despite imagining himself a great authority on the subject. His unsympathetic treatment of the Sioux had made the atmosphere on the North Platte and the Laramie explosive. Katie discovered just how insensitive a man he was when she was brought before him and he had demanded to know where to find Black Moon. Her refusal to provide him with the answers he sought had earned her a hardened enemy. She heard from Jasper Gillette some years later that the General had died of pneumonia, and try as she might to feel a smattering of sympathy for the misguided man, the most she could summon was pity.

She'd been brought to the General's quarters in Old Bedlam by Lieutenant Josh McIntyre, commander of the Eleventh Ohio Cavalry, who had ridden into Black Moon's hostile Oglala village at great danger to himself and his men to deliver the letter from an aunt she hadn't known she had. Little could she know then how her life and his would become entwined. He'd been assigned to escort her to Fort Randall where she boarded a steamship bound for St. Louis. With crystal clarity she recalled what she told him during the long, lonely journey across the plains when it was evident that he was smitten with her. "Don't let your life get tangled up in mine."

He did not heed the warning. On the contrary, his affection for her culminated in courtship when he showed up at her aunt's residence in St. Louis after being relieved of his command due to his sympathetic treatment of the Indians. There was no denying that she had feelings for him, but those feelings paled in comparison to what she felt for Black Moon. She had tried to explain that to him the night he asked her to marry him. The next morning she was gone, leaving for him the strand of love beads Black Moon had given her and hoping he would understand.

She didn't see him again until Black Moon was captured and imprisoned at Fort Laramie. When all hope of rescuing him had seemed lost, the big wooden gate had opened and in rode Lieutenant Josh McIntyre, reinstated to his regiment. It was to Josh she had gone for help. Bitter over her rejection and her departure from St. Louis without even saying goodbye, he nevertheless agreed to help her, proving that beneath the pain of unrequited love beat an honorable heart.

After the dust from the battle on Box Elder Creek had settled, Black Moon confided that he had waged hand-to-hand combat with one of the bluecoats, and it was only the sight of the love beads around the white man's neck that prompted him to spare the white man's life.

In the intervening years Katie had often wondered about the cavalry lieutenant who had put his commission and his reputation on the line to help her. Was he married? Did he have children? Was he happy? Did he think about her and wonder, as she did, what life would have been like had they wed?

As she stood at the window gazing at the activity outside, Katie thought about the other men in her life. Men like her father, the Irishman Tom McCabe, and the trader Jasper Gillette, honorable men who traded fairly with the Indians and viewed them for what they were, just people. And Fire Cloud, Black Moon's older brother and the man she married out of obligation, whose kind heart had led to his murder. But there were also dishonorable men who held life cheap, men like the French-Canadian trapper Henri Chatillon who won her in a game of hands with the Crow, and his squinty-eyed companion Baptiste. And Brigadier General Marcus Worth who viewed all Indians as savages when the truth was they were no more and no less savage than anyone else struggling to survive.

At the sound of faint rustling from behind, Katie's thoughts dispersed like a puff of smoke in a stiff wind.

"You will have to pardon the appearance of things," said the woman who entered the room. Dressed in a gown sewn from Army blue cloth in the style of an officer's uniform, with gold braid and brass buttons in double lines on the bodice, she exuded a commanding and dignified presence. The hem of her dress swished against the gunny-sack carpet as she approached.

"Compared to more established posts like Fort Laramie, we are quite rough here, but coming along. The regimental band is in the process of building a new house for us of fire dried trees. Until then, as good soldiers we shall have to make do. I have asked George, our striker, to brew some tea. George is the enlisted man who acts as the Colonel's attendant. He polishes his boots and carries his laundry to soapsuds row. Here at the house he cooks and cleans and looks after the children. He is dismissed from regular duty, except combat, of course." She smoothed her hair that was parted and pulled back into a bun, saying, "I was in the Colonel's quarters when Captain Brevet

Lieutenant Fetterman arrived. I must confess that I do not like that man. His suggestion for your accommodation was quite unacceptable. It was I who suggested to the Colonel that you be brought here. I hope you don't mind. Until we can find accommodations for you, the Colonel and I welcome you as a guest in our humble home."

"You are very kind, Mrs. Colonel Carrington," Katie replied.

She had already deduced from the embroidered eagle on the woman's bodice that she was the Colonel's wife and addressed her accordingly.

"I see you have some knowledge of rank and protocol," said Margaret Carrington. "I take it you have been at an army post before."

"When I was a girl, my father used to take me to Fort Laramie. I am grateful for your hospitality, although I doubt I will be staying long."

"That was not the impression I got. But never mind. You are here now, and I shall endeavor to make your stay with us as pleasant as possible. But first, we must get you something to wear. Regrettably, the trunk carrying my dresses and evening clothes had to be sacrificed because of limited space in the wagon. I have learned to disregard fashion and clothe myself as best I can." She cast a look down at Katie's moccasins. "I should be able to find something suitable for you."

Excusing herself, she disappeared into an adjoining room and returned a few minutes later bearing a dress of linsey-woolsey and a pair of black leather shoes that laced up inside the ankles. "These should do. The fabric for the dress was purchased from the sutler's store and fashioned at one of our sewing circles. Since we arrived it has been quite hectic, what with teaching the other wives along Officers' Row how to stretch canvas tarps along the underside of their sod roofs and to sew gunny sacks together to serve as carpets." She reached for a tattered newspaper. "This was left behind by a passing emigrant train. It is several months old, but it will provide a passable shade when hung above an unglazed window."

The enlisted man appeared with a tray which he set down on the tea table. "Thank you, George. There's nothing more for you to do today. You can go now."

On the tray was a porcelain tea pot and two cups and saucers decorated with little pink roses and rims and handles edged with gold gilding. Pouring tea into the cups, the Colonel's wife handed one to Katie. "The set was my mother's. There are some things I just could not leave behind. I do the best I can to provide homey touches despite the maddening isolation and confinement of the fort. But..." She expelled a resolute sigh. "The situation is preferable to the alternative. And we did have a lovely time several days ago when the Colonel declared a holiday to mark the completion of the stockade by raising the American flag for the first time. Did you see the flagpole when you rode in? It is quite an achievement, constructed of two pieces much like the mast of a ship, made of lodgepole pine hauled from the wood-cutting area. The round poles were carved into octagons, painted black and pinned together in preparation for the flag. The whole command was in full dress, and we all gathered around with our hair and hats flying about in the wind while the Colonel addressed the crowd, speaking of their hardships, losses and tribulations. Everyone snapped to attention, the officers and enlisted men saluted, and the band played as the first United States garrison flag to fly over the land between the North Platte and Yellowstone Rivers was raised. It was a proud moment, to be sure."

With a brittle smile fixed on her face, Katie sipped her tea and listened to her prattle on. The raising of the Stars and Stripes represented the whites' intention to permanently colonize Indian land, and she could not help but wonder what Black Moon was thinking if, somewhere from the surrounding hills, he could see the red, white and blue flag flapping brazenly in the wind.

In the days that followed, Katie helped Margaret Carrington with the baking, stewing, and sewing, all the while waiting to be summoned to the Colonel's quarters for interrogation.

One day, as they were busy stuffing mattresses with dried prairie grass collected at summer's end, one of the Carrington children's pet antelope found its way inside.

"Shooo," the Colonel's wife said, waving her arms at the beast.

"I'll take care of it," Katie offered. She guided the animal outside where she petted its beautiful head. It looked at her with large, melting eyes. "I know," she crooned. "You would rather be out there running free than caged within these log walls. So would I."

She looked upward, where a red-tailed hawk was circling the sky, wings spread on currents of air. The antelope darted off, and as she turned back to the house, Katie spotted flashing mirror signals coming from the top of a distant rise. An Indian signal. A tremor raced across her flesh, caused not by the cold November air but by the thought that perhaps Black Moon was close by.

Back inside, Katie returned to her seat and picked up her sewing. The wood stove threw warmth over the room, but it failed to chase the chill from her heart. What folly had prompted her to leave the warmth and protection of Black Moon's arms to seek…what? She no longer knew.

"Is it true that you lived among the Indians?"

Katie looked up from her tortured thoughts into Margaret Carrington's inquisitive eyes. "Yes. I was captured by the Crow and taken to their village," she answered evasively.

It was not a lie. A Crow warrior had sneaked into the Oglala village and abducted her when Black Moon was off hunting. Life among the Crow had been filled with treachery, and she'd been betrayed by a Crow woman she thought was a friend when she was cruelly bargained away in a game of hands to the French-Canadian trapper Henri Chatillon. Despite the fact that she was married to his brother at the time, it was Black Moon who had ridden deep into enemy Crow territory to rescue her from the clutches of the drunken trader. But she wasn't about to tell that to the Colonel's wife.

"These are difficult times for all of us," Margaret Carrington said. "The Indians grow more brazen by the day. A sentry was shot by an arrow from the banquet along the stockade. The Colonel turned three howitzers upon the spot, but stopped short of firing. Everyone is on edge. We have become educated to the knowledge of loss. The regimental band provides a great source of comfort. Above all, we women have learned endurance, patience, courage, and duty."

Not unlike a Lakota woman, Katie was tempted to say, but kept her thoughts to herself.

"I must confess, things are becoming quite desperate," Mrs.

Carrington confided. "General Hazen's promised reinforcements have not arrived. The men who left the fort with him are still gone. My husband tells me we have fewer than forty horses." She heaved a beleaguered sigh. "The Colonel sleeps almost not at all and spends his days and nights away from me and the children, lest we see the worry on his face."

A silence as thick as a buffalo robe fell upon them as each woman pondered their predicaments.

The officer's wife had learned to be strong in the face of danger and separation from family and friends. Although she embraced the Army as part of her identity, she was sometimes troubled with doubt about her husband's mission when it included the destruction of Indian lives. Nevertheless, she was pleased to be part of a movement that foreshadowed the arrival of civilization on the Great Plains.

The Lakota warrior's wife had learned resilience in the aftermath of personal tragedy and loss, and the more she saw of the regimental world of Mrs. Colonel Carrington, the less she wanted any part of it. Her thoughts whirled. If she could somehow get away and warn Black Moon of Captain Fetterman's plan... If she could convince one of the civilians at the fort to help her... If, if if. She could just hear McCabe saying that *if* was the most useless word in the English language because it had nothing to do with what was. She had to come up with a plan that did not rely on *if*.

The paralyzing silence was broken by a knock upon the door. Mrs. Carrington placed her sewing aside and went to answer it. "The Colonel is asking to see you," she said to Katie when she returned. "Corporal Higgins is here to escort you."

Katie rose, squared her shoulders, and followed the waiting soldier out into the chill air to the post commander's headquarters.

Chapter 18
Little White Chief

Colonel Henry Carrington looked more like a schoolteacher than an army officer. Being a skilled engineer, the Yale educated lawyer had enthusiastically undertaken the mission to occupy Fort Reno and build two new forts along the Bozeman, incurring the wrath of the Sioux.

So, this is the man the Indians call Little White Chief, Katie thought as she watched him shuffle through the papers on his desk.

After the council at Fort Laramie this past summer, word had spread through the Oglala summer camps along the Tongue and the Powder about how the meeting with Red Cloud had gone poorly. Black Moon had refused to attend the council. Instead, he had called a war council, and later that night, as they lay beneath the robes, he had confided his bitterness to her.

"The Great Father sends us presents and wants a new road, but Little White Chief sends his soldiers to steal the road before we say yes or no. We will make the Sun Dance. Then I will ride to the *Sahiyela* and ask them to join us to fight the intruders."

After the Sun Dance was held high up on the Tongue River, she watched Black Moon ride off to council with the *Sahiyela*, the Northern Cheyenne. The Cheyenne elders were opposed to any conflict with the whites, but by the middle of *Wipazuke Waste Wi*, the

Moon when Berries are Good, Carrington had begun construction of Fort Phil Kearny, and everything changed.

Katie recalled that Jasper Gillette had said that the Colonel's men did not particularly like him. From bits and pieces of hushed conversation she heard around the fort, his lack of aggression in several Indian skirmishes had earned him the disrespect of his officers. Perhaps, she dared to think, that trait might work in her favor.

Stacking the papers into a neat bundle and placing them aside, he removed his spectacles, laced his fingers, gazed at her from across his desk, and stated, "You, madam, are an enigma."

"In what way?" she politely inquired.

"I do not know quite what to make of you. On the one hand, an enlisted man who served under General Worth at Fort Laramie says you are the wife of a renegade called Black Moon. On the other hand, Captain Fetterman tells me you are the wife of an emigrant." He tapped his fingers together. "Now, which is it to be?"

"Ned only said I am his wife because of Captain Fetterman's threatening manner toward me," she said truthfully.

"Ned?" he questioned.

"Ned Jeppsen. The man I was traveling with on the wagon train, a farmer from Minnesota. The Captain would not permit him to accompany me here. He was ordered to remain at Fort Reno."

"Fetterman is a hot-headed fool and has long been a thorn in my side," Carrington admitted. "But that is beside the point. Let us get to the heart of the matter, shall we?"

"Of course, Colonel," Katie replied obligingly. "What is it you would like to know?"

"Will I get the truth from you?"

"You have my word."

"To begin with, what is your name?"

"Kathleen McCabe. My father was the trader Tom McCabe. He and my brother and all of Little Thunder's band of Brulés were killed by Colonel Harney on Blue Water Creek eleven years ago."

"Ah, yes, that was a mess. And what did you do after Colonel Harney dispatched—"

"Massacred, Colonel," Katie tersely corrected. "You asked for the truth, did you not?"

"So I did."

"After Blue Water I found a home among the Oglala."

"As Black Moon's wife?'

"Not at first. But eventually, yes."

"And where is Black Moon now?"

"That I cannot tell you."

"Cannot or will not?"

"Cannot. I left the Oglala to return to St. Louis. That was where I was headed when the wagon train was attacked by Red Cloud. Ned and I made it to Fort Reno, and the rest…well, here I am. As for Black Moon, I have no idea where he is."

"Why were you returning to St. Louis?"

"To claim an inheritance," Katie replied. "My aunt left her entire estate to me when she died. Perhaps you have heard of her. Virginia Devlin Beauregard."

The colonel stroked his chin. "The name sounds familiar. Beauregard," he said, turning the name over in his mind. "Would that be Abner Beauregard?"

"Why, yes."

"My family is from Connecticut, but I seem to recall my father speaking of an Abner Beauregard he met when he had occasion to travel to Mississippi on business. Being an abolitionist, of course he found the situation down there intolerable, but when he returned home, he spoke admiringly of Colonel Beauregard. Apparently, they never had occasion to meet again. So, your aunt left you an inheritance and you were going to St. Louis to claim it."

"Yes." She hoped he would not probe too closely into that subject, for then, despite her assurance of truthfulness, she'd be forced to lie. For if she were to reveal that she intended to use some of the money to buy arms and ammunition for Black Moon, the Colonel would not be quite so amiably disposed toward her.

"Well, you can understand how that it is quite impossible. I cannot spare any troops to escort you safely to the railroad with the Indians constantly harassing my soldiers and raiding the wood and supply parties. I'm afraid you will have to remain here. Meanwhile, I will speak to Captain Fetterman and ask him to leave you alone. He is full of bluster, but that is common among officers. Sometimes I wonder if Captain Fetterman's contempt of the fighting abilities of the Sioux is just bluster on his part. Things are getting bad. Soon it will be all-out war."

Something Josh McIntyre said to her a long time ago came back suddenly to haunt her. "And in the end, victory will not be determined by who is right, but by who is left."

The Colonel rested his elbow on the arm of his chair and placed his chin in his hand. "My wife speaks well of you."

"She is a remarkable woman," Katie said. "While you men are busy in your departments of labor, she is busy baking and sewing and making the best with little fresh meat other than juiceless wild game, not to mention her constant efforts to lift the spirits of the other women who no doubt feel they have arrived at the end of the earth."

"I know how hard it is on her," he conceded. "Not only is this the first time she is away from urban comfort, but she must serve two masters, the ideals of her upbringing and the authority and regulations of the United States Army. I am sure the life she envisioned for herself is vastly different from the life she shares with me on the frontier."

"She spends much of her time worrying about you."

"A woman's lot, I'm afraid." He rose from his seat. "Corporal Higgins will escort you back now. I cannot promise anything fancy, but I will see what I can do about getting you a house of your own."

"Any place whose roof does not leak and is not inhabited by snakes and mice would suffice."

He thought for a moment. "The Weaver house, yes. It belonged to one of the civilians who met with an unfortunate accident at the saw mill."

So it was that Katie found herself in a house constructed of green logs that shrank as they dried, leaving gaps in the walls that allowed the cold wind to come in. On days when the woodcutting detail was able to make it to the pinery and back without being attacked, there was an extra log to throw into the small wood-burning stove for warmth. But on the nights when the stove was empty, she sat shivering and missing the warmth of a Lakota lodge and the arms of a strong

Oglala warrior holding her close.

Where was he? What was he doing at this very moment while she was feeling so dreadfully alone and thinking of him?

Her thoughts were filled with him—his strength, his gentleness, his body, the lingering scent of sage in his long, dark hair, his belief in what he was fighting for. If there was some way for her to make it to St. Louis and get the funds to help him and then return to him, she would find it, for she could not bear the thought of living without the man she loved. But if staying permanently in St. Louis was the only way to help Black Moon in his cause, so great was her love for him that she would sacrifice her own happiness to do it. Perhaps in the spring, when the rivers thawed, she might escape from these log walls and make her way toward her destiny, whether that lay in St. Louis or in a Lakota lodge.

And what about Ned who she'd last seen at Fort Reno? How was he faring? Dear, kindhearted Ned who sought a better life for himself and his family and got only misery for his effort.

As the days marched inexorably toward winter, Katie's thoughts turned more frequently toward escape. The only question was, how?

CHAPTER 19
GIVE ME EIGHTY MEN

Two weeks later, a dinner party was held at the Colonel's house. Under the supervision of Judge J.T. Kinney, a former Chief Justice of Utah who oversaw the business interests of the fort sutler, it was an elaborate affair, with canned lobster, tinned oysters and salmon, elk steaks with jellies, pineapples, tomatoes, sweet corn, peas and pickles, and puddings, pies, plum cake, jelly cake, and coffee for dessert.

Katie sat at the table that was dressed with a white cloth and flickering candles, feeling like a foreigner when, in reality, she was the only person in the room born and raised on the plains. To the men and women sitting around the table she was a curiosity, and except for Captain Fetterman, whose dark eyes scrutinized her from across the table with disdain, they all seemed eager to hear of her experiences living among the Indians.

"From what I have learned about you, Miss McCabe, you spent a good deal of time in St. Louis," Fetterman said. "It is unfathomable that you would leave civilized society to return to this savage place."

"Unfathomable to you, Captain," Katie replied. "Not to me. I was born and raised here. This is my home."

"No self-respecting white woman would choose to live among the Indians, yet by your own admission, you did so by choice."

"We all make choices in life. That was one of the better ones I made."

"Captain Fetterman is of the opinion that a company of regulars can whip a thousand Indians, and a regiment can whip the entire array of hostile tribes," said the Colonel. "What do you think, Miss McCabe?"

"I think anyone who is of that opinion knows nothing about Indian warfare, and even less about the Sioux," she answered.

"We are a curious lot," the Colonel remarked. "We view ourselves as elite members of American society. An aristocracy of merit, if you will. Take Captain Fetterman here. He is the son and nephew of West point graduates."

Feigning a smile, Katie said, "I am impressed. I wish I was as impressed by your mission."

"We are here," said Fetterman, "on a noble mission."

"You are here," Katie responded, "because two years ago Colorado militiamen massacred more than two hundred peaceful Cheyenne on Sand Creek. As a result of that, the Indians have taken revenge all across the plains. Surely, you did not expect them to stand by and watch their friends and relatives slaughtered. And so the government responds by building forts along the Bozeman. And the Indians attack. Do you not see the cycle you have created?"

"What are you suggesting?"

"Only that a little understanding goes a long way."

"At this very moment the carpenter is constructing pine coffins for the two officers who were killed and butchered in the latest raid on the wood detail. The bugler had no time to signal the attack. You might imagine how difficult it was for the soldiers who handled the mutilated bodies afterwards to understand, or how difficult it is for their widows to find any understanding amid the sound of hammers and the grating of saws."

"Now, William," the Colonel interjected, "this is not a subject we should discuss in front of the ladies. You will get your chance to fight the Indians. Until then, let us enjoy this splendid meal." There was no mistaking the order behind the soothing tone of his voice, and the subject was immediately dropped.

Later that evening, as the women engaged in quiet conversation and the men enjoyed their Havana cigars, the Colonel found Katie standing alone by the fire. Casting a subtle nod toward Fetterman, he lowered his voice, and said, "He is a hungry soldier, eager for advancement and not about to let our cordial prewar relationship stand in the way of his own ambition. He is also contemptuous of the fighting abilities of the Indians."

"He should not let his contempt for the fighting abilities of the Indians mislead him into underestimating the strength of men willing to die to protect their land," she said.

"You cannot reason with him over it. There is no telling where his recklessness will lead."

"You are not like him," Katie observed.

"That's the difference between old-school military and the new breed of soldier, ones like Fetterman who are steeped in warfare. After the war he and I both lost our volunteer brevet rankings and reapplied to the Regular Army's Eighteenth Infantry. I reverted from general to colonel and he reverted from colonel to captain, a slight which he carries to this day."

"It is obvious that he does not like you."

"His dossier bulges with honors and citations, whereas mine is filled with connections and contacts who have great political clout. I cannot say I blame the man. While I, my wife and children departed for the west with the Eighteenth, he was assigned to recruiting duties."

"Yet here he is, ready to take on the entire Sioux nation."

"If I have learned anything at all in my six months among the Sioux, it is that the strategies and tactics used at Manassas and Bull Run do not apply out here. Besides," he said with a sigh, "The nation is war-weary. It recoils at the notion of more conflict, particularly with the Indians. Not to mention that the Quakers have turned their attention from emancipation to our treatment of the tribes. But between you and me, the real reason for any shift in Indian policy is budgetary. Washington is simply not interested in throwing more money into another Indian campaign. Although, the size of your inheritance might change some minds. Oh, yes, I did a little digging," he said in response to the look of surprise that registered on Katie's face. "Your aunt was a very wealthy woman, and now, so are you."

"Why Colonel Carrington, are you suggesting that I use my inheritance to fund the Army's Indian campaign?"

"Not at all, my dear. The pending treaty between the United States and the Sioux that was entered into at Fort Laramie some months ago renders it the duty of every soldier to treat all Indians with kindness. But I dare say, every Indian who is wronged will visit his vengeance upon any white man he may meet, and I assume that includes your husband."

"My husband wants only that his people be fed and clothed and safe from harassment. And to live the wild and free life they have always enjoyed on land that is, and always has been, theirs."

"Ah, yes, well that is up for debate, isn't it?"

"I don't think debate will solve this problem," Katie said. "Only warfare will. Do not underestimate the men you are fighting, men like Red Cloud and Crazy Horse."

"And Black Moon."

"Black Moon most of all."

"What is he like?" Carrington inquired.

"Why do you want to know? So that by knowing him better you might defeat him?"

"No," he truthfully replied. "It is just the curiosity one warrior has for another."

"It is interesting that you call yourself a warrior. From what I have learned about you, Colonel, you did not see combat during the war."

His stance stiffened. "No doubt you have heard my men talking. It is true that I spent my time behind a desk. I am an administrator, not a combat leader. Nor am I as robust as Captain Fetterman, owing to a sickly youth." His stooped posture and graying hair attested to that. But the deep-set rheumy eyes that appeared to be perpetually weeping stared back at her with military grit. "Nevertheless," he added, "it would be a mistake to underestimate my devotion to duty."

"Black Moon." The mere utterance of his name sent waves of emotion rippling over her. "How shall I describe him? He is kind and generous and fair-minded. I see you are surprised by that. Nevertheless, it is true. He is also a humble man, but proud and stubborn. He is a devoted son, and he was a loving father."

"Was?" the Colonel questioned.

Her gaze dropped to the planked floor. "We had a child. She died soon after birth."

"I am sorry for your loss," he said.

Struggling with the memory that still haunted her, Katie lifted her gaze and stared forthrightly into the Colonel's watery eyes. "He is a whirlwind that can grow into a tornado when provoked. He is a quiet man, but there is an air of strength and self-assurance that lies just beneath the surface. He reminds me of something my father used to say. Never antagonize a mountain lion. If the Sioux had ten thousand more like him, all the Captain Fettermans in the world would not stand a chance. He has never been involved in any of the massacres on the trail. It would be a mistake, however, to underestimate his devotion to duty."

"I am not sure I like having my words echoed back at me," Carrington said. "But I admire your courage for speaking them. And now, if you will excuse me, I must return to my other guests."

After he had ambled off, Katie sensed a presence behind her and turned to find the dark eyes of Captain Fetterman assessing her. "The Colonel may admire your courage," he said, coming forward, "but I find it misplaced."

"I have no wish to engage in verbal combat with you, Captain."

"And what is it you do want?"

"Simply to leave this place and continue on to my destination."

"The rivers are fast icing over and the trails are growing more treacherous by the day. It looks like you will be here at least until the spring thaw."

"And you, Captain? What is it you want?"

"To bring the fight to the enemy. Give me eighty men and I can ride through every one of those savages' villages up there on the Tongue."

"If you will excuse me, Captain, it's late and I'm tired. I'll say goodnight to our hosts and return to my little house now." At this point, even a lumpy mattress of dried grass was preferable to his company, Katie grumbled to herself as she walked away.

In the days that followed, as word of Katie's St. Louis inheritance spread throughout the garrison, she found herself the recipient of invitations to readings, games, and quadrilles, and engaged in endless chit-chat with the officers' wives. Fort Phil Kearny was a far cry from St. Louis; nevertheless, the never-ending stream of social gatherings reminded her of the whirlwind year she'd spent in the big house overlooking the Mississippi River. The feeling of not belonging was the same. The acute loneliness was the same. The perpetual longing for Black Moon, the need to feel his arms around her, to breathe in the leather and musk that clung to his skin, to hear the sound of his deep voice at her ear, were the same.

She marveled at the difficulty these women had in adapting to life on the frontier. Those whose fingers were accustomed to piano keys now found themselves roasting and boiling, baking and stewing. In the absence of servants, they were obliged to do the sweeping and dusting, darning and stitching. If one looked closely, one could read the despair and disgust on their faces, expressions they masterfully hid from their husbands as they sought to make their homes neat and genteel. As with the women she'd met in St. Louis, she found herself wondering how long any of these army wives would last if they had to do the work of a Lakota woman. Had any of them ever known the kind of freedom she had known? How many of them had ever experienced the passion she had come to know in the arms of a dark-eyed warrior?

St. Louis and Fort Phil Kearny were not so very different, after all. There, the long, windy shouts of the steamboats filled the air. Here, it was the bugle calls—Reveille, assembly call, stable call, mess call, drill call, and any other call depending on the preference of the commanding officer, and finally ending the day with Taps.

As the days passed, she often visited with Margaret Carrington, where the advantage of being an officer's wife was evident in the supply of wood for the stove. On a cold, windswept day in late November, as they sat at the kitchen table making hard biscuit from flour, salt and water, the Colonel's wife glanced toward the doorway and mused, "I wonder where George is this morning."

A short time later, at the sound of the front door opening and closing on its hinges, she said, "There he is now. We will soon have a lovely pot of tea. My goodness, George, we were beginning to worry about you."

"George is under the weather," a masculine voice spoke from the doorway. "I left him huddled before the cast-iron stove in the barracks."

Katie's movements froze. She knew that voice. Fingers sticky with flour and water, she turned slowly in her chair and found herself face to face with Ned Jeppsen.

"Those barracks are fit to be torn down," Margaret Carrington complained. "I'll take the matter up with the Colonel. We're finished here, Private. Why don't you brew us a pot of tea? We'll be in the parlor."

Wiping her hands on the front of her apron, Katie rose and followed her from the kitchen, not daring to look back at Ned.

For the next hour she engaged in small talk, scarcely able to contain her excitement. What on earth was Ned doing here? And dressed as a soldier, no less! Later, as she prepared to leave, praying her emotions did not show on her face, and with as much casualness as she could muster, she ventured, "Would you mind lending me your striker for a while? My wood stove is empty and I could use a pair of strong hands to haul in some logs."

"Not at all, my dear. I'll send him over just as soon as he's finished here."

Bending her head against the bitter bite of the wind, Katie hurried back to her little house. The breath shot out of her mouth in white bursts, crystalizing with the cold air upon impact, while her heart pounded with sudden hope.

CHAPTER 20
HOPE

"Ned!"

She rushed to him and threw her arms around his neck, burying her face against his chest, not caring that his frayed woolen jacket scratched her cheek.

He held her a little too tightly for a little too long. Feeling suddenly uncomfortable by the strength of his embrace, she gently disengaged herself. With a raw sigh, he let her go.

Holding him at arms' length, she gathered her composure and fired questions at him. "What are you doing here? How did you get here? And where did you get these clothes?

"Shhh." He placed a finger against her lips to silence her breathless questions. "There's time for that later. It's freezing in here. I brought wood."

He went back outside and returned with an armful of logs. Kneeling before the cast iron stove, he got a fire going. "It should warm up in here soon." He got up and looked around. "I hate the thought of you living in a place like this."

"It's small and drafty, but the Colonel's wife was able to collect some pieces of furniture from the other officers' wives, and the post carpenter made a bedstead for me. The mattress is stuffed with dried prairie grass. It's a little lumpy, but it's considerably more comfortable than the inside of a wagon."

Ned smiled. "I guess anything is better than that."

Green eyes stared back at him questioningly. The expression on her beautiful face was one of uncertainty, fear, and hope. She reached for his hand and led him to a settee whose brocade covering was worn thin with age.

He could not help but feel that she was meant for so much more than a ramshackle house on an army post or an Indian lodge somewhere out on the plains. If she would only let him, he would build her a cozy, two-story home in Minnesota and fill it with the best furnishings his money could buy. He didn't have much left, but there was enough to get started, and they could build their future from there. He wanted to tell her how he felt, but before the words could even form on his tongue, she spoke.

"You must tell me how you got away from Fort Reno when Captain Fetterman said you were to stay there."

Placing his hopes on hold, he explained, "I persuaded the post blacksmith to help me. He gave me this jacket."

"Might he have gotten one of rank higher than Private?" she asked with a laugh. "Corporal, at least."

"I couldn't be choosy. This one has served me well. It enabled me to fall in with the wood detail and no one noticed me. That's how I got out of one fort and into this one."

"That was a very dangerous thing for you to do."

"No one who came from Fort Reno recognized me."

"I meant you might have been killed. The Sioux attack the wood trains nearly every time they go out.

"I was lucky, I guess."

"That explains how you got out of Fort Reno and into Phil Kearny, but it doesn't explain how you managed to make it here on your own."

"I wasn't exactly alone."

She looked at him quizzically. "I don't understand."

"When I escaped from Fort Reno with the blacksmith's help, my intention was to get to the Oglala winter camp at Bear Butte and give

Black Moon your message."

"You would do that for his people?"

He looked longingly into her eyes. "I would do that for you."

"Ned, I—"

"Anyway," he cut in, sparing her the necessity of letting him down and himself the disappointment of hearing it, "I was following the Belle Fourche and was washing up in the river when I spotted some Indians, Sioux, I guess, and I had to leave my clothes behind. So, there I was, near naked and freezing my…well, freezing, when along comes your trader friend."

"Jasper Gillette?"

"And he wasn't alone. Black Moon was with him. Apparently, the trader went to Black Moon's village to tell him about the attack on the wagon train, and as soon as Black Moon heard about it, he took off to find you."

Katie's heart skipped a beat. Yes, that was the man she knew, brave and strong and protective. The one who would risk any danger to himself to save her. Oh, how she loved him!

"Your friend went on to find the winter camp to give them the warning, while Black Moon and I followed the regiment here."

"You and Black Moon rode together? I can just imagine how that went."

"Not so bad, if you consider that we didn't speak a word to each other and I slept with one eye open."

Rolling her eyes at his sarcasm, she asked, "Where is he now?"

"Out there, up in the hills where I left him."

So close, Katie thought. He was so close. "I wish I could get out of here," she said desperately, "but I'm being closely watched. Colonel Carrington treats me like a guest, but I know too much about Black Moon for him to let me go."

"Are you under arrest?"

"They won't call it that, but what would you call being confined and unable to leave?"

"Is there anything I can do?" he asked urgently.

"You can get out of here as soon as you can. Stay away from the post commander's quarters, and whatever you do, don't let Captain

Fetterman see you."

"I can't leave you here alone," he protested.

"They're not finished questioning me. But don't worry. I can hold them off for as long as I have to."

"And then what?"

"Hopefully, come spring they'll let me go. I still have the weight of the Beauregard name behind me, not to mention all that money."

"And where will you go?"

"On to St. Louis."

"Katie, what's in St. Louis? I mean, what's *really* in St. Louis?"

She gave him a secret smile. "The less you know, the better."

"I can slip in with the wood detail and make it back to Black Moon and let him know you're here."

"Do you think you can make it? I hate to think what would happen if they caught you."

"It's so cold, my spit freezes before it hits the ground. We used to call this no-neck weather back in Minnesota. All these men can think about is keeping warm and staying alive. With my head down and my hat pulled low, sure, I can make it."

"Have you had a good look around?"

He nodded. "The troops carry mostly Sharp muzzle loading carbines and a few Spencers and Springfields. The regiment is stretched to the limit. By my count, Carrington is down to under three hundred and fifty officers and men."

"Black Moon always said that to defeat an enemy it is necessary to know as much about him as you can. You must tell him what you have seen here."

"But he doesn't speak English. How will he know what I'm saying?"

"Find a way to make him understand. He'll know what you're saying. Don't let his quietness fool you. His strength is his ability to think."

"That can also be our biggest weakness," Ned sourly remarked, "especially when we humans think we're better than all other living creatures."

"The Indian does not place himself above other beings," Katie said. "Every creature has its strength. The hawk has keen eyesight. The wolf has fangs. The pronghorn has speed. Humans have the ability to think and to plan, and Black Moon has honed that ability sharper than any blade."

"Do you think he'll attack the fort?"

"He's too smart for that. But he and Crazy Horse will continue their attacks on the wood train. It's only a matter of time before something really bad happens, and I can't help but think that Captain Fetterman will be somehow involved. Under the Colonel's direction he leads the cavalry and a squad of mounted infantry up the wood road each day to relieve the train and drive the attackers across the creek. There's a rumor circulating the fort that Fetterman will replace Colonel Carrington as the battalion's commanding officer. All he needs is one good Indian fight to impress the War Department."

Linking her arm in his, she turned him toward the door. "You should go now before Mrs. Carrington begins to wonder where you are." She paused at the door to give him a sly look. "Is George really sick?"

He smiled knowingly, a twinkle playing at the corners of his eyes. "I gave him a few dollars to let me take his place. The enlisted men only make thirteen dollars a month, so he was happy to do it. He's the one who told me you've been spending a lot of time at the Colonel's house, so I took a chance you'd be there today." He gazed strongly into her eyes. "I'm glad I did."

Reaching up on tiptoes, she placed a kiss on his cheek. "So am I."

A gust of wind blew the door back on its hinges when she opened it to let him out. She watched him tuck his chin down and hurry away, wondering when…or if…she would ever see him again.

CHAPTER 21
THE WHITE WOLF

Morning broke cold and gray. A stiff breeze prowled the land as Black Moon sat before a small fire among the sage and rocks, gazing down upon the soldier town. The sun had risen and fallen three times since the white man went down to the fort and still he had not returned. What was he doing down there?

Black Moon did not have to speak words with this white man to know he was no different from all the others. What was it about the *wasichus* that they were not content with what they had or who they were? They wanted more land even if it meant stealing it. They came from the east in long lines of rolling wooden houses searching for something Black Moon did not understand. They were so intent on being different from what they were, whereas he had no wish to be anything other than what he was. He wondered if any of them ever stopped to talk to the wind or listen as it whispered over the grasses and sang through the cottonwoods. They wanted to die in a land far from home, but this, this place of sprawling prairie and sacred hills that was his home was where he wanted to die, facing westward where the bones of his grandfathers and their grandfathers and all the people of the Buffalo Nation were scattered and one with the land.

Turning away from the hated log walls of the fort, Black Moon gazed at the panorama and took a deep breath. To the north a succession of round-topped red buttes followed one after the other, blending with the uneven horizon. To the west lay the Tongue River and the little green valley where his people sometimes made their summer camp. Beyond that, rose the Shining Mountains and the greasy grass river, the one the whites called the Little Big Horn.

Not a day went by that the sight of all this did not make his heart beat faster. The only thing that stirred his heart in such a way was his green-eyed woman.

She should be in their lodge right now, cooking a big pot of elk meat instead of living at the soldier town where he could not reach her. And he should be sitting before a warm fire waxing his bow string and watching her from the corners of his eyes, secretly thrilling to the graceful movement of her slender body and the firelight dancing along the long red strands of her hair and caressing her smooth brow and cheekbones, instead of out here alone and imagining it.

With a snort from his bay gelding, Black Moon let the memory slip from his mind and turned his attention to the direction in which his pony was looking intently. Rising from the fire, he blew on his hands to warm them as he watched a party of mounted bluecoats moving along the road used by the wood cutters from the fort on Buffalo Creek. He knew that the bluecoats did not come this high on the slopes, so there was no reason for him to hide. Nevertheless, he untied the elk skin case that held his rifle from the neck rope of his pony and held it in the crook of his arm as he watched the bluecoats ride slowly toward the pine-covered foothills.

Nearly three moons had passed since he and Crazy Horse had led the raid that resulted in taking two hundred mules and horses, yet the Long Knives stayed. All during the summer moons the wood trains were attacked, and still they stayed. It seemed that nothing could drive the white intruders out. Crazy Horse complained that they did not have enough guns and ammunition to drive them out, but Black Moon knew that no amount of guns and ammunition would mean a thing if the Long Knives would not even come out of their fort to fight. It would take a big fight to convince the Long Knives to abandon their fort and leave.

The bay gelding's nostrils flared as it tested the wind, alerting

Black Moon that something was afoot. Peering out across the foothills, he saw Crazy Horse and his warriors swoop down a long, steep slope. Upon being spotted, the Long Knives took out after them with rifles booming. Crazy Horse led the Long Knives on a good chase, with one objective in mind—ambush. When the fighting was over, two Long Knives lay dead.

At any other time Black Moon would have been riding with Crazy Horse, but not today, not when the Long Knives had his woman.

The sound of hooves galloping hard in his direction startled him. Whirling, he saw the white man returning at last.

Ned reined his horse up short and jumped down. Gesturing to the place in the distance that was filled with the smoke of battle, he said breathlessly, "Fetterman." Scarcely able to catch his breath from the close call, he panted, "I thought I was gonna die out there."

Black Moon may not have understood the words, but he recognized fear when he saw it and was obliged to privately admit that it took a certain amount of courage for the white man to join the wood train and risk the wrath of Crazy Horse. Yanking his water pouch from his saddle, he tossed it to him.

Ned deftly grabbed it in midair and drank in long swallows.

When Ned had his fill and tossed the pouch back, Black Moon uttered one word that sounded like an animal growl from deep in his throat.

"Katie."

Ned nodded toward the fort. "She is there."

Then, using hand signals and scratching out drawings in the earth with a stick, Ned did his best to convey to Black Moon what he had learned about the fort and Katie's imprisonment.

Later, as the sun dropped behind the jagged mountain ridges to the west, the two men sat before a small fire, eating the rabbit Black Moon brought down with a swift arrow and skinned and gutted. Ned could not stop his teeth from chattering. He'd never been so cold, and he could not help but wonder if his uncontrollable shivering was caused by the weather or the uncertainty of what tomorrow would bring.

Seeing the white man's discomfort, Black Moon got up and

removed the buffalo robe tied behind his hide saddle and tossed it to him. When the night sun was high, and while the white man dozed, he sat long into the night, staring into the darkness. How was he going to get Katie away from the Long Knives?

From watching the soldier town from this vantage point, he had observed wolves gathering around the slaughter yard. Each night the bluecoats threw meat out to them. Soon after the wolves ate the meat, they were dead. The meat had been poisoned so that the bluecoats could take the pelts of the wolves for robes.

Like the Lakota, the wolves were free spirits. They were fiercely loyal to their mates and families, capable of outwitting their enemies, steadfast, and protective. From the wolf, Black Moon had learned to observe and scrutinize everything a second time, to adapt quickly to unusual circumstances and to avoid unnecessary battles.

He recalled the time two winters past when he'd been badly wounded by a bluecoat's bullet and taken to a Cheyenne winter camp for healing. There, he had dreamed of the wolf, the patron of all warriors, but not just any wolf, one that was big and white, with eyes as blue as the summer sky. In his dream the great white wolf loped down from its high place and spoke to him, saying, "The warrior will find the way."

Katie had found him in the Cheyenne winter camp and, mistakenly thinking he had taken another woman for his wife, had run off, only to be thrown from her pony. He found her half-buried beneath the snow. Beside her frozen body was a wolf's paw print almost as large as a grown man's hand. Later, she told a story about a white wolf coming to lie beside her, keeping her alive with its warmth, telling her, "Do not be afraid. The warrior comes."

As Black Moon sat long into the night, an animal cunning seeped into his being. Back then, the white wolf's message was clear. They would always find their way to each other. And now it had given him the answer to his question.

The next morning Ned was startled awake by a rough hand on his shoulder.

Using hand signals, Black Moon instructed him to wait for the wood train and go back with it to the fort. "*Anpètu Wi,*" he said, gesturing to the sun rising in the east. Then he made the setting-sun motion.

"Nightfall." Ned nodded with understanding.

"*Peta.*"

This time Ned stared back.

Motioning to the ashes of last night's fire, Black Moon repeated, "*Peta*," and jabbed a finger toward the log walls of the fort.

"You want me to start a fire at the fort to create a diversion," Ned exclaimed with sudden comprehension. "Yes. I'll do it."

Black Moon strode to a secluded grove of willows and watched grimly as the wood wagons rolled through the west gate of the fort for their four mile ride to the pinery. He counted their numbers, then sat back to wait. The sun had nearly reached middle sky when he spotted them returning. Again, he counted their numbers. This time, there was one more rider among the escort.

Black Moon's grudging respect for Ned's courage was overshadowed, however, by a darker emotion. It was obvious to his keen eyes that Ned was in love with Katie. Courage or not, he thought icily, if the white man tried to take his woman, he would pay with his life.

Although the sun brought some warmth, the air of *Waniyetu Wi*, the Winter Moon, had a sharp bite. A lone hawk rode on a high wind. Somewhere in the distance came the thin bark of a coyote and the drumming of a sharp-tailed grouse as Black Moon sat on the crest of a hill, working his plan over and over again in his mind.

As twilight stretched across the land, his back stiffened when he saw the bluecoats tossing the poisoned meat out into the growing darkness.

It was easy enough to track one of the dying wolves into the thickets. He found it beneath a snake berry bush. After skillfully skinning it, he uttered a silent prayer of thanksgiving to the wolf for letting him have its pelt and tied a small bundle of sage in the branches.

Night fell. The air was cold and a thick layer of clouds hid the face of the moon. With his pony picketed, he pulled the wolf hide, head to tail, up over himself and crawled to the stockade.

A sentry patrolled up and down the banquet along the stockade, every so often calling "All's well". Black Moon silently nocked an arrow on his stout ash bow and waited, tense and alert, for the signal.

Chapter 21
A Pact of Fire

Taps, the last bugle call of the day, sounded as Colonel Carrington paced back and forth across the puncheon floor of the commander's quarters with hands clasped behind his back.

"Your actions yesterday have resulted in the deaths of an officer and an enlisted man," he fumed.

The light of an oil lamp fell across the face of Captain Fetterman. There was no hint of remorse in his eyes over yesterday's failed Indian fight, only a look of utter contempt which he did not bother to hide. "The Lieutenant took it upon himself to pursue the Indians," he said tersely. "If I had known what his intentions were, I would have ordered him to remain with his men."

"It is your duty to maintain tactical control of your command," Carrington fired back.

"All these Indians know how to do is ride and shoot their arrows. Their fighting ability is non-existent."

"Tell that to the two dead men."

"We need to organize an offensive against them," Fetterman insisted.

"It would be wise to keep in mind that this enemy is different from the one you fought during the war. They are unpredictable. Besides, we are not here to fight Indians, Captain. We are here to protect the road." At the look of disdain that crossed Fetterman's face, Carrington said, "For weeks you and others have questioned my authority, as well as my experience and my honor. Brigadier General Cook of the Department of the Platte issued orders stating very clearly that I am in command here, and that means that my orders are to be followed. Therefore, effective immediately, I am reassigning you. You are hereby relieved of field command until I say otherwise. Is that understood?"

Despite the intensity in his eyes, Fetterman said evenly, "Understood, sir."

Snapping to attention and bristling over the chastisement, Fetterman left the commanding officer's quarters. Outside, he drew a cigar from his breast pocket. Striking a match on the sole of his boot, he lit it, and coaxed spirals of pewter smoke upward to mingle with the frosty air.

The Regimental Band provided drummers and buglers for drills, ceremonies and combat commands during the day, but in the evening they gathered at the bandstand surrounding the flagstaff to serenade the post with popular tunes of the day. On this cold November night the sweet strains of *Beautiful Dreamer* floated through the garrison and out into the deep reechoing valley.

As Fetterman made his way along the walkway that divided the quadrants of the parade ground, he spotted a familiar figure standing before the bandstand.

"Beautiful dreamer, wake unto me. Starlight and dewdrops are waiting for thee."

Katie felt a tightness in her throat at the familiar voice that murmured the lyrics from the shadows.

"A lover serenading his beautiful dreamer who is most likely dead," Fetterman said as he approached. "It speaks of home, so far distant and in so wild a place as this." He came to stand beside her. "It's quite a departure from *Oh! Susanna* and *Camptown Races*."

She drew her shawl tighter around herself, partly to ward off the cold, but mostly from the chill he inspired. "I would not have guessed you to be so familiar with Mr. Foster's verses."

"There's much about me you don't know."

Turning away from the bandstand, she said, "I was on my way back to my house when I stopped for a moment to listen. If you'll excuse me, I'll be going."

He fell into place beside her. "Allow me to escort you home. It's rather late to be out."

"I was with Mrs. Carrington, stitching army blankets procured from the sutler's store into overcoats for the enlisted men."

Fetterman shook his head and said disparagingly, "The recruits come from the proverbial bottom of the barrel. They receive little or no training other than basic drill. Most never even saw a horse, let alone rode one, until they got here."

"That's a rather dim view of the men in your regiment," Katie sourly noted, "considering they are poorly paid, poorly fed, and poorly housed."

"It's better than nothing. But don't feel too sorry for them. They have kitchens in their barracks and live in open bays heated with cast-iron stoves."

"How sensitive of you," she said dryly.

Ignoring the barb, he said, "You misjudge me."

"I think not."

"What I meant is that you misjudge me if you think I will divert from the issue of taking the fight to the Indians," he bluntly replied, shifting the subject to the crux of the matter. "I feel an offensive against the Sioux is imperative, and I have made that recommendation to Colonel Carrington." He saw no particular need to inform her of Carrington's rejection of his recommendation or of his recent non-assigned personnel status. "Indulge me for a moment, if you will. How long do you think they can hold off the military might of the United States Army? You would be doing your country a tremendous service if you would tell us everything you know about them. Black Moon in particular. How many fighting men he has. Where he hides. You just might save some of their lives."

Katie tilted her chin up at him. "I'm sure you fancy yourself an honorable man, but under that uniform you are hell-bent on destroying innocent lives."

Fetterman snorted derisively. "Careful, or I might begin to think that you consider them human. There could be repercussions for that."

"Humanity is hardly a punishable offense," she said tartly. "In fact, I have not been charged with anything. More to the point, Captain, I am free to leave this place any time I wish."

"And yet you have not. Am I to assume it is my company that keeps you here?"

His sarcasm grated on her nerves. "Don't flatter yourself. It is the weather that prevents me from leaving."

"It would be a shame if you were to leave," he said, his coal-dark gaze moving over her. "You are quite lovely. A rare thing in such a dismal place as this." His hand encircled the back of her neck. "Maybe you have been around that Indian so long that you have forgotten what a white man's touch is like." He drew her closer. "I'm not talking about that farmer from the wagon train. I'm talking about a real man." He brought his mouth toward hers, but she flung her face to the side to avoid his kiss and gave him a mighty shove.

"You take entirely too much for granted," she said sharply as she spun away.

He caught her by the arm and jerked her back around. "Are you saying you prefer that heathen?"

"That is exactly what I'm saying."

"If it's the last thing I do," he said through gritted teeth, "I'll see that renegade destroyed, and then you'll be forced to come to me."

"That, Captain, is something that will never happen."

"We will see about that when I am in command here, when your future is in my hands and you capitulate to my will. Who knows? You might even learn to love me."

"I could never love a man like you," Katie spat.

His look hardened, his jaw flexing beneath his muttonchops. "You will soon learn that I am not a man to be denied, whether it is an Indian war or a woman."

She opened her mouth to protest when, suddenly, the sound of panicked voices rose from across the parade ground. Turning in unison, they saw flames licking the night sky.

"Good God!" Fetterman cried. "The hay yard is on fire!" Releasing her, he darted off.

Within minutes, half-clothed men streamed out of the cavalry and infantry barracks and raced toward the burning hay yard on the western edge of the garrison. The Colonel burst out of his quarters and joined Fetterman, the quartermaster, the blacksmith, the wagon master, teamsters, civilians, the sutler, and even the band members who dropped their instruments and rushed to extinguish the flames. Chains of men were hastily formed to haul buckets of water from the water corral to staunch the fire and keep it from reaching the nearby mule stables.

Pressing her hands over her ears at the frightened brays of the mules and the frantic shouts of men, Katie hurried back to the little house that had become her home these past weeks.

In the frenzy, no one noticed that the sentry patrolling the stockade wall lay dead with an arrow in his back.

CHAPTER 22
RESCUE

She bent to light the wick on an oil lamp, when a hand darted out of the darkness to clamp over her mouth, and a strong arm snaked around her waist from behind.

A bolt of panic shot through her. She struggled against her captor's strength that held her pinned against him. The pressure he exerted grew tighter, threatening to choke the breath out of her lungs. Had the Captain followed her here? Was he about to make good on his promise? Into her mind sprang the memory of that dreadful time after Blue Water when she'd been dragged into a grove of pines by two bluecoats who attempted to rape her, and later how she fought off the brutal lust of the French-Canadian trapper Chatillon.

With every ounce of strength she possessed she twisted and kicked and clawed at the hand that held her screams trapped in her mouth.

Over the stench of smoke and the strong musty smell of burning bales of hay from the compound came the scent of sage close at hand, and amidst the shouts and hollers from outside a familiar voice spoke at her ear, its warm breath brushing against her cheek.

"Why do you shake like a frightened long-ears?"

She froze. Those same words had been spoken to her long ago, when she had huddled in a dark cave in the aftermath of the Blue

Water tragedy, staring across the fire into the hostile eyes of a Lakota warrior.

The blood left her face. Relief and emotion washed over her. She sank back against the solid wall of his chest, and as the hand slipped from her mouth, she answered as she had done that fateful night.

"I am no rabbit. Do not call me that."

"I will call you whatever I please." His deep voice echoed what he had said to her that night, only this time it was softer, with no hint of the malice that had sent chills down her spine back then.

Turning slowly in his arm, she looked up into the dark eyes that once had frightened her and now filled her with desperate hope. "And what do you call me now?"

"*Mitawa*," he whispered, caressing her hair with gentle fingers.

The word filled Katie with an aching love. Yes, she was his own. Just as he was her own. They had come such a long way since that night in the cave, their journey having taken them through absence and misunderstanding, love and loss, and bringing them to this moment. When all else was uncertain, only this, the solid shape of him, was the one true thing she could believe in. Pressing her cheek against his chest, she held him tight.

Black Moon embraced her longer than he should have, for danger stalked all around them. It was only the frantic shouts of the white men outside that drew an animal-like growl from deep in his throat and made him push himself away from her. "We must go," he said brusquely.

The sight of him, so unexpected in this place, held Katie to her spot. He was so beautiful and solemn, his midnight eyes trained on her face, his hair falling long and loose over the shoulders of his hide shirt, his well-formed mouth bearing a grim smile.

She stared at his impassive face. He looked so confident, so assured, while everything inside of her was on the edge of panic. Her voice, caught in emotion, rushed from her lips in an urgent whisper. "What are you doing here?"

"I have come for what is mine."

She felt herself crumbling at the possessive tone of his voice. She shuddered with longing, her fingers aching to touch the brown skin beneath his hide shirt. His strong musky scent infiltrated her senses, making her heady with immediate desire. Nevertheless, she frowned up at him through the darkness. "You have put yourself at great risk."

His mouth curved downward in a frown. "Do you want me to go?"

"Yes."

A sliver of pain pierced his heart. Was she turning him away? Did she really want to remain here in this place of log walls and white men?

He received his answer when she reached up and took his face between her hands, and drawing his head to hers, she kissed him, whispering against his lips, "But I want you to take me with you."

Even now, in the midst of turmoil, and with danger stalking all around them, his flesh stirred and he could not stop the thundering drumbeat of his heart caused by the press of her body against his, the fresh winter smell of her hair, and the suggestive tone of her voice. If they were anywhere else, he would have laid her down and covered her body with his and taken her with all the power and love that were in him. But time allowed only for a kiss, brief but thorough.

Dragging his lips from hers, he said roughly, "Woman, you tempt me too much."

She aimed a killing smile up at him. "Do you not want me?" she teased.

"Come," he said thickly, turning her toward the door. "I will show you later how much I want you." While the Long Knives were busy trying to put out their fire, the fire that raged inside of him would have to wait to be quelled.

Black Moon hurried to the door, pulling Katie along with him. Cracking open the door, he poked his head out and scanned the scene. Men were racing about, some coming dangerously close to Katie's little house that stood not far from the hay yard. Ducking back inside, he said urgently, "We must find a way to throw them off our trail."

"I have an idea," Katie exclaimed. "Whenever a column of soldiers returns, instead of taking their horses to the barns, they turn them loose in an open area in the middle of the buildings after unsaddling them. If the horses can be made to scatter—"

Black Moon did not wait to hear any more. Snatching the army blanket from Katie's bed, he went again to the door and peered outside. Relying on instinct, he sprang into action. Grabbing Katie's hand, they rushed to the place where he had traversed the stockade. A short distance away was a supply wagon. Pushing her down behind the wagon, he ordered, "Stay here," before darting off.

He made it to the Long Knives' big horses without being seen and moved swiftly and silently through the herd, waving the blanket at them and letting out a low growl to imitate a bear. Already spooked by the smell of smoke, the startled horses bolted and broke past the buildings at the opposite end of the compound. Upon seeing this, some of the bluecoats dropped their buckets and hurried off to round up the panicked horses.

Black Moon raced back to Katie. With the bluecoats scrambling to put out the fire and stop their stampeding horses, he used his formidable strength to push the wagon close to the stockade wall. Hoisting Katie onto the wagon, he climbed up behind her and then leapt onto the top of the stockade. He held his hand down to her. She had to reach up on tiptoes, but when her hand was grasped firmly in his, he pulled her up alongside him. Without hesitating, he jumped down and rolled to break his fall. Springing back up, he raised his hands to her.

"Jump!"

But Katie was frozen to her spot, her stricken gaze riveted to a spot a few yards away where the crumpled form of the sentry lay with an arrow protruding from his back. Through the darkness she recognized the narrow green bands around the shaft. Black Moon's mark.

His voice, hushed yet emphatic, forced her to tear her gaze away. Leaning over the stockade, her heart rose in her throat. The drop looked much further than eight feet, and in her heightened state of panic, considerably more dangerous. Gathering her shawl around her, and with great effort, she gingerly put one leg over the top of the stockade and then the other. Fear clutched at her, of the soldiers, of being discovered, of the precipitous drop to the ground. She felt her lungs laboring under the weight of it.

"Katie."

Black Moon's voice barking out her name cut through the paralyzing web of fright. She cast a petrified glance back over her shoulder. The fire brigade was fast getting the flames under control. If she didn't act now, it would be too late. Her heart rose in her throat as she sat there for several treacherous moments, her hair whipping about in the stark November wind.

Katie knew what she had to do. Forcing her shaky limbs to obey, she braced herself. But just as she was about to jump, she cried out as the hem of her dress caught on a splintered log. With a mighty tug, she tore her dress loose. Over the roar of her heart she did not hear the fabric rip. Placing her trust in Black Moon's strong, capable hands, she jumped.

He caught her before her feet even touched the ground and used his strength to guide her safely to an upright position. So relieved was she to find herself standing and unhurt that she burst out with nervous laughter.

He gave her a cross look, and pulled her forward, but Katie dug in her heels, refusing to budge.

"We cannot leave Ned behind." She struggled to be free.

"It is too dangerous to go back. He will find his way out."

"What if he cannot? What if Captain Fetterman recognizes him from Fort Reno? We have to go back."

Black Moon issued a low grumble under his breath. "There is nothing to be done."

"You don't understand," she protested.

Dark hints of anger appeared in his eyes. "Enough of this," he said forcefully. Ignoring her objections, he swept her up in his arms. Tossing her over his shoulder like a sack of flour, he darted off into the darkness with Katie beating at his back.

Black Moon plunged through the bristly soap weeds, and only when the fort appeared in the distance behind him as a dark shadow against the night did he release her.

She landed on the cold ground with a thud and jumped to her feet. Oblivious to the sharp bite of the Winter Moon, she threw her head back, and with her hair streaming in the wind glared up at him and breathlessly declared, "I will not be treated like a child."

"Then do not act like one," he angrily replied as he stalked away.

For several moments Katie just stood there, bubbling with anger. She cast a disdainful glance back at the log walls of Fort Phil Kearny. As much as she hated to admit it, Black Moon was right. It was too dangerous to go back. Looking away from the fire's orange glow against the night sky, she grudgingly followed him through the shadows.

They found the bay gelding where he had tethered it to a low-hanging branch. His strong hands went around her waist to hoist her onto the pony's back. He jumped up behind her, and her breath quickened when his arms went around her and she felt the warm, solid shape of him pressed to her back. His hands on the jaw rope were quiet and firm, and years of horse mastery were evident in the subtle, almost imperceptible, way he urged his pony into a gallop.

High up into the hills they rode, away from the fort, away from the soldiers, away from Ned. Katie vowed she would never forgive Black Moon if anything happened to Ned.

CHAPTER 23
THE STAR THAT ALWAYS STANDS IN ONE PLACE

Black Moon hobbled his pony's feet a stone's throw away. Gathering some kindling, he set about getting a small fire going using his flint and striker. Out of dry brush he fashioned a heat reflector to direct the fire's heat in one direction and to hide the glow of the fire from unwanted eyes, and then spread a layer of dead leaves and brush over the cold ground.

An uneasiness hung between them as they settled in to wait out the rest of the night. With only one buffalo robe for warmth, they sat side by side with the robe wrapped around their shoulders. It reminded Black Moon of the time when the sting of being stripped of the bighorn shirt and his honor as Shirt Wearer had been so great that he had galloped off into the driving snow to be alone with his bitterness and regret. There had arisen behind him the sound of someone riding hard after him. It was Katie, who had seen past his anger to the pain beneath and who told him that she would love him even if he wore no shirt at all. That day, the snow had turned into a blizzard, and as they huddled together beneath his buffalo robe, even though she was his brother's wife, they had succumbed to their insatiable desire for each other.

As they sat now in tense silence before the crackling fire, he flexed his fingers, wanting desperately to touch her. But he was nursing his anger over her leaving him and forced himself to curb the impulse. She wanted only to do a little trading, she had said, but if he had not risked his own life to rescue her from the soldier town, would she be sitting here with him? Would she have returned to him as she had promised, or was it just so many empty words spoken in a moment of weakness?

So much around him was changing. When he was a boy, the buffalo covered the earth like a giant robe stretching from one horizon to the other. Now, the buffalo scouts had to travel farther to find them. Hide hunters came, killing the buffalo, first taking only the tongues, then the hides that they piled as high as lodges. Some of his people were living on the agencies, no longer living the wild and free life. Even the sacred *paha sapa*, the heart of all things, was changing as more and more white men came into Lakota country. There was a time when he could ride for days without seeing another human being. Now, soldier towns dotted the land. First, it was the one on Dry Fork that the whites called Fort Reno. Then, the one on Buffalo Creek. Was Katie's love for him changing, as well?

Somewhere out in the frozen distance the resonant song of a wolf rode on the wind, offering faint reassurance that some things stayed the same. He reminded himself that some men waited a lifetime and never found the kind of love he found with this green-eyed woman, but if he lost Katie, there would be no wolf call loud enough nor strong enough to offer reassurance to his broken heart. He knew better than most that there were certain unavoidable realities in life, and that the wounds suffered by the heart were the most grievous of all.

The sound of Katie's stomach grumbling brought Black Moon's head up from his brooding thoughts.

"With the new sun I will hunt for food."

"What about Ned?"

"When your white man comes out with the others to get the wood, he will know where to find us."

"We must help him get back to his people," she said.

He was staring coldly into the fire, his proud, unflinching profile etched against the orange glow of the flames. "And will you be going with him?"

When so much was uncertain, Katie did not dare to think beyond the moment. "I do not know what I will do," she answered, although in truth, she did not envision a future for herself with Ned Jeppsen.

"Do you want to go back to that place in the east?" he asked.

She shrugged, brushing his shoulder with hers. "I do not know."

"Is there anything you *do* know?" he questioned irritably.

"I know that I love you."

He turned to face her then. An expression of anger and pain twisted his handsome features. "And you show your love for me by leaving?"

"I do not know where I belong. I thought the only way to find out was to go back there, but I see now that I was wrong."

He gave an angry laugh. "And perhaps I was wrong to come and get you."

"Please try to understand," she said in a softly beseeching voice.

The robe fell from his shoulders and the flames danced this way and that as he sprang to his feet. "You ask too much of me." He stomped away. Stopping suddenly, he turned back to her. "Why did you say you wanted me to take you with me?"

It had happened so quickly. One moment he was not there and the next moment he was. Had it been a moment of weakness caused by the sight of him, the smell of sage in his hair, and the promise of what his touch could do to her that had prompted her to ask him to take her with him? "I know only what is in my heart."

"And do you know what is in your white man's heart?"

"I do not know what you mean."

"Do you think I do not know that he loves you?"

Her eyelashes lowered. "Oh, that."

"Yes, that. He told the soldier chief at Dry Fork that he is your husband."

"He only said that to protect me."

"Or perhaps he said it because he wishes it."

She peered up at his imposing form. Under his steady glare, she ran out of evasions. "All right, he is in love with me. I cannot help what he feels."

"And you?" he questioned. "What do you feel?"

Throwing the robe off her shoulders, she got up and went to him. "How can you think there could be any other man for me after everything we have been to each other?" She reached for his hand, but he flinched away. "Will you let your anger stand in the way of what you want?"

"What I want and what I can have are not always the same things."

"You want me," she said. "I can see it in your eyes. "And you can have me. I have always been yours for the taking." This time when she reached for his hand, he did not pull away. "You said you would show me later how much you want me." She placed his hand on her breast and felt his fingers twitch. "I would ask my husband to show me now."

"You play with my heart like it is a toy," he grumbled.

"No. I am the toy. And you can play with me any way you wish."

He was stunned by her boldness that made her say such a thing when he really should not have been surprised at all, for she had never been quiet and demure like proper Lakota women. For several moments he glared at her, trying to decide between his heart and his mind. Which should he listen to? His mind told him to remember that his priorities were his people and the land and his fight to protect them both, and that he should hate her for playing with his emotions like this. He glanced quickly toward the west where the Thunder Beings lived, the direction of power. But looking back at her, he felt his power weakening and he knew that his heart was rapidly winning this battle.

Grabbing her hand, he pulled her back to the bed of leaves and pushed her down upon it. Ordinarily, he exhibited a measure of control in his lovemaking, owing to his size and strength over her. But not now. Not when he was trying so hard to hate her and wanting nothing more to do with her, all the while loving her and wanting her and unable to imagine living another moment without her.

He knew her body was too slight for the whole of his weight, yet he was all animal power and urgency as he came down hard over her, pressing himself against her length and hearing her breath faltering under his weight. There was no denying his hunger. His mouth ravaged hers as if he were starved for its taste. His teeth raked across her lips and his fingers dug into the curve of her waist.

If it was his intention to hurt her, he was succeeding, but she reveled in the power he had over her. Her body throbbed for more. She lost herself in the feel of him. She dug her nails into his shoulders. No one but him could make her feel like this—mindless and aching. Each time with him was like the first time, and every kiss was as if it would be their last.

With his mouth locked on hers, he tore impatiently at her calico dress, the one she had gotten at the sutler's store and whose seams she now heard ripping and did not care. She lay naked and trembling beneath him. The winter wind blew overhead, but a desperate heat raced between them, and her flesh felt singed everywhere he touched. There rose in her an overwhelming need to be possessed, to be taken and claimed and made to feel that she belonged only to him.

She ached for the feel of his naked flesh against hers, but when she attempted to push the buckskin shirt up over his head, he threw her hands off him. Lifting his hips, he loosened the rawhide ties on his leggings and pushed his breech clout aside, and forcing the space between her legs to widen, he came into her without ceremony.

She could not stop him, and if it had not been her husband who she loved more than life itself, she would have fought his invasion instead of moaning his name to the wind with a desperate hunger that shook her to her core.

She whimpered a little at the aggressive power of his body as he thrust into her. Her head fell back as she surrendered to his conquest.

He took her the only way he knew how, giving up control and thrusting with potency. With an explosive tremor he burst within her. He gave a final shudder, and with a rush of breath at her ear, collapsed against her.

He lay there for a few moments before rolling off to the side, pulling the buffalo robe up over her nakedness as he did. As fiercely as the need had whipped through him before, it was with a gentler touch that he brushed her hair behind her ear and asked, "Did I hurt you?"

It did not matter to Katie that her skin was chafed by the buckskin shirt and leggings that he had not bothered to remove, or that her mouth felt bruised from the savagery of his kisses, or that he sated his own pleasure with no regard for hers. What mattered was that he wanted her and needed her, and if the look in his eyes was to be believed, that he loved her. She shook her head and nestled against him.

"I know I did. I acted like a selfish boy who thinks only of himself. I will have to make sure to give you enough hides to tan, otherwise, I would fear for my own hide."

"One of the fiercest warriors among the Lakota is making fun of himself?" Katie chided.

"It is not good to take yourself too seriously," he said. "Perhaps I also take others too seriously."

"Others? Like who?"

"Your white man," he grudgingly admitted. "For all of his faults, he is not a bad sign-talker."

"He has been a good friend to me. I could not bear to lose him." She sat up and hugged her knees. "I have already lost so many."

With the tip of his finger he traced the line of her spine. "The old ones say that heartbreak falls into every life as surely as snow falls in winter and life moves in a circle," he said. "But there is one whose loss will never be accepted as a part of life. Her journey was like a shooting star that flashes across the sky and is over much too quickly." He hadn't meant to say that. The words that hovered perpetually in his mind had slipped out before he could stop them.

Katie tensed. This was a loss they did not speak of, one that cut so deeply the spirit never healed.

He went on in a sad, reflective tone, talking mostly to himself. "She would be approaching her sixth winter. Now she runs and plays in the Land of Many Lodges. It is a wonderful place filled with good things. The buffalo and other animals roam the land and all things that ever existed live forever. She lives there now with my mother and my brother."

His words trailed off as the memory returned of that cold, cruel winter when he had erected a scaffold of four forked posts with a platform no higher than his chest and tied to it a buffalo-hide bundle no bigger than a child's toy. But it was not a child's toy. It was a child. His child. From the support poles he hung the stuffed deer-hide doll he had made for her. Then he had clambered up onto the platform and held the tiny bundle in his arms, his tears freezing as they fell from his eyes. Back at the village, while his family members underwent the *wacekiyapi*, the worship ceremony, walking solemnly, weeping and singing of their grief, he had stayed out in the cold with his arms wrapped around his daughter. The snows were deep and the winter wind howled, but still he stayed, his hair crusted with ice, using his body to keep her warm as she traveled the spirit trail.

He had been taught that death was a part of life. Sooner or later everyone died, as did his cousin Hail Storm, his brother Fire Cloud, his mother Pretty Shield, and his friend Lone Horn. He was not afraid of his own death. Dying gloriously in defense of the people was an honor for every Lakota fighting man. But where was the honor or the glory in the death of a child? The gut-wrenching impact of that tiny bundle atop the scaffold was a hard, unbending truth that challenged his faith in the goodness in life.

Days had passed in which he had ignored his hunger and thirst. Finally, when there were no more tears left to shed, he climbed down from the scaffold and returned to the village. There, he saw that the women had hacked off their hair and gashed their arms in the Lakota way of mourning. But Katie had not. Nor had she keened or even cried. She seemed incapable of accepting comfort or giving it. Instead, she had retreated behind a shield of inconsolable grief. His attempts to speak of their loss were met with resistance. It was not good to keep all that sorrow buried inside, but if that was her way, who was he to question it?

As time passed, things seemed to return to normal. Katie fixed their meals, prepared the dried meat, tanned the hides he brought back to her, mended his torn moccasins, and cared for Little Storm as tenderly as the boy's true mother would have done. At night, beneath the robes, she opened herself up to him and fired him up with the depth of her passion. But as the seasons went by something began to change. She seemed restless and guarded. Often, she jumped astride her pony and rode out onto the prairie alone. Sometimes, he would catch her looking off at nothing in particular with an expression of unbearable heartache on her face, and he knew she was thinking about the little one they lost.

Katie shifted and turned her face away to hide from him the tears that threatened to spill. She had tucked away the memory that was too painful to recall. Was it the thought of losing Ned, or the loss of her mother to cholera and her father and brother to an attack by soldiers that caused the memory to surge back after all these years? Or perhaps it was Black Moon's quiet voice that made her remember it as if it had happened only yesterday.

The baby had been born along the Yellowstone when the snows had come early. In the days leading up to the birth one of Black Moon's grandmothers had fashioned two sand lizards, chosen because the little creatures were hard to kill, out of hide and decorated with red and white quills. One was to hold the child's cord after birth. The other was to be worn around the child's neck when she began to walk to guard her against the forces that might harm her. As the time neared, her mother-in-law had laid down a clean square of deerskin to catch the baby and driven a study stake into the ground at the rear of the lodge. When the pains began in earnest, she had squatted at the stake, grasping the top and pressing her knees against it. Her mother-in-law placed the newborn on the deerskin, cut the cord and drew it through a puff ball, dusting it with the fungus powder before fitting it over the navel. The infant had been swaddled in a strip of deerskin to hold the puff ball in place, cleansed with sweet grass soaked in warm water, wiped with buffalo grease, wrapped in a blanket, and placed at her breast.

Katie had noticed right off that the baby had difficulty drawing breath. It was not until two days later that she knew the tragic extent of it when she cradled in her arms a child whose heart was no longer beating. There would be no feast for naming the baby, no cradle gifts, no giving of gifts to family and friends. Apparently, those little sand lizards were not so hard to kill, after all.

To the Lakota, bearing a child was the fulfillment of a woman's role, and there had been nowhere for her to turn except toward the unbearable truth that she had failed. Like a kettle when the hot stones are dropped in to make the water boil, her tears had bubbled up inside of her, yet she had forced them back. In her grief she had accepted solace from no one, not even her husband, and had simply been incapable of offering him the comfort he needed, which she did not have to give.

As she huddled there lost in remembering, Katie was unaware that her shoulders had begun to shake until her whole body was wracked with sobs that she could not control. The tears that had been held back for so long burst forth like water through a broken beaver dam, and the wails that had been locked in her throat split the frosty stillness.

Startled out of his own tortured thoughts, Black Moon reached for her and pulled her close. Pushing back the hair from her face, he sought to wipe away the tears that rolled down her cheeks, but they were so many that all he could do was fold her to his chest and let her weep against the soft buckskin of his shirt.

He held her like that for a long time, his own tears falling against the top of her head.

They held each other delicately, like two broken things. Gradually, her sobs eased, and she caught her breath in great gasping gulps. It was a long time before she could speak. Turning her face up to his, with starlight glistening in her tear-shiny eyes, her voice eked out from a place somewhere deep inside of her.

"She was so little."

Black Moon tried to steady his own voice, but failed. "So little, but so big in our hearts."

"She looked like her father. The same dark hair and eyes." She choked back a sob. "I named her Kathleen."

He had not heard the name before tonight, and despite his vow never to speak the white man's language, he asked, "What is this Kath-leen?"

"It was my mother's name. You do not mind?" She took a deep breath, and knowing how he felt about the white world, prepared herself for his reaction.

He tucked her quivering head beneath his chin, and in a voice as gentle as a summer wind across the prairie, he said, "I do not mind. I called her *Wichapi Owanjila*. You do not mind?"

"The star that always stands in one place," she repeated. "I do not mind."

"She will always stand in one place inside of me. Here." He touched his hand to his heart.

"You never said."

"There were no words to say it." *And you were not ready to hear it or speak of it.* He looked off into the darkness, and in a voice scarcely audible, confessed, "I still see her face."

"It was so hard for me to speak the words I carried in my heart," she said. "Can you forgive me for my silence? I never meant to keep you out of my sorrow. I just could not—"

He pressed the pad of his finger to her lips. "There are times when I can feel the heartbeat of Mother Earth, and it is in the silence between those beats that I find peace. Silence is good, and sometimes it is necessary."

For many heartbeats they clung to each other, feeling the cold air on their faces and breathing in the scent from the pines, the silence all around them growing deeper. And for the first time since that terrible winter, they mourned the loss of their newborn together.

Chapter 24
Trouble Will Come

It was late when Captain William Fetterman knocked on the Colonel's door and entered. Snapping to attention, he saluted.

Carrington glanced up from his papers and offered a weary salute in return. "Is the fire sufficiently out?"

"Yes sir. We were able to save several bales, but we'll have to send to Fort Reno for more before the overland trails freeze and the horses and mules starve."

"I'll send a detail out in the morning. What of the men?"

"They're in the barracks," Fetterman replied.

"They worked admirably to extinguish the blaze. I'll address them after mess."

When Fetterman did not budge, the Colonel raised his eyebrows and asked, "Is there more, Captain?"

"Yes sir. The woman is gone."

"The woman?"

"Black Moon's woman."

"What do you mean she is gone?"

"Just that. She is not in her dwelling. I saw her just before the fire broke out. When the flames were under control, I went to check on her and she's not there."

"Perhaps she is staying with my wife," Carrington suggested.

"No sir. Even though the hour is late, I took the liberty of going to your home to see if Mrs. Carrington and the children are all right, and Mrs. Carrington has not seen her since yesterday."

The Colonel stroked his chin. "Well, that is one less thing we will have to worry about."

"She could have provided vital information on that renegade, Black Moon."

"That was not likely," Carrington responded. "Perhaps your impression of her differed from mine. I got the distinct impression that she was tolerating us until she found a means of escape."

"Well, she found it," Fetterman said. "And in the process, we lost almost all of our hay, and one of our sentries was found atop the stockade wall with an arrow in his back." Fetterman pressed his point. "That fire was no coincidence. I tell you, this is Black Moon's doing. Sir, if you would reinstate me to my command, I can track him to his village and wipe them out. On one of my reconnaissance missions, I spied a village about thirty miles north of the Tongue. There could not have been more than a dozen or so warriors. That's where he's bound to be."

Carrington rose from behind his desk and stomped to the door. Pulling it open, he ordered his aide, "Tell Jim Bridger to come at once."

A short time later there came a knock on the door. A tall man, still muscular for his advanced age, entered and took the seat to which Carrington gestured.

Turning to the old man, Carrington said, "I'm sorry to call you out so late, Jim. What can you tell me of the village north of the Tongue, about thirty miles from here?"

Stifling a yawn, the old man replied, "Sioux. Maybe some Cheyenne. They run with the Sioux."

"Captain Fetterman here says from what he observed there did not appear to be more than dozen or so warriors. Is that usual?"

"For a winter village, maybe. They break up into smaller villages come the winter months. But if the Captain saw only a couple dozen warriors, you can bet there's more he didn't see."

"How many?" Carrington questioned.

"More'n likely a thousand if you count all the villages on the Tongue."

Carrington turned back to Fetterman. "That would make it difficult to ascertain precisely which village Black Moon is in. Mr. Bridger has spent a lifetime acquiring his knowledge about the Indians, so I am inclined to believe his assessment and deny your request to track Black Moon." Sliding his chair back, he got up, went to the stove in a corner of the room, and opening the stove, put in two pieces of split wood.

Fetterman threw up his hands. "Sir, we have the strength to take the offensive."

Returning to his desk, Carrington turned to the old man. "Jim? Do you have an opinion on the subject?"

Bridger pursed his lips. "Why go lookin' for trouble? Give it time and the trouble will come to you."

"You expect things to get worse?" the Colonel asked.

"The way things are goin', they sure as hell ain't gonna get better. And from what I hear, Black Moon is riding with Crazy Horse. Those two can stir up a heap of trouble."

"If we wanted to find Black Moon, where would you suggest we look?" Fetterman asked.

"His people usually make a winter camp up around Bear Butte."

"There, you see," said Carrington, turning to Fetterman. "He's not even in the area."

"'Cept I also hear that this year he stuck around. If you're lookin' for Black Moon, chances are, you'll find him at Crazy Horse's camp up on the Tongue."

Carrington contemplated the situation based on Jim Bridger's knowledge. The old mountain man's experience reached back to the twenties. His conversational knowledge of French, Spanish and a few of the native languages enabled him to trade with the tribes and keep his scalp. He'd been married three times to Indian women, one the daughter of a Shoshone chief, and fathered five children. His discovery of an overland route that came to be known as Bridger's Pass shortened the Oregon Trail by more than sixty miles, and as recently as two years ago he had blazed the Bridger Trail, an alternate route from Wyoming to the Montana gold fields that avoided the dangerous Bozeman. Bridger had more than forty years of exploring, trapping, hunting, and guiding throughout the west under his belt, and the Colonel was not about to ignore his advice.

"Thank you, Jim," Carrington said. "I will take everything you said under advisement."

When the old mountain man got up and left, Fetterman said, "Sir, about my reinstatement."

Turning a bespectacled look on him, Carrington said, "I will consider it. Until then, Lieutenant Powell will lead the escort of the wood train in the morning. That's all, Captain."

When Fetterman was gone, Carrington removed his spectacles and rubbed the place on his nose where they perched. What Fetterman did not know, and what the Colonel was reluctant to tell him, was that General Cooke had issued a direct order to turn his earnest attention to the possibility of striking the hostile bands by surprise in their winter camps. It was precisely the fight Fetterman was looking for.

Outside, Fetterman turned his collar up to the cold. The wind stung his face as he stomped back to his quarters.

"William!"

Turning, he saw Lieutenant Powell darting toward him from across the parade ground.

"That was a close call," Powell said. He was panting, and his face was smudged with smoke. "We were lucky to get the flames out or we might have lost the mule stables. I saw you come out of Carrington's office. Has he reinstated you to your command?"

"Not yet," Fetterman icily replied. "But he will when he has need of me."

"Damn. I guess that means I'll be going out with the wood detail in the morning. I hope we don't run into any trouble."

"Old man Bridger says there's more than a thousand of those heathens out there," Fetterman grumbled. "I don't care if there's a million. I've seen firsthand the dismal ability of those Sioux as combatants. An organized offensive against them would do the trick. But nothing will change until we have a new post commander."

"A man like yourself, you mean?"

"Why not? Before I left Omaha I was informed that the Frontier Army plans another reorganization. General Cooke said the 2nd Battalion will become the center for the new 27th Regiment and that I will replace Carrington as the battalion's commanding officer."

"Cooke said that?"

"Not in so many words. But he strongly hinted it. And the first order of the day will be to go after Black Moon."

"That's if you can find him."

"Bridger says he's with Crazy Horse up on the Tongue about thirty miles from here. It shouldn't be too hard to find the village."

"What has you so riled up against Black Moon?" Powell asked. "Red Cloud and Crazy Horse are just as bad."

"Let's just say he has something I want."

"Would that be a red-haired woman?"

"What makes you say that?" Fetterman said, irritated.

"I saw the look in your eyes when you were talking to her at the Colonel's house. That little lady has worked her way under your skin."

As much as Fetterman hated to admit it, Powell was right. Katie McCabe had indeed gotten to him. Not just because she was beautiful. Of that there was no doubt, and he was, after all, a man with a man's hungers. But more than that, it galled him to think that she preferred that Indian over a man like himself. The idea that a mere savage could outsmart and outfight an officer of the United States Army was an affront to him. "If it's the last thing I do," Fetterman vowed, "I'll rub out that damn Indian."

"How do you plan to do that?" Powell asked.

"The way to get to him is through the woman. She's gone, and the carpenter will have to make a coffin for the sentry we found dead with an arrow in his back. Black Moon must place great importance on her if he risked his own life to sneak in here to get her. If I can get my hands on her, that Indian will walk right into a trap."

Powell looked at the man who outranked him in length of service. "Let's get this uncorked." From beneath his coat pulled out a bottle of whiskey. "Come on. I'd say we both can use it."

CHAPTER 25
DUST CLOUD

Ned never considered himself to be much of a risk-taker. It wasn't until an early spring day in Minnesota, when he turned the cows out to pasture, that he looked out across the farmland and wondered what lay beyond his immediate world and ways. Was farming the way to make a better future for his family, or did the future lie down untrodden paths and into perilous territories? Was he willing to risk his life and the lives of his wife and children on a wagon train heading west and face rushing rivers, deep canyons, high mountains, and Indians to carve out a place for them? The answer had come with a steep cost.

It had all happened so fast, one tragedy following on the heels of another and then another, and now, here he was, lonely and far from home, with all his dreams having crumbled around him. And then the unthinkable happened. He met Katie McCabe, and just when it seemed there might be hope to rebuild his life with her, he was left with the dismal reality that she was another man's wife.

He could not blame her for loving a man like Black Moon. Black Moon was a fighter, a leader of his people. Reckless and dangerous, he was like the quiet thunder rolling over the prairie bringing the promise of the storm to come. What could a simple farmer like himself offer a woman like Katie whose heart was as wild and unpredictable as this land? If there was any solace to be derived from any of this, it was the thought that at least she was safely away from this place and back with the man she loved.

With the enlisted men asleep in their beds, he snuck out of the barrack, hoping that a walk in the cold night air would help clear the confusion swirling in his head. He was thinking of home and all he had lost and all that might have been when he spotted Captain Fetterman emerge from Colonel Carrington's quarters. It was only the unexpected appearance of Lieutenant Powell that diverted Fetterman's attention, enabling Ned to duck unseen between the buildings that housed the officers' quarters and the post commander's quarters. He huddled there, blowing warm breath into his cupped hands, wishing the two officers would hurry along so that he could get back to the barrack where the open bay was heated by a cast-iron stove.

But as he stood there shivering and listening to their conversation, Ned's frozen fingers clenched into fists of rage. Fetterman was going to use Katie as bait to snare Black Moon. Equally obvious was the Captain's intention to have Katie for himself. Katie was not some prize for the taking. With a gasp of disgust, Ned put his head down and hurried back to the barrack.

The next morning, with his Kentucky percussion rifle in the crook of his arm, Ned joined the escort. Word around the fort was that Carrington had relieved Fetterman of his command, and with Lieutenant Powell leading the escort, there was no need for him to ride with his cap pulled down over his forehead.

Although it was easy enough slipping in with the wood train escort and convincing the enlisted men that he was one of them, he was constantly looking over his shoulder for Captain Fetterman who was sure to recognize him from Fort Reno, and he didn't want to think about the consequences if it were discovered that he had started the fire in the hay yard.

How long could he keep up the charade? He wasn't cut out for life as a frontier soldier. His only hope was to join a wagon train, a prospect he found daunting considering all that overland travel entailed. On the westward journey he'd seen enough sickness, accidental gunshot wounds, drownings at river crossings, lightning strikes, and blinding heat to last a lifetime. Some stretches of the Oregon Trail had been so rough that the wagons bumped along hard enough to churn milk into butter. It had been a trip fraught with peril and personal tragedy. On the journey east he'd barely escaped an Indian attack. Still, if joining a wagon train was the only way to get away from the fort, he was willing to do it. Westward, eastward, it did not matter in which direction it was headed, he just had to get away from Fort Phil Kearny. But the Bozeman was already icing over, making wagon travel too treacherous, and with months to go before the trail could be traveled, Ned's hope of joining a wagon train was rapidly slipping away.

With every dead or wounded trooper, every horse or mule stolen, and every ambush by Indians, tension at the fort was mounting. The soldiers bickered among themselves. The troop was rapidly disintegrating under the weight of petty feuds. The outlandish cost of a full uniform at one hundred dollars and seventeen dollars for a new pair of boots was impossible for a trooper to afford on his paltry pay. Since Ned wasn't on the enlistment rolls, it was pay he would not receive. He still had some money left in his pocket, enough to entice an emigrant family to let him join them, that is, if he could hold out until spring, and if Fetterman didn't recognize him before that, and if he wasn't killed in an Indian attack. All things considered, Ned could feel his luck running out.

The escort was edgy as it made its way over the icy trail. They were about half-way along the four-mile journey to the pinery when a thin column of dust was spotted on the Bozeman in the distance.

Lieutenant Powell came cantering back along the escort line and fell in beside Ned. "What's your name, soldier?"

Ned answered tentatively. "Jeppsen, sir."

"And you?' he asked of the trooper riding beside Ned.

"Hobbs, sir."

"I want you two to ride up into those hills and see if you can get a look at whatever's making that dust cloud and report back to me."

"You think it's a war party, sir?" Hobbs asked nervously.

"It's probably just some riders along Bozeman."

"I can go alone, sir," Ned offered, thinking slyly that it would be a good chance for him to make a break for it.

"If it's Indians, you'll be glad for the company. You'll go together," Powell said, dashing Ned's hope.

CHAPTER 26
LIKE MIST ON THE RIVER

Cold gripped the land under a brightening sky.

Katie pushed the buffalo robe aside and sat up. Shivering against the cold, she glanced down at the calico dress whose seams were torn from Black Moon's lust. Her body felt bruised from his urgent possession and her lips were still red from his forceful kisses. But thoughts of last night under the robe with him brought a flush to her cheeks and a renewed hope that everything would be all right between them.

She saw him squatting before a fire. Beside him was the rabbit he had brought down with an unerring arrow while she'd still been sleeping. She watched as he removed his knife from its beaded sheath at his belt, and work quietly and skillfully to skin and gut the carcass. Steam rose from the warm blood as it stained the snow.

He was such a part of his surroundings. He and the land were one. Just as their bodies had been one last night. But it was more than their passion for each other that made her feel awakened. It was the release of a long-held memory. For the first time in a long time she felt an easing from the burden of grief. The loss would remain with her forever, but the long-held pain of it had receded like mist on the river in early morning to reveal a bright, sparkling ribbon of hope.

Rising, she pulled the hide along with her. Wrapped in the heavy robe, she joined him by the fire. With one hand clutching the robe, she held her other hand above the flames to warm it, and said, "I am hungry."

Black Moon put the skinned rabbit on a spit and hung it over the fire. "There is a good long-ears roasting here. Soon there will be food to fill you."

She placed a warmed hand lightly on his shoulder. "It is not food I want."

He looked up at her. She was smiling in that way that made his heart lurch in his chest and caused his man part to stiffen. He rose slowly and turned to face her. "I cannot know what you want unless you tell me." He was playing with her, forcing her to tell him what he already knew.

"I want to feel your hands on me."

"A proper Lakota woman would not say such a thing."

"I am not a proper Lakota woman," she responded. "I do not wait for things to come to me."

"I have noticed."

"Do you object?"

"Only when you leave me to find out where you belong."

"This is where I belong." She allowed the robe to slip from her body. Standing naked and shivering before him, she took his hand and placed it against the mound between her legs. "And this is where you belong."

His fingers flexed against the dark curls. "I do not know," he roughly teased. "Perhaps I should go in search of something better. That is what you did, is it not?"

"I went in search of something, yes. But not of something better. There could be nothing better for me than this." She moved her hips forward, pressing herself against his hand.

"Is this all I am to you? A means to your pleasure?"

"I would be lying if I said you do not bring me pleasure. But last night the pleasure was all yours. Am I not deserving, as well?"

She drew in a sharp breath and trembled when his fingers pushed past the curls.

"Are you cold?" he asked.

"Not when you are touching me like this."

He moved his thumb over the source of her heat. "Is this what you want?"

"Oh, yes."

"I am out of practice," he taunted. "When my woman left me, my skill grew rusty. Is this how it is done?"

She was gasping now, her breath coming out in white bursts against the frosty stillness. "Like that," she rasped. "Yes."

As his motions increased in intensity, it drew from her the wetness that made it easy for him to slip a finger into her. Winding his free arm around her waist, he pulled her hard up against him. Her back arched and she felt the deep vibrations from within his chest against her breasts.

Cupping her breasts, he lowered his face to the cleft between them. "These are for the child," he rasped. "Not for the man to taste."

She swallowed a gasp, her voice muffled against his hair. "That has never stopped you before." Clasping his head in her hands, she brought his face to one nipple hardened by cold and desire. "It is yours."

He tried to go slow, but the taste of her drew an urgent response from him. Tugging at her nipple with his teeth, he closed his mouth over it and suckled, not as a child, but as a man with a man's desperate hunger.

Soft moans escaped her and her body tightened. It hurt a little, but it was a glorious pain that moved through her entire being. His probing fingers and deep kisses were driving her beyond reason. Without thought, acting now solely on instinct and desire, she plunged her hand between their bodies, and pushing aside his breech clout, wrapped her fingers around his hardness. In between soft gasps, she said, "You asked that I tell you what I want." Her fingers tightened, drawing a groan from him. "This is what I want."

She released her hold on him, extricated herself from his provocative fingers, and walked toward the bed of dried grass.

His mouth went dry at the sway of her hips. Sweeping the robe up from the ground, he followed after her.

Reclining back against the bed of dried grass, she propped herself up on her elbows and said, "I want to look at you."

With a crooked smile on his face, he began to undress. "You are a wicked woman."

"I am a woman who thrills to the sight of her husband's body."

When he stood before her as naked as she was, her eyes traveled over his well-knit form etched against the blue sky, from the broad shoulders, to the arms heavily muscled from years of drawing taut bow strings, the veins showing in the early-morning sunlight, to the slender hips and corded thighs, and coming to rest on that part of him that held no secrets, her eyes widening with appreciation at the hardness that strained against the daylight.

Lifting her eyes to his, she found his gaze strong and heavy upon her, unbridled passion sparking in their dark depths. "Are you finished looking, or would you have me stand here in the cold?" he asked.

Her gaze swept over him in a final all-consuming look. "I am finished looking."

He dropped to his knees in the space between her legs. "And now?"

"Now I would have you inside me, filling me up with your heat."

"And with my love."

He came down over her, molding the lean length of his body to the slender shape of hers, pulling the buffalo robe up over their heads.

To the red-tailed hawk that flew overhead on currents of air rose the sounds of whimpers and moans, of whispers of love and wordless murmurings of passionate accord, of feminine cries and masculine groans.

Afterwards, they lay wrapped in each other's arms in the warmth of the robe. Katie turned her head to the side and nuzzled his neck, tasting the salt of desire and satisfaction on his brown skin. She ran her hand across his smooth chest, grateful that there were no Sun Dance scars to mar its muscled perfection. He claimed he did not need the rigors of the Sun Dance to prove himself to the Great Mystery. While others drove pegs into their flesh and hung by thongs from the Sun Dance pole until the pegs broke loose, tearing the flesh, he proved his supplication in all that he did and all that he was.

His voice drifted into the cold stillness like a feather on the wind.

"The autumn hunt yielded plenty of meat. The children play even in the cold. I taught Little Storm the snow-snake game since the ice on Beaver Creek is thick and solid."

Katie gave him an inquisitive look. Beaver Creek was a small east tributary of the Tongue River, far from where Black Moon's Oglala traditionally made their winter camp. "You have moved to Beaver Creek?"

"I, my father and mother and Little Storm and my aunts and cousins."

"I thought you would have led the people to *Mato Paha* to wait out the winter moons."

"Swift Bear led them."

"Why not you?"

"It is easier for me to keep an eye on the bluecoats from here."

"You mean it is easier to attack the Powder River Road," she muttered. "And the wood trains that leave the fort each day."

"I do what must be done," he said.

"And Crazy Horse?"

"My young friend has never shown much interest in planning hunts or deciding where his camp will move, but now that the talk is about killing whites, he has made his voice heard."

"Does he know of the soldiers' threat against the children over the age of seven? The trader was bringing this news to the camps at *Mato Paha*."

"He knows. Riders came from the *paha sapa* to tell of it."

Katie was relieved to know that Jasper Gillette had made it to the Oglala winter camp with the news of Fetterman's threat. "What will he do?"

"Whatever it takes to keep his people safe."

"There is something about him that is unsettling," she said. "It is as if his spirit is scarred."

"It is said that when Crazy Horse was born, because of his light hair and fair skin, his father accused his mother of being with a white man. My father says that Crazy Horse's parents were both Lakota. His father was Oglala and his mother was Minniconjou. But she could not bear the shame of the accusation and hung herself from a cottonwood.

Crazy Horse's relatives sought to hide the manner of her death from him, but a child kept from the truth is often unable to put the event in its rightful place and carries it as an unhealed wound throughout his life. His father took another woman for his wife, and over the years Crazy Horse has enjoyed a good relationship with his new mother and her children. If there is something that saddens him now, it is pining for a woman he cannot be with."

"You mean Black Buffalo Woman. Whenever we have visited his camp I have seen his feelings for her in his eyes. But I have also seen another look in his eyes. It is fierce and uncompromising. It is the same look I have seen in your eyes when you speak of the whites."

"We both want to drive the *washicus* out of our country," he said.

"Yes, in that way, and in others, you and he are the same. You both take the lead in battle and are first to meet any challenge, you are both familiar with loss, and I think he must have dark thoughts and doubts just like you. But he is not nearly as good-looking or well-built as you are."

He smiled broadly. "You think I am good-looking?"

She gave him a playful punch on the shoulder. "Do not get too full of yourself. And do not ever let me find you pining for another woman."

"Ho!" he cried. "I have learned my lesson well."

He was referring, of course, to Pine Leaf, the Cheyenne girl who had nursed him back to health when he'd been struck down by a bluecoat's bullet.

Drawing Katie's hands to his mouth, he kissed her open palms. "These are the only hands I will ever allow to touch me."

"Even if you lay dying?" she teased.

He plucked a piece of dried buffalo grass from her hair. "Even then."

They lay there like that, discovering and rediscovering each other as the sun rose over the hills and sent its light deep into the gullies.

After a while, Black Moon extricated himself from her embrace and got up. "We cannot lay here all day," he said. Swiping his buckskin shirt off the ground, he pulled it on over his head, then drew on his leggings and slipped his breech clout into place. "Tell me about

Little White Chief," he said as he slid his feet into his moccasins. "What kind of man is he?"

Katie shimmied into her calico dress and pulled on her black leather shoes. Clutching her shawl tight around herself, she said, "He asked the same thing about you."

"What did you tell him?"

"That you are a humble man."

He gave a little grunt. "Anything else?"

"That you know where my pleasure lies and how to stroke and caress my body to make it hum."

"And what did he say to that?"

"That I should not tell his wife or she might want to find out for herself."

Black Moon offered his most modest look. "Then I would have no choice but to show her."

"And I would have no choice but to take my skinning knife to you."

He laughed. It was good to see her like this again, with merriment in her voice and mischief brightening her eyes.

"There seems to be some goodness in him. I do not think he wants a war. He is here only to protect the Powder River Road. But he is not the one you should worry about," she said, her tone turning serious when she came to stand beside him. "The danger comes from the one called Fetterman. You must be careful of that one. There is something in his eyes that frightens me. He is an ambitious man looking for a fight." She stopped short of telling him about the Captain's advances and of his threat, for fear of Black Moon acting recklessly.

"What is his place?" Unlike the Lakota who did not choose one to lead the others, he knew enough about the Long Knives to know that some held rank over others and that the markings on their uniforms told which ones were the leaders.

"He is called the field commander. When the wood wagons go out each day, he leads the soldiers that protect them."

Black Moon walked to the edge of the ridge and watched the clouds building to the west, the kind of thick gray clouds with quiet thunder in their bellies that threatened snow. He sniffed the wind and caught the scent of stale smoke coming from last night's fire at the soldier town. As he stood there, something in the distance captured his attention. It was too far to make out, so he strode to his hide saddle, removed the far-seeing glass from his pack and returned.

Katie came to stand beside him. "What do you see?"

Holding the glass to his eye, Black Moon said, "The bluecoats have left the soldier town to go for wood."

Sweeping the glass in a wide arc to scan the horizon, he stopped suddenly when something else came into view.

"What is it?" she asked.

"Two are riding away from the others." He shook his head. "They will not be long for this world."

"Why do you say that?'

"There." He stretched out a buckskin-clad arm, pointing to a spot in the distance. Fanned out across the top of Lodge Trail Ridge was a line of mounted warriors. "Crazy Horse will make short work of them."

CHAPTER 27
A SINGLE ROUND BULLET

Nearly a day's ride south of the Tongue River camp, Claw, Running-water Woman and Little Storm made their way along the Bozeman Trail on their way to visit relatives camped just north of Crazy Woman Creek, hoping to get there by sundown.

Running-water Woman glanced nervously at the log walls of Fort Phil Kearny that rose in the distance. From here, the only thing she could make out clearly was the upright pine pole, taller than any lodge pole she'd ever seen, from whose top hung the large cloth banner of the Long Knives.

"What does it mean?' she asked of the banner that flapped about in the wind.

Claw shrugged beneath his buffalo robe. "Maybe it tells the story of how they came into our land."

"When I was a little girl, a white man stayed at our village over the winter," she said. "My father welcomed him into our lodge and my mother cooked for him and gave him warm clothes to wear. When he left, Grandmother Hawk reminded us of the Lakota legend about the giant whose hunger was so great that he ate everything and everyone, even those who had befriended him. Old Grandmother Hawk was right. The white man is like the giant."

"Will the white men come out of their fort and eat us?" Little

Storm asked.

Seeking to reassure his grandson, Claw said, "Do not worry. The Long Knives mostly stay in their fort. They come out only to go for wood and are afraid to wander too far from the Powder River Road. You see up there?" He pointed to the north, where small dark specs dotted the crest of Lodge Trail Ridge. "Lakota scouts. If there is trouble from the Long Knives, we will be warned of it."

That seemed to settle Running-water Woman's nervousness, but what the travelers did not know was that at that very moment they were being watched by two mounted bluecoats.

Having reined their horses to a stop on the crest of a hill, Hobbs had the field glass raised to his eye and trained on the dust cloud on the Bozeman. "It's just two old Indians and a kid," he concluded. "Let's get back to the escort."

"You go on," Ned told him. "I'll keep an eye on them a little while longer."

"When Lieutenant Powell told the two of us to go together, I expect he meant for the two of us to return together." He swung the field glass southward toward the wood train and the line of troopers riding escort. "The distance from them is increasing, and I don't like it. We'd best be getting back."

Ned gazed out over the open land. The flat prairie met suddenly with the dark, jagged ridges of the Bighorn Mountains that reached for the sky. There was so much wide open space here that it seemed anything might happen at any moment. Everything about this wild country was sudden and unexpected, from the blazing heat of summer, to the unrelenting cold of winter, to the sudden death that came at the hands of the elements or the Indians. As he turned his horse's head away to catch up with Hobbs, he saw dark forms spilling out of the surrounding hills. A chill shot up his spine.

"Indians!"

The two men drummed their heels into their horses' flanks. With powerful lunges, the horses stretched out into a gallop.

At the first rifle blasts that shattered the stillness, Claw leaned over and grasped the braided jaw ropes of his wife's and grandson's ponies and tugged them into the thickets on the side of the trail. He jumped off his pony in one smooth motion, pulled them down with him, pushed them to the ground and ordered, "Stay down!"

Peering through the tangled thickets he saw a group of mounted warriors swoop down on two fleeing bluecoats. One bluecoat went down in a flash, a bullet tearing through his chest and slashing its way out his back. A scream tore through the air as the second one's horse stumbled and fell, landing less than twenty paces from where the three travelers were hiding.

Thrown to the ground, the bluecoat went down on one knee and positioned his rifle at his shoulder, but before he could get off a good shot, a bullet propelled him backwards. Somehow, he managed to get to his feet. He staggered a few steps and fell behind a large clump of sagebrush.

The warriors swept by like a dark wind, racing toward the wood wagons and the escort. In the lead, Claw recognized the slender form of Crazy Horse crouched low over the neck of his pony.

From the direction of the wood train came rapid return fire. A bugle call sounded and the cavalry charged forward. Bullets whizzed and arrows twanged. But the attempt by Crazy Horse to lead the bluecoats on a chase and into an ambush was not working on this day. Raising his muzzleloader into the air, Crazy Horse gave out with a piercing war cry, jerked his pony's head around, and took off back into the hills, his warriors fanned out behind him.

When the rifle fire ceased and the thunder of pony hooves receded, Claw stood up and looked out over the thickets. The white man had crawled out from behind the sagebrush and was kneeling, bent over, clutching his arm and wailing in pain.

Running-water Woman stood up beside her husband and gasped to see blood spurting from the white man's elbow. "We must do something."

"He is a white man."

"He is a man."

Claw watched his wife surge forward. Turning back to Little Storm, he said, "Stay put," and rushed after her.

The white man had collapsed face down. When they reached him, they saw the ground all around him splotched with blood.

"What of the other one?' she asked.

Claw glanced around and spotted the other bluecoat a stone's throw away and went to look. Returning to Running-water Woman he said, "That one is dead. The bullet went through his chest and came out the other side. The hole in his back is big enough to fit two fingers."

"This one is alive," she said.

"I can see that," Claw responded sourly.

Gingerly, they turned the white man over. For several moments they stood frozen, staring down at the unnatural angle of the forearm and the sharp edge of bone that sliced through the sleeve of his blue jacket. Kneeling, Running-water Woman took out her skinning knife and slit the sleeve for a better look.

She forced down a gag.

The white man's forearm was barely attached to his upper arm and hung by shattered threads of skin and muscle. He was very pale and losing much blood as he slipped in and out of consciousness.

Running-water Woman took a deep breath. "This wound is very bad. We must stop the bleeding."

"Why is it our place to help a bluecoat?" Claw asked impatiently.

A moan erupted from deep within the wounded man's chest, and in his delirium his voice emerged as a strangled groan.

"Because this one is a friend."

"A friend to who?" he scoffed.

"It is your son's name he calls."

He clamped a hand over his wife's arm, demanding her attention. "How do you know what he says?"

"I speak the white man's language."

Claw stared back in disbelief.

"Hurry," she said sharply, pulling away. "Get some water and something to wrap the arm with."

Not knowing what to make of this news, Claw hurried to his pony. From a small rawhide bag tied to his saddle he took out a strip of brain-tanned hide. Grabbing his water flask, he returned to Running-water Woman and watched as she knelt over the white man, poured water over the nearly severed arm and then wrapped it in the tanned hide.

"The hide is filling with blood," she said. "We must turn back and get him to the medicine man."

Calling out to Little Storm to bring the ponies, Claw lifted the white man in his arms. With a grunt, he hoisted him onto his pony, a tall, muscular bay Black Moon had stolen from the Long Knives last spring, and climbed up behind him. With the wounded man slumped over in front of him, he nudged his pony to the white man's horse that was standing nearby, and grasping the reins, they rode out, careful to stay off the trail in case the bluecoats took their revenge against any Indians they could find.

As they rode on in silence, questions swarmed like angry hornets in Claw's mind. Who was this white man who claimed Black Moon as a friend? How was it possible that Black Moon was friends with one of the Long Knives? Looking down at the blood on his pony's withers, he wondered how a single round bullet could cause so much damage to a man's arm. And aiming a curious glance at his wife, he voiced the one question that seemed to bother him the most.

"Why did you not tell me you speak the white man's language?"

Running-water Woman grimaced at the blood on her hands and answered, "You did not ask."

Chapter 28
Too Easy to Hate

"Where is Ned?" Katie asked anxiously. "Do you see him?"

Black Moon swept the glass in a wide arc over the land below. The dust was still settling in the aftermath of Crazy Horse's attack. The Long Knives had picked up their wounded men and were heading back to the fort. "He is not with the others."

She breathed an uneasy sigh of relief. "At least he was not killed in the attack. That must mean he is still inside." A sudden terrible thought occurred to her. "Was it Ned who started the fire?'

Lowering the glass, he said, "It was the only way for me to get inside." He turned away from the battle scene below to see Katie spin on her heels and stalk away. "Where are you going?"

"We have to go back for him. If they find out that it was Ned who started the fire, there is no telling what they will do to him."

He caught up to her in several long, panther-like strides and caught her by the arm. "There is nothing we can do for him."

She gaped at him. "Nothing?" she echoed. "How can you refuse to help? And do not tell me it is because he is a white man. Did he refuse to help you because you are Lakota?"

"He did not do it for me," Black Moon asserted. "He did it for you."

"That may be, but we would not be standing here now if not for him."

He turned on her fiercely. "Why should I care what happens to him? The *washicus* are all the same. They are like a prairie fire that consumes everything in its way. And the Long Knives are the worst of all. They do not fight for honor. What they do not like they kill. Killing is all they know."

Katie met his intense gaze. "He is not one of the Long Knives," she argued. "And he is not like other white men. He is a good man, and we must help him."

"I will not risk your life or my own by sneaking back into the soldier town to get him."

"You said he will know where to find us. We will wait," she said stubbornly. "Maybe with the new sun he will come out with the others."

"And if he does not?" he challenged.

"Then we will leave." The fire in her eyes softened into a pleading look. "If you will not do it for him, then do it for me."

Despite the white man's feelings for Katie, Black Moon was obliged to admit that he had proven himself to be a brave and honorable man. His fingers relinquished their hold on her arm. Looking down at the ground, he kicked at the dirt with his moccasin. When his gaze came back up to hers, the look on his face changed. The savage frown had faded away, revealing the unblemished handsomeness that never failed to steal her breath away.

For several moments he said nothing. Finally, in a softly grudging voice, he relented. "We will wait."

She moved toward him and pressed her cheek against his buckskin-covered chest. When so much around them was in a state of upheaval, his arms going around her felt natural and right. This was where she belonged. Not in St. Louis or anywhere in a white world that sought to destroy this one. But here, in the arms of her husband, the Lakota warrior who set her world on fire with the strength of his kiss, the one who had killed for her and who would die for her.

Weighed down by sadness and uncertainty, and grappling with her darkest forebodings, Katie's voice emerged as a muffled whisper against the skin of his shirt. "I am afraid."

His warm breath fanned the top of her head. He held her, using the strength of his embrace to calm her fears as he had done so many times in the past, his fingers smoothing her hair.

The rhythmic, comforting brush of his fingers slowed and then stopped. She tilted her face up and looked at him.

Black Moon was staring off into the distance, his face shadowed by a faint frown as he surveyed the valley. The land lay silent. The Long Knives were gone, having barely escaped the wrath of Crazy Horse who was right when he said the *wasichus* made it too easy to hate them.

As a boy, he had watched the wagons going west along the Shell River Road, the one the whites called the Oregon Trail. What began as a wisp of smoke from the smoldering embers of a fire had grown into a mighty flame that threatened to destroy the entire Buffalo Nation. Bearded men came from the east beyond the Great Muddy River, tearing up the trails with their iron-rimmed wheels and killing the buffalo. Many came up the Great Muddy in houses that floated on the river, stopping to trade or take on wood and bringing the running-face sickness that wiped out entire villages. The traders called it smallpox and stayed away.

A small trading place along the Shell became the soldier town called Laramie. Men in blue coats came to live there, and because they carried knives as long as a man's arm they became known the Long Knives. And with the arrival of the Long Knives things got much worse.

He would never forget the mutilated bodies of women and children that Woman Killer Harney left at Little Thunder's camp on Blue Water eleven winters ago, and two winters ago a peaceful Cheyenne village was attacked at Sand Creek.

Why did they come, Black Moon wondered bitterly, leaving the carcasses of their dead animals to rot in the sun, changing the names of the trails, and building their soldier towns that looked like scars upon the land? The soldier towns and the Holy Road had become a part of Lakota life. The old ones sat around council fires scratching their heads and asking how it had all come to be. Perhaps, they said, all the wagons would eventually pass through on their way to the west and no more whites would come. But Black Moon did not share their foolish notion. The only way to get rid of the *wasichus* was to drive them out.

His gaze moved along the creek beds and the groves of pine, oak, and willows. To the north, Lakota scouts were fanned out across Lodge Trail Ridge, waiting for bluecoats to leave the protection of their fort. With today's ride to the pinery cut short by Crazy Horse's attack, they would be forced to come out with the new sun to go for more wood or freeze inside their log houses. The only question was whether Katie's white man would be with them.

CHAPTER 29
THE STILLNESS OF DEEP WATER

At the camp of Crazy Horse a group of young boys were playing the *pte-hes-te* game along the bank of the frozen river. Little Storm's *pte-hes-te* resembled a large arrow. It had been made by his uncle who had wedged a long stick into the open end of a buffalo cow horn and then split feathers and wrapped them on the stick with sinew in much the same way he made his own fast-flying arrows. Holding the *pte-hes-te* by the stick, Little Storm swung it back and forth over his shoulder as his uncle had shown him, and then flung it across the icy ground. It was no surprise that his *pte-hes-te* went farther and faster than those of the other boys when he had Black Moon as his teacher.

But playing the *pte-hes-te* game was not the only thing the boy learned from his uncle. At the age of seven he was becoming skilled with his bow, having learned by shooting arrows through a willow hoop that Black Moon rolled along the ground. Black Moon's teachings took the boy up steep mountain slopes and across bushy creek bottoms where he watched the rhythms and moods of the land and came to recognize the spirit that dwelled in the vast endless space that was the prairie and learned that the creatures living upon it had lessons to teach him.

He learned that the hunter and the hunted had much in common, that men and animals alike lived to sustain the lives of others. The grass fed off the earth, the buffalo, deer, and antelope fed off the grass, the wolves and men fed off the buffalo, deer, and antelope. He was taught that whenever his arrow took the life of an animal, even one as small as a prairie yapper, to offer a bundle of sage as a gift for the animal that gave its life, and that the spirit of a killed buffalo was honored by placing its skull facing east to meet the rising sun.

His uncle also taught him lessons about men, as well. "Do not look too long at the enemy's eyes," Black Moon had cautioned. "He will feel your stare and know you are looking."

He also learned the value of patience. "It takes patience to wait for a deer to come within the range of your bow," his uncle told him. "Shooting too soon will result in a sure miss, and the family of a hunter without patience does not have enough food to eat or new hides to sew." And about determination. "As long as you try, do not be afraid to fail. Even the true-dog fails at his kills more often than he brings down game. His strength is not in his great fangs but in his determination never to give up."

Little Storm heard the stories the others told about his uncle, and even at his young age, he sensed that Black Moon's determination never to give up extended beyond his hunting ability. From watching his uncle the boy learned that while every man was a hunter, not every man was a warrior. Black Moon was not flamboyant and boastful like so many of the warriors. Unlike the others, there was a stillness about him. It was like the stillness of deep water. Little Storm would not soon forget the time he had accompanied his uncle to the Shell. For a long time they sat on a hillside watching a line of wagons moving slowly westward. Little Storm had never seen the *canpagmiyanpi*, the wood that rolls. He had glanced at his uncle to ask about them, but the words froze upon his tongue. Although Black Moon sat calmly, saying nothing, it was clear from the fierce look in his eyes and the savage frown upon his face that much was going on beneath the calm surface.

Little Storm had been too young to remember his mother's face. Katie told him about her, what a sweet girl she was, and how she had gone on a journey into the light of the next life and was now with his father. For as long as he could remember, Katie was the only mother he had known. Talk around the camp was that Black Moon had gone after her to bring her home. Each day the boy looked toward the horizon, hoping to see his uncle and his mother returning.

On this cold day in the Middle of Winter Moon, the scouts signaled from the top of a rise overlooking the Oglala camp that someone was coming.

The dogs announced the arrival of the riders in the circle of lodges. Shielding his eyes against the glare of the sun off the snow, Little Storm recognized the bay gelding. "*Leksi*! *Ina*!" he called excitedly to his uncle and mother. Throwing down his *pte-hes-te*, he raced toward them.

"*Tonska*," Black Moon said, smiling broadly and addressing the boy as his nephew as he rode toward him. Grasping Katie by the elbow, he lowered her to the ground. The smile was big upon her face when she dropped to her knees and opened her arms to receive the boy. "*Chinkshi*," she crooned, calling him son and pressing kisses to his face.

Black Moon watched their reunion. It pleased him to see the happiness sparkling in Katie's eyes and to hear it ringing in her voice once again. Tapping his heels to his pony's flanks, he moved on past them.

Katie glanced away from Little Storm to see Crazy Horse step out of his lodge into the bright winter sunshine. Black Moon dismounted to greet him. The smile faded from her face as she watched the two men talking, and although from this distance she could not hear their words, she knew by the somber looks on their faces that they were discussing a serious matter. Something was wrong.

"Go play," she said, urging Little Storm back toward the other boys. She watched him run off, then marched to where Black Moon and Crazy Horse had their heads bowed together.

"I have been watching the Holy Road," she heard Crazy Horse say as she approached. "There are not so many of them traveling now, but when the warm moons come, there will be more. And the more wagon people who come will need more Long Knives to protect them. They do not belong here. This is our land. The only way to rid them from our land is to kill them." Upon seeing Katie standing there, he acknowledged her with a brief glance. "I hope you do not think my words are meant for you."

She gave him a conciliatory little smile and would have let it go at that, but the guarded look the two men exchanged told her there was more to their hushed conversation than emigrant travel on the Holy Road.

"What is it?" she asked.

Silence hung over them like a cold fog.

"What are you trying so hard not to tell me?"

Mumbling something, Crazy Horse disappeared back into his lodge.

Drawing a stiff breath into his lungs, Black Moon said, "Your white man is here."

"Ned! Where is he?"

"In my mother's lodge."

Katie turned abruptly away, but Black Moon caught her by the arm before she could take another step, warning, "You will not like what you see."

CHAPTER 30
GOOD FRIENDS

Katie scratched at Running-water Woman's lodge and entered. In the far corner, beyond the fire glowing in the center of the lodge, she saw a figure bundled beneath a buffalo hide robe. Nearing, she gasped to see Ned lying there unconscious.

"I have given him the yellow medicine to make him sleep."

She tore her stricken gaze away and looked into the dark eyes of the medicine man. He was a slender man in his fifties whose gray hair hung over his shoulders in two thin braids. From beneath the robe hanging loosely over his shoulders she saw old Sun Dance scars on his chest, evidence of years of supplication to *Wakan Tanka*. Turning to Running-water Woman standing nearby, he said, "Would you boil a kettle of water for me?"

Running-water Woman hurried away and swung a small metal pot of water from a tripod above the flames of the fire, carefully lifted hot stones from the simmering coals with a forked stick, shook off the ashes, and placed them in the water.

A low moan came from the beneath the bundle.

"That is a good sign," the medicine man said. "It means he is still on this side."

Kneeling at Ned's side, Katie said, "He is so pale, and his breath is so shallow."

"That is to be expected considering what had to be done," said the medicine man.

She turned a questioning glance up at him.

Leaning forward, he grasped a corner of the buffalo robe and pulled it aside.

A horrified gasp tore from Katie's throat.

"I could not save his arm," he said flatly.

The stump at the end of Ned's left arm was wrapped in rawhide. Having been applied while still wet, it had dried and shrunk, slowly tightening around the stump.

Katie stared down at the rawhide covered stump and swayed, feeling sick.

Having followed Katie inside, Black Moon came up quickly behind her and grasped her by the elbow to steady her. "Come away," he urged.

She pulled back. "No! I will not leave him."

Black Moon exchanged a troubled look with his father who stood nearby. "He will wake eventually," Claw said, "and perhaps it will be good for him to see her when he does."

The anguish in Katie's eyes was hard to ignore. A shadow moved across Black Moon's face as he took a step back. He was not surprised that Katie wanted to remain with the white man. It was nothing more than her worry for a friend, he tried to convince himself as he left the lodge.

Running-water Woman returned with the heated water she had poured into a buffalo horn cup. The medicine man spilled some of the yellow medicine into the cup and handed it to Katie. "When he wakes, give him this. He will not want it, but you must make him swallow."

Katie remembered the medicine as the arrowleaf plant. Her mother used to collect it on the prairie, pulverize the leaves into a tea, and make her and Richard drink it to relieve the congestion of winter colds. Once, when Richard fell off his horse and broke his arm, their mother made him drink the arrowleaf medicine made from the crushed roots to help him sleep.

Taking the cup into her trembling hands, Katie asked, "Will he live?"

"I think he will heal. Do not let him pull off the rawhide covering."

"How will he will react to the loss of his arm?"

"That is hard to say," he said as he gathered his things. "I will come back tomorrow to check on him."

When the medicine man was gone, Katie looked up into the watchful eyes of Running-water Woman and smiled weakly. "*Pilamaya,*" she said, thanking the woman. And because she was not permitted to address her father-in-law, she said, "Please tell my husband's father how grateful I am."

Claw acknowledged Katie's gratitude with a nod of his head, and with a grunt, left the lodge.

"How does he come to be in your lodge?" Katie asked, nodding toward Ned.

Running-water Woman sat down beside her. "We were riding to Crazy Woman Creek when our warriors attacked the rolling wood of the Long Knives. This one and another one got in the way. When we went to check on him, he was losing a lot of blood and mumbling. I understood his words and knew he was a friend of your husband's."

"So, you gave up your secret to help him. Claw must not be very happy that you speak the white language."

"He was not pleased. But I cannot unlearn what I already know."

"When he is strong enough, we will move him to my lodge." Remembering that she had been gone since before Black Moon moved to this camp, and since it was the woman's place to erect the lodge, Katie added, "If I have one."

"Your husband has not been living with the pony herd. His aunts put up a lodge for him. It is at the end of the circle. But you are welcome to stay here as long as you want."

In coming to the aid of a white man who, for all intents and purposes, was the enemy, taking the chance of incurring her husband's anger, and now, by offering her lodge, Running-water Woman showed the typical Lakota value of *wawokoye*, a generous and caring spirit without expecting anything in return.

Katie reached up and drew one of her mother-in-law's proper married-woman braids over her shoulder. "You are a good friend."

Running-water Woman's eyes strayed to the white man asleep beneath the robe. "That one will need all the good friends he can get."

Katie expelled a beleaguered sigh. Ned was a stranger here, and a hated one to many. She was the only good friend he had. It was up to her to do everything in her power to help his body heal and his spirit survive.

CHAPTER 31
MOON OF POPPING TREES

The wind slid off the mountain slopes, carrying a bitter chill. Overhead, hawks and eagles prowled the skies, and although the whistle of a bull elk could be heard from the foothills, nothing moved upon the frozen land. Inside the lodge at the end of the circle the fire was kept fueled day and night, and it was warm.

Two days after Black Moon and Claw carried Ned inside he awoke from his induced sleep. In the gentlest words she could find, Katie explained to him what had happened. That night she heard him weeping softly to himself. Since then, he had not spoken a word to anyone.

"Not at all?" Running-water Woman questioned early one morning at the water's edge.

Katie shook her head and bent to fill the paunch with water through the hole that had been hacked into the ice. "He eats and drinks, but only because I plead with him. He goes out at night to relieve himself, but during the day he stays under the robe."

"What does your husband say?"

"Nothing. He spends his days with Crazy Horse, and after sundown he goes to the council lodge."

"There is much for them to talk about," said her mother-in-law. "I remember when the white man called Bozeman pounded stakes into the ground and we all laughed. But we stopped laughing when more whites followed the stakes to the gold diggings up north, west of Crow lands. Now the old men and the leaders of the fighting men are wondering how to solve this problem."

The encroaching emigrants were not the only problem, Katie thought as she made her way through the freshly-fallen snow back to her lodge. What was she going to do about Ned?

He was sitting up when she entered the lodge. Upon seeing her, he quickly laid back down and pulled the robe up over his head.

She had tried to be patient with him, but after so many days of this, even her patience had its limits. "Sooner or later you'll have to talk to me," she said. "I can wait. Meanwhile, you can lay there and listen to what I have to say." Putting the paunch aside, she set about mixing a bowl of dried and pounded elk meat together with the dried chokecherries she had gathered over the summer. Adding some rendered fat to hold the mixture together, she kneaded it with her hands, casting a look over her shoulder at the mound in the corner.

"Bravery is born of the wisdom of life and death as well as one's honor," she said as she worked. "It is not blind or reckless and can come from the depth of our being in times of need. This is your time of need, Ned. Your vulnerability in spite of your circumstances can help you defy even the worst odds."

A movement beneath the robe told her he was listening. "You lost your arm," she went on. "It is a terrible thing. But you're not stupid, are you? What you did with two arms you can learn to do with one. You are one of the lucky ones. The people I saw massacred at Blue Water will never again see the sun rise. You still have your eyes and will see it every day. They will never again feel the warmth of the sun's rays on their faces or the cold air nipping at their cheeks. The old ones say that a man can have knowledge without wisdom but he cannot have wisdom without knowledge. This injury has given you a knowledge that many men don't have. You can learn from it and put it to good use, or you can let it destroy you. The choice is yours."

From the corners of her eyes she saw him pull himself to a sitting position. "Well, that's a start. Tomorrow we'll go for a walk outside. It will do you good to get out from under those robes and back into the world. Or you can lay there and wither away. Think about it and let me know what you decide."

He cleared his throat.

"I'll take that as a yes," Katie said, smiling to herself. "Are you hungry?"

His voice, so long untested, scratched at the back of his throat. "Yes."

Into a bowl she spooned some elk soup seasoned with wild turnips and brought it to him. Noticing that he was careful not to let the robe slip down past his left shoulder, she said, "I have seen worse wounds, but I don't remember when I've seen a more sorry-looking man." His cheeks were hollow, there were dark circles under his eyes, his hair was disheveled, and many days' growth of beard spiked his face. Watching him wolf down the food, she said, "At least your appetite is good."

When he finished eating, she gave his fingers a little squeeze as she took the bowl from his hand.

"I don't remember how I got here," he said.

Katie shrugged. "Maybe it's not so important that you remember how you got here, only that you are here among friends."

Ned gave a little laugh in spite of himself. "Does that include Black Moon?"

"I think so."

"But you don't know for sure."

"He hasn't been spending much time here," she admitted.

"Because of me?"

She didn't answer.

Since Ned had come to stay with them, Black Moon had made no move to touch her beneath the robes, turning over with his back to her and falling asleep instead. Each morning, she braided his long, black hair and watched him eat a bowl of elk stew before he donned his heavy hide shirt and went out. For a man who was reticent by nature, his silence was deafening. But it was more than Ned's presence that darkened Black Moon's mood and set Katie's nerves on edge. Beneath his remoteness she sensed a tension she recognized only too well. It was that tense quietness that came every time he was preparing to ride off to war.

Katie's dark forebodings were disrupted when Ned leaned back against the soft fur of the robe and said absently, "I've lost track of the month."

"It's December," she said. "The Lakota call this the Moon of Popping Trees because the air is so cold it causes the tree limbs to crack."

"You wouldn't know the date, would you?"

She threw some sticks onto the fire. As they spit and sputtered, she got up and went to a rawhide bundle in the corner. Untying the thongs, she pulled out a piece of tanned hide. "At the fort I knew the dates because the Colonel's wife had a paper calendar pinned to the wall in her house. I've been keeping this calendar since we got here." She unfurled the hide for him to see. "This is the day Black Moon rescued me from the fort. And this is the day your arm was...well..." Her words trailed off awkwardly.

"Cut off," he said morosely.

"How does it feel?" she asked.

"I think it's healing. There's some pain, a throbbing mostly, and it itches under the rawhide. Sometimes I think I can feel my fingers," he said, adding bitterly, "but that's not possible, is it?"

"Ned, you must have hope that things will get better. That you'll be able to—"

"To what?" he cut in. "Go back to farming in Minnesota?" He gave a short angry laugh. "There's no future for me in farming. One bad winter three of my cows froze to death. Two years ago the locusts devoured the wheat crop before it was ready to be picked. Would you believe that one year we were saved from starvation by the cat that brought a freshly killed rabbit each morning?" He drew in a ragged breath. "Even when I had two arms it was hopeless."

"So maybe you're fated for something other than farming," Katie said. "This land is filled with opportunity. My father used to say a hard-working man can always find a place for himself. Who knows? Maybe your future lies in Oregon where you were headed when you left Minnesota."

He slanted a quick look at her and ventured, "Or St. Louis, where you were headed when we met. We could go together."

She gave him a tender smile. "It's a tempting offer, and I'd be lying if I said I don't often dream of it. But it's just a dream. This..." She spread her arms wide, gesturing around them. "This is my reality."

"And Black Moon," he added.

"And Black Moon."

"Katie, there's something you should know. Back at the fort I overheard Fetterman talking about getting Black Moon. Even more than Crazy Horse and Red Cloud, he hates your husband."

"I said things to him that must have made him feel inferior to Black Moon," she confessed. "I'm afraid I am the cause of his hatred."

"Men hate what they don't understand," he said.

"That's true, but I shudder to think where Fetterman's hatred will lead."

"It's understandable that you would be afraid for Black Moon."

"It's not Black Moon I am afraid for. He is a warrior. Protecting his people and his land isn't something he decided one day to do. It is ingrained in his being and as essential to him as the air he breathes. Fetterman aspires to be more than he is. Black Moon does not wish to be anything more than what he is. He simply wants to be. He walks a difficult path, one he was bound to walk, through the vision he had as a boy. You may look at Black Moon and wonder how a man who is quiet and humble in the village can be such a force on the battlefield. It's not something he talks about, but I see it every time he rides off to war with a lightning streak painted on his pony's withers. The lightning is the symbol of the Thunders. Black Moon is a Thunder Dreamer and must live his life as an example to others. I guess you could say his life is not his own. That is a strength more powerful than all the Fettermans in the world. Besides, word around the fort was that Carrington relieved Fetterman of his command, so it's not likely he poses any immediate threat."

"If I have learned anything at all," Ned said, "it's that nothing is predictable, nothing is certain, and anything can happen at any time. I used to think that unfortunate things happened to the other man." He looked down at the rawhide covering the stump of his left arm. "But

I've come to the realization that I am that other man."

She saw him slipping back inside of himself, and in an effort to lift his sagging spirit, she pointed a finger at the calendar she had drawn on the hide with a quill and paint, and said, "Look. It's almost Christmas."

"And in two days it will be the twenty-first," he said. "The first day of winter according to the Farmer's Almanac. Except for the cold and the snow, it never was a very eventful day back in Minnesota."

Katie rolled up the hide and put it aside. "No, I don't suppose December twenty-first will be a day of much importance."

CHAPTER 32
THE ROAD TO WAR

The firelight glanced off the angles of Black Moon's scowling face as he stalked about his mother's lodge.

"She hardly knows I am there," he complained. "All she does is look after him. It is natural for a man to have more than one woman in a lodge, but not for a woman to have more than one man."

Claw leaned back on his latticed backrest of willow rods, listening to the frustration and anger in his son's deep voice. Knowing how fiercely Black Moon loved Katie, it was easy to understand how he might feel threatened by her friendship with the white man. But that was not the only reason Claw wanted to see the white man gone.

"As soon as he is strong enough he should leave," Claw advised. "The people are not comfortable with a white man in their midst. The Cheyenne who live among us lost their families at Sand Creek two winters ago. Now, even the sight of a white man, especially a Long Knife, brings back bad memories of that terrible time for some of them."

Black Moon shook off his hide shirt and sank into a cross-legged position before the fire. "It is true that the Long Knives killed anything that moved that day and did bad things to the bodies of the dead ones, but he is not a Long Knife."

"He was wearing the blue coat when we found him."

"Only as a trick to get in and out of the soldier town. He is a farmer."

"It will be hard for him to be a farmer with only one arm."

"If anyone can do it," Black Moon said, "it is him."

"If I did not know better, I would say that you like this white man."

Expelling a frustrated sigh, Black Moon said evasively, "Sometimes it is hard to hate him."

"Crazy Horse has no trouble hating him," Claw remarked. "He is one of those talking openly about having the white man here."

"He does not know him."

"And if he did, do you think he would change his mind about him?"

Black Moon shrugged. "He is a strange one. Despite his contempt for white people, he seems to bear no bad feelings against Katie."

"That is because she is your wife, and he has no wish to get on your bad side. He is young yet, just past his twenty-fourth winter, and he aspires to be like you."

"He is making a name for himself by leading the attacks on the bluecoats and raiding their wagons when they go for the wood."

"Crazy Horse may lead those raids," Claw said, "but we all know that you are the one who plans them. Leadership is not just how a man performs on the battlefield. A leader must prove to others that something can be done so that they will attempt to do it."

Deep in thought, Black Moon nodded as he rolled a lead bullet around in his palm. "Many winters ago the peace-talkers of the *wasichus* told us that all they needed was enough room for their wagon wheels, and we thought that meant they were only passing through our country. But they stayed and built their soldier towns and the Long Knives came to protect them." His voice dropped low, like the warning growl of a cornered wolf. "The young men must understand that the whites are not honorable enemies. Fighting them is not for honor or victory stories told around the fire. It is to wipe them out. With the new sun I will ride with Crazy Horse. After all they have done to our people, the spirit of revenge will be riding with us." He rose and shrugged into his hide shirt. "I must go. The others are waiting in the council lodge for me to lay out an ambush plan."

Claw nodded his approval. Perhaps the warpath was what Black Moon needed to distract him from his woman seeing to the needs of another man, and a white one, at that. Claw could not help but think of everything Black Moon had gone through for the woman he loved—her marriage to his brother, her abduction by the Crow, a long and painful absence when she went east, her recent absence and capture by the Long Knives, and now this friendship with the white man that provoked Black Moon's jealousy. Was there to be no end to the obstacles those two faced?

Black Moon returned to his lodge after meeting with the others in council to find Katie still awake. Tying the inside flap to prevent the cold from following him in, he took off his hide shirt and sat down before the fire.

"I have saved some elk stew for you," she said. She rose from her spot and spooned some stew into a bowl and returned with it to sit beside him.

The sound of snoring coming from beneath the robes in the corner assured Black Moon that the white man was asleep. In a hushed voice he said, "I will ride out before first light. I have chosen nine decoys to lure the Long Knives into an ambush. I will lead them."

Her shoulders slumped and in a voice heavy with resignation, she said, "You must do this brave thing."

Black Moon chuckled. "I do not know how brave I am."

She gazed into his coal-dark eyes and smiled. "I do. I will have your heavy hide shirt and mittens ready."

Licking the meat from his fingers, he took her hand in his. "When many others were against me, only you stood by my side. Your belief in me has given me the strength to do what I must do."

"It is the heart afraid of losing that cannot win," she said softly, repeating the words she had said to him on the eve of the battle that cost him the bighorn shirt and stripped him of the honor of being a Shirt Wearer.

"The heart can lead us to places we do not plan to go," he said. "When you came to live with my people, I tried to tell myself that you were my enemy, but my heart led me to loving you."

The fire cast Katie's lowered lashes into shadows against her cheeks. "But sometimes the heart can play tricks on us. I was looking for something that is not there. I was thinking about what my life was like before I came here. It was heavy on my mind."

"Yes," he said, "you seemed to go someplace inside of yourself that I could not go."

"But I realized that the answer to who I am and where I belong in the world is not out there, or even here. The answer is inside of me."

A lump formed in Black Moon's throat as he listened to her softly whispered words. "Do you want to go back to the white world? If that is what you want, I will not stop you."

"No," she said, her voice firm. "I know who I am. I am the daughter of the trader, Tom McCabe. And I know who I was meant to be. The wife of the brave and good man I see before me."

Black Moon's heart beat faster. "And I was meant to be the husband of this brave and beautiful woman I see before me. Like stars in the sky, so many they can never be counted, you are the one bright star *Wakan Tanka* has singled out just for me."

In the lingering light of the fire she saw his smile, a faint curve of his lips. A hot need welled up inside of her to give herself up to him, to every kiss and caress, to the pleasure that blossomed between her thighs and the desperate desire to make him a part of her.

Cupping his face in the palms of her hands, she whispered, "*Mihigna.*"

Black Moon thrilled to the sound of her woman's voice calling him her husband. He cocked his head to one side and listened to the sounds coming from the corner. Satisfied that the white man was sound asleep, he drew Katie into his arms. He laid her back, covered her body with his, and drew the robe up over them.

Katie breathed in the scent of winter and sage in his long, dark hair and wriggled her hip beneath the warmth of his palm.

"*Mitawin,*" he mumbled, his breath hot and harsh against her neck.

"Yes," she breathed, "I am your woman. I have always been your woman, from the first time you took me beneath the shaggy leaf trees to this very moment. Yours. Completely yours."

She was moist and hot and ready for him when he pushed her elk skin dress up past her hips, slipped in between her open legs, and thrust into her.

Burying her face in his shoulder, she wrapped her legs around him and drew him in even deeper. There was an urgency in his lovemaking and in her desperate surrender to his conquest. But it was more than mindless passion that drove them. It was the thought that hovered over them like a cold, dark wind that with Black Moon riding off to war with the new sun, this might be the last time they were together like this.

That night the drums pounded as Black Moon lay awake unable to sleep. Katie lay beside him, the sound of her breathing familiar and comforting to a man with much on his mind. With the new sun he would lead his warriors against the Long Knives. He thought about the one called Fetterman that Katie had told him about. An ambitious man looking for a fight, she said.

If Fetterman wanted a fight, Black Moon was ready to give him one.

Chapter 33
Hundred in the Hand

The morning broke sharply cold. Black Moon disentangled himself from the womanly body next to his and rose from the warmth of the robes. For several minutes he stood gazing down at Katie still sleeping, her hair fanned over her face like the red glow of the setting sun. Bending, he brushed a strand away from her cheek to better see her flawless beauty in the pre-dawn darkness.

Eleven winters had passed since the first time he had gazed into her splendid green eyes from across the fire, and she was still the most beautiful thing he had ever seen. Despite every tragedy and hardship she had been through, she retained a resilience that came from an unbreakable spirit and a courage that many men did not possess. Life for a white woman among the Oglala was hard, and although she had chosen willingly to be here, he knew that the thought of the white world she left behind was forever in the back of her mind. He also knew how hard it was for her to watch him ride off to war.

With the new sun he would go against the Long Knives, with no assurance that he would return. He worried that without him, even with Claw and Running-water Woman and Little Storm, Katie would feel lost and alone here. Long into the night he had pondered over what to do. By morning he had reached a decision. Glancing at the white man asleep in the corner, he drew in a deep breath and went to him.

Ned felt a rough hand on his shoulder shaking him awake. His eyes blinked and snapped open to see Black Moon kneeling over him. The old animosity was gone from those dark eyes, replaced by a determined look.

With quick and graceful motions Black Moon signed his intent. By now, Ned knew enough sign language to know what Black Moon was telling him. He was riding off to war with the Long Knives. Ned nodded his solemn understanding. But what Black Moon signed next took him by surprise.

Pointing a finger at Katie's sleeping form with one hand, Black Moon then poked a finger at Ned with his other hand and brought his two hands together in signs that were plain to read. If he did not return, Ned was to take Katie away from this place.

Ned was stunned, not just by the thought that Black Moon's love for Katie was so great that he would do anything to keep her safe, even if it meant entrusting her to a white man, but by the knowledge that it was not just any white man, but one he considered a friend. Ned didn't think Black Moon thought of him as anything more than a nuisance, until now. He answered with a shaky nod of the head.

Black Moon emerged from his lodge before first light to see that snow had fallen overnight. He smiled slyly to himself. The snow had most likely covered the tracks left by the scouts watching the Long Knives. That would make his plan easier to put into motion.

The others showed up bundled against the relentless cold. From his quiver Black Moon handed each of the nine chosen men an arrow marked with a narrow green band on its shaft.

Crazy Horse took his arrow and went off by himself. Black Moon found him among the pony herd.

"My little brother is worried about something," Black Moon said. "Is it the coming fight?"

Crazy Horse caressed the medicine bundle he wore from a thong around his neck. "I am prepared to thump death on the nose," he said, "but we do not have enough bullets."

"How many do you have?"

"Four."

"That is a good sign," Black Moon responded. "Four is the medicine number. There are four directions, four stages of life, four seasons, four parts to everything that grows from the ground—the root, the stem, the leaves and the fruit—four kinds of things that breathe—those that crawl, those that fly, those that walk on four legs and those that walk on two legs. The Great Spirit has caused everything to be in fours, so four bullets is a sacred thing. Besides," he wryly added, "we have enough arrows."

"And you have made a good plan," Crazy Horse said.

"The plan also has four parts. The signal, the trap, the decoys, and the fight. It will work if we stick to it. We will be watching from our hidden places, and when the Long Knives go down close to Prairie Dog Creek, I will give the signal for the ambushers to close the trap behind them. Remember, Lodge Trail Ridge is the thing. The decoys will bring them down off the ridge. That is when we will attack them. Come," he said, slinging an arm over Crazy Horse's shoulder, "let us get going. We want to be at Little Goose Creek by the time the night sun is high so that we will be ready when daylight comes."

As they threaded their way back to the others, Crazy Horse could not help but notice that Black Moon kept glancing back at his lodge. "You are worried that she is alone with the white man?"

"I know you do not like that he is here," Black Moon replied. "But remember, my friend, the Great Mystery also made the white man, and not all of them are bad. From the look on your face I can see you are surprised by what I say. Do not misunderstand my words. It does not mean I like the *wasichus*. It means only that there are some among them who are good. My woman's father was a good man who traded fairly with our people. The one who sleeps in my lodge may have only one arm, but he has courage. Without his help I could not have rescued her from the Long Knives. It is plain to see he cares for her. That is why I have asked him to take her back to her own people if I do not return from this battle. It is the only place where she will be safe from the hard times that are coming." Knowing Crazy Horse's introspective nature prompted him to add, "I know you think long and hard on these things. But now is not the time to think. Now is the time to act."

Crazy Horse's laconic face broke into a grin. "It is a good day to be alive."

"Whatever we do is for the people, not for ourselves," Black Moon said. "Only the Earth lives forever. Today may be a good day to be alive, but tomorrow will be a good day to die."

***

Early the next morning Captain William Fetterman barged into Colonel Carrington's quarters, his overcoat unbuttoned and gloves in hand, and gave a hasty salute.

"Sir, the wood detail is under attack!"

"Is that the signal from Pilot Hill?" Carrington asked of the continuous daylight lookouts stationed at the top of the hill.

"Yes, sir."

"It's probably just a few braves stirring up trouble," the Colonel responded. "Lieutenant Powell can handle this. Have the bugler blow assembly."

"Sir, I respectfully request permission to lead this mission based on my senior rank."

Clearly annoyed, Carrington threw a coat over his shoulders and went out into the cold December air without answering. Finding Lieutenant Powell at the far end of the parade ground about to mount his horse, he said. "The Captain is asking to lead the mission."

Powell took his boot out of the stirrup. "I agree with Captain Fetterman, sir."

Turning to Fetterman, Carrington gave him a heated look. "Very well, Captain. You will lead the mission. But you are to support the wood train. Under no circumstance are you to engage the Indians or pursue them over Lodge Trail Ridge. Those are my orders, Captain. Lieutenant Grummond will follow with the 2nd Cavalry."

After Carrington had stomped back to his quarters, Powell said, "Good luck, William. And remember, Lodge Trail Ridge and no further. You're already on Carrington's bad side."

Fetterman smiled. "I will not pursue them over Lodge Trail Ridge, but you can bet Black Moon will be with them, and between here and there I aim to teach him a lesson he will never forget."

The bugler's call sounded over the garrison. Mustering his soldiers, Fetterman mounted his horse, and the column, riding four abreast, exited the sally port.

***

Black Moon sent several hundred of his fighting men off to hide in the ridges and gullies from Prairie Dog Creek to Lodge Trail Ridge and then joined Crazy Horse and the other decoys to wait astride their warhorses behind a thicket. As the sun rose in the morning sky, the column of mounted soldiers appeared, with the walking soldiers not far behind. At the signal, the ambushers sprang into action.

The frigid mountain air rang with the sound of gunfire. Lashing his pony into a gallop, Black Moon slid off its right side, and with his left leg hooked over the pony's back, got off a few shots from his rifle into the ranks of oncoming soldiers. Despite the snow covering the uneven frozen ground causing his pony to slip and slide as he rode within firing range of the soldiers' guns, back and forth he rode in front of them, taunting them with his closeness before sprinting away, leading them farther away from the fort and well beyond the walking soldiers.

In the midst of the gunfire Crazy Horse dismounted and began to calmly scrape ice from the bottom of his pony's hooves. Another of the decoys stood on his pony's rump and then dropped back down and galloped away. Each antic drew the column of soldiers closer to Lodge Trail Ridge.

Crazy Horse reined his brown and white paint in close to Black Moon's bay gelding. "My fingers are so numb they can barely hold my weapon."

"I will ride up that slope at the back of Lodge Trail Ridge and get a small fire going so that we can warm our hands," Black Moon shouted.

When the decoys gathered around the small fire Black Moon built with his flint and striker, he told them, "We will keep to the wagon trail. The Long Knives will stay on the trail they are familiar with. Keep up the tricks. If they think we are poor shots and do not know what we are doing, they will follow. Then we will kill the snake."

***

The breath shot out of the nostrils of the big army horses in white bursts that crystallized upon impact with the frigid air as the officers parleyed.

"They're disorganized and don't know what they're doing," Fetterman asserted. "There's just a few them. I'm telling you, we can dispatch them to Kingdom Come."

"Remember what happened two weeks ago," Captain Frederick Brown cautioned. "This could be another ambush."

"It looks like that one's waiting for us to make our next move," said Lieutenant George Grummond, nodding toward the lone Indian who sat astride a muscular bay horse within gunshot range.

"That's Black Moon."

Fetterman yanked on the reins and wheeled his mount around to focus his steely gaze upon the Indian. "How do you know it's him?" he demanded of the corporal who made the claim.

"Because I saw him when I was garrisoned at Fort Laramie. He brought his people in to the agency because they were starving over a real bad winter. Someone said he threatened to kill General Worth so they arrested him and threw him in a cell. It was my job to bring him food. He escaped, but not before killing the guard. Yeah, that's him, all right."

"He probably thinks we're not going to chase him across Lodge Trail Ridge," Fetterman said. "Well, I've got news for him."

"William!" exclaimed Brown. "You heard Carrington's orders.

We're not to pursue over the ridge."

"I'll take the responsibility. The cavalry will follow and the infantry will bring up the rear." He cast a stony look at the others, daring them to contradict his order. "What's today's date?" he asked demandingly.

"The twenty-first," Brown soberly replied.

"A day to go down in history."

Raising his arm, signaling for them to fall in behind him, Fetterman led his command eastward and then north up the Bozeman Trail to the summit of Lodge Trail Ridge.

***

Black Moon lashed his pony into a gallop. Hunched low over the bay's neck, he raced across the flats leading to Prairie Dog Creek. Joined by the other decoys, they formed two lines, swinging wide and then crisscrossing on the opposite side of the creek. As Black Moon had planned, this was the signal to attack.

The earth seemed to come alive as the waiting ambushers spilled out from the gullies. Surprised by an overwhelming force of Indians, the soldiers' advance stopped. They fought hard as they retreated up the ridge, but wave after wave of mounted warriors cut off their escape. Rifles boomed, bullets whined, and the sky darkened with arrows. The sun had not even reached middle sky by the time it was over.

Black Moon sat astride his bay pony and looked out across the field of battle. There were no breath clouds forming over the bodies of the bluecoats. He was not surprised. The outcome of the battle had been foretold when an old man with the power to see into the future had been asked if there would be a victory, and he rode into the hills and returned to say he had a hundred soldiers in his hand.

***

Several days later, Colonel Carrington stood at the window staring out at nothing in particular, hands clasped behind his back. Removing the spectacles from his face, he rubbed his weary eyes, and asked, "What is the count?"

"Eighty," the corporal replied. "Forty-eight from the Eighteenth Infantry, twenty-eight from the Second Cavalry, one unassigned armorer, and three civilians."

Carrington let out a beleaguered sigh. "What about Fetterman?"

"From the position of the wounds in the left temples, sir, it looks like both he and Captain Brown saved their last bullets for themselves."

"And the bodies?"

"Stripped naked. Most were mutilated. Why'd the Indians do that to the bodies, sir?"

"They hate us."

"But it's not right."

Turning away from the window, Carrington went to his desk and leaned back in his chair. "It's no less than what Colonel Chivington and the Colorado Militia did to the Cheyenne on Sand Creek in sixty-four. Was it right for Chivington's men to do what they did? Perhaps men are defined not by what is in their hearts but by the deeds they do." He gave a weary dismissive wave of the hand. "That's all, Corporal."

When he was alone, the Colonel stared listlessly down at the names of the dead scrawled on the paper the Corporal had presented to him. What had prompted Fetterman to disobey orders and cross Lodge Trail Ridge when, in a few short weeks, the Army Reorganization Act would go into effect and Fetterman would become a member of the 27th Infantry, thus freeing himself from a commanding officer he detested? Why would he risk a stain on his record? Carrington shook his head with dismay. Was it for the glory, or was Fetterman just a hotheaded fool? Whatever the case, fate had caught up with Captain Brevet Lieutenant-Colonel William Fetterman on the twenty-first of December.

Carrington lifted his weary gaze and looked at the calendar on the wall. It was Christmas Eve.

CHAPTER 34
A RELUCTANT FRIENDSHIP

"Little Storm." Katie called the boy over to her lap and unfurled the strip of hide. "Do you see this date? It is a day when the white people celebrate the birth of the baby Jesus. You remember, I told you about him and how he was born in a stable with only the breath of the animals to keep him warm."

From where he sat in the corner sharpening a knife blade, Ned remarked, "I thought the Indians don't celebrate Christmas

"They don't," Katie said. "Not in the sense that we do. The single most important constant in Lakota life is belief and dedication to a higher being they call *Wakan Tanka*. It is similar to our belief in God. Those living near Fort Laramie have been exposed to Christian teachings, so it's possible that some of them celebrate the holiday. I taught Little Storm about Christmas because a day will come when it will be important for him to know the white man's ways. My father used to say that nothing stays the same. The people who are Little Storm's enemies today may be the ones he must rely on tomorrow."

Ned had said nothing to Katie about Black Moon's wish that they leave this place together should he not return. But it had been five days since Black Moon rode out at the head of an army of warriors. The mood of the entire village was one of apprehension as they waited anxiously for the warriors to return, and despite Katie's effort to give the appearance that everything was fine, he felt her tension keenly.

Katie nudged Little Storm off her lap and watched Ned run the knife blade back and forth across the stone that was wedged between his knees. "You're getting very good at that."

"It's amazing what you can get used to when you have no choice. The only thing I think I'll never get used to is not having someone to share my life with. What woman would want a man with only one arm? She'd probably think she'd be doing all the hard work herself."

"Not a Lakota woman," Katie said. "They're used to hard work."

"Are you suggesting I should take an Indian woman for my wife?"

"I'm suggesting you should take for your wife a woman who will love you for the good man you are and who isn't afraid to share the hard work. And if that's a Lakota woman, then so be it."

It was hard learning how to do things with only one arm. Shooting a rifle was out of the question, but Katie had shown him how to load her six-shot pistol and had taken him outside to practice shooting it. He saw the disapproving looks from some of the others, but Katie assured him that since he was a guest in the lodge of the *blotahunka*, the war leader, they dared not voice their displeasure at his presence among them.

With Katie's help, Ned was slowly beginning to realize that beneath the war paint and the drama of their ceremonies and the nightly beating of the drums, they were just people, after all. He saw the love that mothers and fathers bestowed on their children and the pride that women had in their husbands, sons, and brothers. "The Lakota family has no beginning and no end," Katie had explained. "A man might lose his parents or his wife or his children, but he cannot lose his family."

There was much to learn about these people. Still, the thought of taking an Indian woman for a wife was preposterous.

Ned cleared his throat. "Katie, there's something I've been meaning to tell you. Before Black Moon left, he asked me—"

A sudden clamor rose from outside, staunching Ned's words.

Katie jumped up and ran from the lodge, with Little Storm on her heels.

Hoisting himself up, Ned followed. Throwing aside the flap, he peered outside, and for the time being, the throbbing in his arm was forgotten as he watched a group of mounted men ride into camp.

With faces painted, rifles, bows and lances held high, the warriors circled the camp, once, twice, three times, to the excited trilling of the watchers and the wailing of those whose loved ones were slung across their ponies' backs.

Two warriors rode at a leisurely pace behind the others. One was Crazy Horse, whose light-skinned face mirrored the pain of having lost a good friend in the fight. Jerking on his pony's jaw rope, he left to go off by himself.

The other was Black Moon. His braids were undone, and his hair streamed behind him like black ribbons waving in the wind. He looked wild and magnificent, with no humor in his expression, just the battle-weary remnant of perfection. Tied in front across his hip were his unstrung and encased bow and quiver of arrows. His rifle case was tied to his pony's neck rope. But the deadliest weapons he carried, the ones that could not be seen, were the strong heart and iron will.

A deer hung across his pony's withers. While the others had boasted and painted their faces in preparation for the victorious ride back to the village, he had stalked the buck, bringing it down with an arrow to its chest.

Katie ran to him, her moccasins making squeaking sounds in the freshly fallen snow.

Unloading the gutted carcass for others to collect, he slung a leg over his pony's neck, jumped down, and opened his arms wide to receive her.

Watching from a distance, Ned loosed a long sigh of relief that Black Moon was alive, yet it was not without a touch of envy that he watched Black Moon pull Katie possessively into his embrace and place a deep, lingering kiss on her lips. Then, hoisting Little Storm up onto his shoulders, he and Katie walked hand in hand toward the lodge.

Ducking discreetly back inside, Ned was waiting for them when they came in.

Katie went immediately to throw more kindling onto the fire.

Tossing a glance back at Black Moon, she said to Ned, "This is the best Christmas present I could have received."

Black Moon swung Little Storm off his shoulders and deposited him gently on the ground. Nudging him toward the entrance, he said, "I see a boy who wants to go ice sledding."

"Will you come with me, *leksi*?"

"No," his uncle replied. "I will stay to speak with our guest."

"It is very cold outside," Katie said. "You must bundle up. Here are your heavy coat and mittens."

When the boy went out to play, she scrutinized Black Moon from head to toe, looking for any injuries he might not admit to having so as not to worry her. "You are unhurt?" she asked.

He nodded.

As he slid the heavy stone-headed war club that he used for close combat from his belt, she did not fail to notice the discoloration it carried and was relieved that it was not his blood staining the head of the club. He hung it from the tripod just inside the entrance, along with his bow, otter skin quiver, and the case that held his rifle.

She saw a shadow move across his face and shuddered slightly. Something was bothering him. "After you have eaten, I will braid your hair," she offered. She hurried to fill his bowl with soup from the kettle hanging over the fire.

Black Moon stripped off his heavy hide shirt, peeled off his leggings, kicked off his moccasins, and sat down before the warming flames clad only in a breechclout.

Katie turned toward him with the bowl of soup in her hands, and froze. The orange glow of the fire flickered across his bare chest, accentuating his broad shoulders and well-muscled arms, sharpening the strong line of his jaw, and etching his high cheekbones. He was what every Lakota man was bred to be, a hunter and a fighting man, and the sight of his strong, browned body caught the breath in her throat.

For a moment, the presence of the white man in the corner was forgotten, and all that existed in the world was the two of them as black eyes fixed strongly on green and a look of unbridled desire raced back and forth between them.

Katie placed the bowl in his hands. The heat of his fingers against hers felt like a prairie fire, scorching her down to her core. She ached to touch him, to run her palms across his smooth, unscarred chest and up and down his strongly muscles arms. And she would have done so if they were alone, but they were not.

Black Moon forced his gaze from hers and took a sip of soup. Nodding toward the white man who sat in the corner sharpening a knife blade with his eyes carefully averted, he asked,"Where did he get that knife?"

"I gave it to him. It is just my old carving knife."

Rising, Black Moon went to his saddle bag and took out a knife sheath. From it he removed his hunting knife whose stone blade was fastened to a carved wooden handle. Setting the blade aside, he returned to the fire and dropped into a cross-legged position. "Even an old carving knife must have a good place to stay."

"Ned," Katie called softly, "why don't you come and sit by the fire?"

Grateful for the distraction from the longing looks he witnessed between them, Ned put the knife down and joined them.

At the sheath Black Moon held out, Ned gave Katie a look of uncertainty.

"He is giving you this gift," she explained. "Your friendship has pleased him."

Reaching forward, Ned accepted the gift. The knife sheath was made of deer skin. Along the top of one side was a band of stained porcupine quills in white, black, yellow, red and blue, with a fringe of tin cones that jingled. "How do you say thank you?"

She answered, *"pilamaya."*

Ned looked at Black Moon forthrightly and repeated the word.

"It is customary to give a gift in return," Katie said.

"But I have nothing to give," Ned replied.

Katie thought for a moment. "Yes, you do." She got up and went to the place where Ned slept and rummaged through his things. She returned with the blue soldier's jacket the blacksmith at Fort Reno had given him. "You're not likely to be needing this."

"What would he want with that?" Ned exclaimed.

"It's not for him. Well, it is, but he won't keep it. He is a Thunder Dreamer. The vision he had when he was a boy told him that his would be a life of sacrifice. That's why he wears plain clothes and does not adorn himself the way the others do. He gives away most of what he has. That knife sheath is the fanciest thing he owns. It belonged to his brother, which is why he kept it. Besides," she added with a chuckle, "he'd die before he'd ever wear something like that. He'll give it to Little Storm to play with. Go on. Present it to him."

Ned was relieved that she had not chosen his Kentucky percussion rifle to give, just the worthless, threadbare army jacket.

Black Moon looked at it with disdain, gave a grudging nod, and laid it aside. Then, addressing Katie, he spoke in Lakota.

"He wants me to translate his words," she explained.

The fire crackled brightly, throwing its heat across their faces as Black Moon's deep voice filled the lodge.

"There was a time when our enemies were honorable men. We knew who they were. We fought them. We respected their fighting skills. But times have changed. Sometimes I question whether the Long Knives are human beings. Do they think they love their children more than we love ours? Do they value the land upon which they live more than we value the land upon which we live?"

He picked up his short-stemmed pipe and into its bowl he put a pinch of red willow tobacco. Offering the pipe to the sky, the four directions, and the earth, he poked a short stick into the flames and lit the pipe. In moments the sweet-smelling tobacco filled the lodge and drifted upwards, spiraling out into the cold winter air through the smoke hole.

Drawing in a breath of smoke, he went on. "There was a time when the buffalo were so many they shook the ground when they ran, but the hide men came with their big guns and took only the hides and left the carcasses to rot on the prairie."

He turned the pipe and offered it stem-first to Ned.

"It is an honor that he smokes with you," Katie said.

As Ned drew the tobacco into his lungs, Black Moon continued in a low, steady voice. "The white man called Bozeman staked out a trail heading north to the diggings west of the Elk River. It did not matter that it cut through the heart of Lakota hunting grounds. The log walls of the fort on Buffalo Creek went up to protect those seeking that thing the whites call gold. Many Lakota have died fighting the Long Knives and the whites who come up the Powder River Road."

It was here that Black Moon's voice hardened and a look of contempt flared in his dark eyes. "No matter how much we fight them, it seems we cannot drive them out. We do not have enough guns and ammunition. If we had the papers the whites use in their trades, we could buy all the guns we need, but the only place I know where so many of those papers exist is far to the east in the place called St. Louis."

As Ned handed the pipe back to Black Moon, a sudden clarity flooded him. He understood now why Katie had been so intent on getting to St. Louis. It was to buy the arms Black Moon needed to fight his war against the soldiers. He glanced at Katie and received a sly little smile as confirmation.

"The Long Knives came in wagons filled with their belongings and built the fort while their leaders were pretending to ask our permission," Black Moon went on. "Before we could say yes or no, during the Moon When the Sun Stands in the Middle, the log walls rose on Buffalo Creek." He drew in a deep breath and let it out slowly through pursed lips. "I do not enjoy killing white men, but if it is the only way to drive them out of Lakota country, I will do it.

"Is it difficult for you, being married to a white woman?" Ned asked.

"She has made her choice," Black Moon answered. "The feelings in her heart are Lakota, although her thoughts are sometimes in the world she left behind. She is a contrary, impossible woman, but I would not have her any other way." He stole a glance at Katie, his look softening. "It is not difficult loving a woman such as this."

Katie blushed as she repeated his words.

"The battle," she said to Black Moon, deflecting the subject away from the look of embarrassment she saw on Ned's face. "Tell us about the battle."

"The Long Knives had two chances to stop what was coming. One was when the soldier chief who led saw our decoys. We were like a mother sage grouse that pretends to have a useless wing and cannot fly and stays a few jumps ahead of the coyote who chases her. We pretended to be frightened and disorganized as we stayed just ahead of the bluecoats. Their other chance was lost when their leader ordered his men off Lodge Trail Ridge to pursue the decoys. That was when we sprang the trap."

Ned swallowed hard. "What happened?"

"It was a hard fight," Black Moon said. "Our ponies were slipping on the frozen ground. Many Lakota and Cheyenne were wounded. We counted less than fifteen killed."

"And the soldiers?" Ned asked.

"All killed. Nearly a hundred, I think. It is as the old man said it would be."

"What old man?" Ned questioned.

Katie explained about the man who said he could see into the future who returned from the hills claiming he carried a hundred soldiers in his hand.

"The battle of the hundred in the hand was not an easy victory," Black Moon said.

Ned's voice emerged a shallow whisper. "Fetterman?"

The firelight glanced off Black Moon's shoulders when he shrugged. "I do not know."

A paralyzing silence fell over them, broken only by the crackle of the fire. Black Moon leaned forward and dropped a bit of prairie sage onto the coals. White smoke billowed upwards toward the smoke hole. Gazing into the flames, he saw images from the battle, of men fighting and dying, and could still hear the whine of bullets and the boom of rifles. "We won this battle," he said at length, "but it will not end here." He gestured toward Ned's arm. "How is it coming along?"

"It hurts a little, and it itches, but otherwise..." He gave a negligent shrug.

In a flat voice Black Moon said, "With the new sun we will build the scaffolds to hold the bodies of the brave men killed in the battle. Be thankful you are still here and not in the spirit world. It would be good for you to leave here as soon as you can, but the trails are frozen and the winter is hard, with more snow than we have seen in a long time, and you would not get very far. We will have a lodge put up for you to live in until the snows melt."

With that, Black Moon rose and went to his sleeping place. He was weary down to his bones. He took a long shuddering breath. He needed Katie beside him, the warmth of her woman's body, the sound of her voice, the brush of her breath against his flesh. He wanted to reach for her hand and thrust himself on her, drawing upon her strength and womanly wisdom to tell him that what he was doing was the right thing. He watched her by the fire. Her flawless profile was etched against the orange glow of the flames. He longed for her smooth skin and lean, firm flanks, and even from here he caught the scent of her, hot, raw and strong.

She and the white man were speaking in hushed voices in a language he did not understand. He knew she was struggling to get back to the Lakota world she had known before a restless wind had blown her off her path. Is that what they were talking about? Was she still uncertain as to where she belonged? Sinking back down against the soft fur of the buffalo robe, he closed his eyes, but he did not sleep.

Sadness and uncertainty weighed heavily upon him. Despite the recent victory, the Long Knives would not stop. They wanted to place every Lakota left alive on the agencies. Many years ago, when his people were starving over a long, hard winter, and Good Deeds, Little Storm's mother, was ill and would have died without the white man's medicine, he did the only thing he knew to keep them from perishing by bringing them in to the agency at Deer Creek. There, he witnessed the miserable lives the people were living, with hunger and restrictions and treachery all around them. As a warrior, he accepted that it might be his fate to die fighting. To face the Long Knives in battle was one thing, but Black Moon knew better than most what life would be like for those left behind at the mercy of the Long Knives, and he vowed that neither he nor anyone he loved would ever be forced onto an agency.

The old ones said the future was a visitor without a face, but Black Moon knew its face. It had blue eyes and a beard.

Four days later the victory dances began. The drums beat long into the night and the flames of the fire in the camp circle reached high, as if to touch the stars.

As usual, Black Moon took no part in the dancing, but that did not stop the old men from singing in praise of his bravery and his leadership. From where he and Katie watched from beyond the glow of the camp fire and ring of dancers, he muttered, "I do not lead. If others follow, it is because they choose to do so."

"If others follow," she gently corrected, "it is because you are the one leading."

"When they took the bighorn shirt from me, I ceased to be a leader."

She reached for his hand through the darkness. "With or without the shirt you have always been true to who you are. Once a leader, always a leader."

CHAPTER 35
A JOURNEY ENDS AND A NEW ONE BEGINS

Winter slid into spring. In the Moon When the Buffalo Calves Are Red, the women struck the lodges and packed everything onto pony drags. Crazy Horse and his people moved from the Tongue, south to the Elk River to join with the Minniconjou and Hunkpatila bands.

With the parfleches filled with meat and *wasna*, Black Moon, Katie, Claw, Running-water Woman, Little Storm, and Ned set out to meet up with the Oglala who had wintered at Bear Butte. Days later, the summit of Bear Butte appeared in the distance, and the lush slopes of the *paha sapa* swelled on the horizon.

"This is where Black Moon was born," Katie said to Ned who rode beside her on his Minnesota mount. "The Lakota call this place the heart of everything that is. In July, the bands will come together here for the Sun Dance. No one knows how many Lakota have been laid to rest in these mountains. Over the years their flesh and bones have become one with this place. The people do not own this place. It owns them."

Ned gazed upon the hills. Seen from the plains the mantle of green pines faded to a dusky purple that gave the Black Hills their name. He understood now, simply from observing them from this distance, the reverence the Indians had for this sacred place and found it hard to put into words the feeling of awe that came over him.

When the entire band was together again, they settled in a little cottonwood valley near the forks of the Cheyenne River. It was the time of year for hunts and raids, for gathering early vegetables, for painting parfleches and robes, for dances and vision-seeking.

One morning, when the sun was in the morning half of the sky, the scouts signaled that a wagon was spotted coming up the Holy Road from the southeast.

Jasper Gillette guided his wagon past the pony herd to the cluster of lodges set in a circle and all facing east toward the rising sun. In a nearby grove of box elders a group of women were tapping the trees for their sap, while the men led several yearling ponies into the river for breaking, the water cushioning their falls off the bucking ponies. He parked his wagon at a spot at the edge of the tribal crescent as was customary. While his children ran off to play with the other boys and girls, and his Oglala wife and her sister unloaded the wagon and began the work of putting up their lodge, he went off to find Katie.

He found her hunched over a buffalo hide that she had staked out on the ground, scraping the flesh and gristle away with a tool fashioned from a bone tipped with a blade. He watched her for a while. Wearing a deer-hide dress adorned with two rows of elk teeth around the shoulders and calf-length leggings above her moccasins that were decorated with quillwork, she might have been taken for any other Indian woman were it not for the flaming red hair that fell in two braids down her back, errant strands circling her face as she worked.

"Where'd you get that one?" he asked as he approached. "I didn't think there were many buffalo left in these parts."

Katie straightened up and gave him a welcoming smile. "There aren't. The hunters had to travel far to find a herd."

He looked past her to her lodge. "It looks like it wintered pretty good."

Wiping her hands on her dress, she said, "It did. But Little Storm needs new moccasins, and Black Moon can always use new leggings."

"Where is Black Moon?" he asked, glancing around.

"He went hunting with Swift Bear and Ned."

"Ned?" he exclaimed. "You don't mean that young fella you were traveling with on the wagon train."

"He spent the winter with us. I expect he'll be leaving soon, although I can't imagine where he'll go or what he'll do." She shook off the bleak uncertainty of Ned's future, and said. "They should be returning soon. Are you traveling alone?"

"Not this time. I brought my wife and kids and my wife's sister with me. We'll stay here for a spell and then we're heading west."

"Where to?"

"Can't rightly say. Montana, maybe."

"Don't tell me you're going for gold."

"I'm too damn old to spend my days bent over a stream with a pan in my hands," he replied with a laugh. "No, I was thinking maybe I'd build me another trading store like the one the Cheyenne burned down a couple years ago after Sand Creek. Travel on the overland trail will only get heavier. I figure those westward moving whites are gonna need supplies."

"The autumn hunts were good," Katie said, "and Black Moon's arrows never miss, so he should be bringing home a nice fat deer. You and your family are welcome to eat with us. There's plenty to go around."

"That's right kind of you," Gillette said. "We'd be honored. Besides, I'll be wanting to talk to Black Moon." In answer to Katie's searching look, he added, "I bring news from Fort Laramie,"

Later in the day, after Little Storm and Gillette's children had eaten and run off to play outside, Katie welcomed the guests into her lodge. A short time later Black Moon and Ned returned.

Black Moon entered first. Against the fire-lit lodge skins his eyes were bright and his body pulsed with feral grace. The scent of trampled grass clung to his elk hide shirt. Ned came in behind him and set his Kentucky percussion rifle against the hide wall.

"We have guests," Katie announced. "You remember Mr. Gillette. This is his wife, Pretty Owl, and her sister Rattling Blanket."

Black Moon spoke a few words of welcome to his guests before laying his things aside and shedding his shirt.

Ned extended his hand for a shake, and it was then that Gillette noticed that his other arm was missing from the elbow down.

Gillette gasped. "Good lord, son, what happened to you?"

At the impulse of distress that passed over Ned's face, Katie spoke up. "Ned got caught in a fight that wasn't his." She fixed Gillette with a look that warned him not to press the issue. Changing the subject, she said, "I hope everyone is hungry."

Into six bowls she spooned the roasted elk that was simmering in the kettle over the fire.

As they ate, they engaged in quiet conversation. Over the past few months, with Katie's tutoring, Ned had become proficient enough in the Lakota language to get the gist of what was being said, with only an occasional need for signing. He seemed, however, to be less interested in the talk than in the guests seated around the fire, and Katie could not help but notice the way his eyes kept straying to Rattling Blanket, and that she, exhibiting the shyness typical of a Lakota girl, kept peeking up at him, returning his look through demurely lowered lashes.

When the meat bowls were empty, Black Moon took his pipe from its rawhide case and put a pinch of willow tobacco in the bowl. Offering the pipe to the four directions, the sky, and the earth, he took a puff and passed it to Gillette on his left.

"This is a fine-looking pipe," Gillette said of the catlinite pipe that had been polished and finished to a deep red color. He knew why a man of Black Moon's stature smoked a short-stemmed pipe such as this, but showed his respect by giving it the same solemn reverence as if it had been a long-stemmed one. Drawing in the fragrant tobacco, he let it out through his lips and passed it on to Ned.

The talk was of hunting and how rapidly the children were growing. Katie slanted a look up at Gillette. "You said you bring news from Fort Laramie."

Gillette cleared his throat. "They are still talking about the fight from this past winter at Lodge Trail Ridge, the one the Lakota call the Battle of the Hundred in the Hand." He shot a quick look at Black Moon whose expression remained implacable. "Word is that Little White Chief issued orders to Captain Fetterman and Lieutenant

Grummond to relieve the wood train and not to pursue beyond Lodge Trail Ridge. Apparently, as Grummond joined him, Fetterman turned east, away from the wood train, picked up the Bozeman, and then turned north up Lodge Trail Ridge. The garrison watched as Fetterman's command, with Grummond's cavalry out in front, crossed out of sight over the ridge to pursue ten Indians who were acting as decoys. I cannot imagine who they might have been," he added with a sardonic grin. "They rode right into a trap. Fetterman's infantry and Grummond's cavalry were wiped out."

They listened gravely as Gillette's story unfolded. Ned aimed a guarded look at Katie, and then ventured, "Fetterman?"

"Dead. The fools. Fetterman was familiar with decoys so he should have known what they were up to, and apparently, Grummond could never resist the temptation to chase them. Now the government is talking about a new treaty with the Lakota and Cheyenne for next year and maybe abandoning the forts." Gillette gave a rueful shake of his head. "All that, for what?" He dropped his gaze and stared into the fire. "By the time that fort is abandoned, "I will be long gone. Montana. Oregon. It does not matter where I go, as long as I can get myself and my family away from all this killing."

A silence as thick as a winter buffalo robe settled over the lodge. Breaking the tension, Katie said, "I was so busy this morning that I forgot to fill the paunch. Rattling Blanket, would you do that for me?"

The young woman smiled and rose.

"Ned," Katie said, "why don't you go with her?"

Gillette smiled knowingly. Something was afoot in Katie's mind, and it was not hard to figure out what it was.

***

Ned emerged from the lodge Katie and Running-water Woman had erected for him on the outskirts of the tribal crescent. He yawned and stretched his arms up over his head and gazed out upon the land.

It was a beautiful place, where the grass grew tall, blankets of blue sage covered the ground, and the white-bellied pronghorn were plentiful. An eagle patrolled the sky, is wings spread wide to catch currents of air. Spotting a tasty morsel on the ground unseen to human eyes, it folded in its wings and dived out of sight. From somewhere out upon the prairie a bull elk whistled, the thin, wheezing sound carrying far across the land.

On the far bank of the river stood several death scaffolds. Four poles supported the newest platform holding the hide-wrapped body of a warrior who'd been killed in a recent raid against the Crow far to the west. From it hung the symbol of his life, a painted shield whose eagle feathers flicked about in the warm spring breeze. Beneath it lay the body of his favorite war horse. The day the war party had returned with his body slung over the back of his pony, wails and moans echoed throughout the village. The next day the slain warrior's women relatives appeared with their hair hacked short and blood still dripping from the wounds they had slashed on their arms and legs. And in the days that followed, Ned noticed that mothers and fathers held their children a little closer, perhaps pretending that there were no troubles in the world.

Ned's attention was drawn to a place further down the river where Little Storm was playing with a group of boys. He watched with mixed emotions as each boy took his turn donning the blue soldier's jacket, and the one playing the Long Knife was chased by the others with toy bows and arrows. Their mock combat would one day be real, but Ned knew the numbers would shift heavily in the other direction.

Upon seeing him, Little Storm waved from across the distance. Ned waved back.

Over these past months Ned had come to view these people from a completely different standpoint. They were not the beggars, thieves, or savages others claimed they were. They were people. Just people. No different, really, from the ones he knew back home in Minnesota, or the ones who joined wagon trains for the westward migration, or those who turned around and went back east. They doted on their children, laughed at jokes, cried and mourned for lost love ones, told stories around winter fires, and worked hard to make better lives for themselves and their families.

The soldiers had not ventured too far out of Fort Phil Kearny over the winter. The wood train was still under continuous harassment by Black Moon, Red Cloud and Crazy Horse, but with the warmer weather, Ned knew that tensions with the Army would only get worse. Sooner or later, he would have to strike out on his own. Over the winter he'd gone hunting with Black Moon, and with the Oglala's help he had reached the point where he could fire his rifle with the butt wedged between his right shoulder and neck. The first time his bullet brought down a deer Black Moon had given him a resounding slap on the back. But being able to feed himself was one thing. How would he combat the loneliness that was sure to haunt him after he left here?

Winter had released its stranglehold over the land. If only it would release the nagging uncertainty of where he would go. There was nothing to return to in Minnesota, and what kind of livelihood was there for a one-armed man in Oregon? The future looked bleak, even on a day when the sun shone brightly in the sky.

"The days are warm, but the old ones keep an eye out for storms. A blizzard during the spring moon can be bad."

Ned turned to the sound of Katie's voice. Her footsteps were so quiet in the new spring grass that he had not even heard her approach. Just like an Indian, he could not help but think.

Coming to stand beside him, she held her hair back against the breeze and looked across the river at the uneven line of scaffolds. A moment of silence passed before she spoke again.

"The scaffold on the end holds Lone Horn, a friend of Black Moon's, who died in a fight with the soldiers at Box Elder Creek. The buffalo hide shield that hangs from the scaffold is weatherworn and its covering is tattered. The paint has faded, but the figure of a fox can still be faintly seen. He was a member of the Kit Foxes, a warrior society."

"What about those two that are close together?" Ned asked.

"The one in front belongs to Pretty Shield, Black Moon's mother. The other belongs to Fire Cloud, his brother." Her voice echoed the sadness that lingered in her heart over the loss of Fire Cloud. "Did I ever tell you about him?"

"Only that you and he were married for a brief time."

"He was murdered," she said flatly.

"By the soldiers?"

"By one of his own people. A jealous rival of Black Moon's. I don't think Black Moon has ever gotten over it. They were so different. Black Moon is hotheaded. He's a warrior. He knows that the only way to drive the soldiers away is by fighting them. Fire Cloud was a quiet man who advocated for peace. But we all know that peace is not possible. That's why you need to leave here, and soon. Do you know what you will do?"

Ned gave a hapless shrug as he stared out across the rough, broken land.

"You could stay with us," she offered.

He turned to look at her. Her red hair hung long and loose about her shoulders and down her back. A spring breeze flicked up the ends and tossed a strand across her face to tangle in her lashes. He smiled and gave a soft shake of the head. "I don't belong here."

Katie brushed the silken strand from her face. "I suppose you're right."

"My best bet would be to see if I can catch a wagon train heading west. Now that the warmer weather is here, there are bound to be more traveling the Oregon Trail. And then, who knows? What about you?" he asked.

In her quiet talks with Jasper Gillette, Katie learned more than he'd been willing to say openly to Black Moon and the other leaders. "Gillette told me the Bozeman Trail will soon become obsolete as a route to the Montana gold fields and that the government is shifting its focus to a rail line to the north along the Elk River, giving Black Moon, Red Cloud and Crazy Horse the impression that they have won the war when, in reality, things are apt to get much worse."

She shook off her forebodings and said with a lightheartedness she did not truly feel, "If I learned anything at all from Tom McCabe, it was to pick myself up every time I fall."

"That's sage advice," Ned commented.

"Feel free to use it if you need it," Katie jokingly responded.

Lifting her head, she looked up at the pillows of clouds rolling across the sky, and the humor receded into gentle musing. "Clouds, wind, the buffalo, everything is in constant motion. The seasons are part of a never-ending cycle. Even life itself moves from infancy, to childhood, to adulthood, and finally to old age. There is no beginning and no ending to it. It just is."

"Is that Black Moon talking?" Ned inquired. "Or you?"

"It's me, and it was me long before Black Moon came into my life. My father taught me to love the land and everything on it. We lived in our little cabin along the Laramie, but we also knew that this is Lakota land. From the Muddy River to the east, to the Running Water and the Shell to the south, from the Shining Mountains to the west, and the Elk River on the northern border. Lakota land." She heaved a sigh. "Life has a way of leading us to unexpected turns. Who would have thought that I, the daughter of an Indian trader, would one day be the wife of an Oglala warrior, or that a farmer from Minnesota would have eyes for a certain Oglala girl?"

Before Ned could voice his chagrin, Katie went on. "By her age most Oglala girls are already married with children. Gillette said she'd been married only a few weeks when her young husband was killed by a grizzly. It had been an arranged marriage. The boy was from a Sicangu family and a nephew of Spotted Tail. Her mourning period is over, but she has shown no interest in another man. Until now."

"Katie," Ned began in protest, "you don't think—"

"I think Rattling Blanket has been working very hard and would probably like to go for a ride." At his hesitation, her voice became stern. "For goodness sake, Ned, you lost your arm, not your sight. Are you the only one who doesn't see that she favors you?"

"But we're from different worlds," he argued.

Her tone softened. "You have much in common. You both lost loved ones, and you're both lonely. You have nothing to lose and everything to gain. In the Lakota way, a new husband becomes part of the woman's family."

"Husband?" he exclaimed.

"Can you look me in the eyes and honestly tell me you haven't thought of it?" she challenged.

He lifted his head and brought his reluctant gaze to hers. Her eyes were green and bright and filled with affection. "Thought of it?" he repeated. "Hell, Katie, it's all I've been able to think about since the day I met her."

Her laughter flowed over him like water over rocks. "Come on," she said, taking his hand. "I'm heading over there now."

A short while later she and Gillette watched as Ned and Rattling Blanket rode out of the encampment together.

Linking her arm in the trader's, they strolled toward the river.

"I think I know you well enough by now to know that something's troubling you," Gillette said.

"It's what you said about Captain Fetterman."

"How's that?"

She told him about her encounters with the infantry commander and how she had rebuffed his advances. "I can't help but think that if it weren't for me, Fetterman would not have been so obsessed with wiping out Black Moon, and maybe he'd still be alive."

"There's two things that make men do foolish things. Women and war. There's no way of telling which one led him to cross Lodge Trail Ridge that day, and it does no good to fret over it. What's done is done. It doesn't matter."

"You make it sound so simple."

"It is," he said. He placed his hands on her shoulders and turned her toward the land that stretched across the river. "That's what matters. Have you ever seen anything more beautiful?" He took a deep breath, filling his lungs with the sweet mountain air. "I'll never forget the first time I saw this country," he said. "I'd never seen anything so wide and open and unspoiled in all my life."

"It's only May," she said, "and the streams and creeks are already drying into mud wallows. Soon the prairie fires will eat up the land."

"And make way for the tender green shoots to push up through the ash," Gillette added. "Life is a circle, the Indians say. The end of one journey is the beginning of the next."

"The spring brings strong new life."

Something in her voice compelled him to turn his face away from the landscape to look at her. Despite her misgivings about William Fetterman's fate, there was a glow about her that he had not noticed before. And then he saw the way her hands cupped her belly, and he realized what it was.

"Does Black Moon know?"

Katie shook her head. "I haven't told him yet."

"I remember when Pretty Owl told me there was going to be a young one. You could have knocked me over with an eagle feather. Hell, what did I know about being a father? But I learned real quick. Then another one came, and another one, and another one." He laughed. "Who would have guessed that this old man had all that life in him?"

He fell silent as the memories swept over him. Looking back out upon the land, he said, "Yes sir, I knew the first time I set eyes on this place that this was where I'd spend the rest of my life. It took me a spell to find the place where I wanted to settle down, but then I found a little spot on Deer Creek just north of the Shell River and built a toll bridge across the Platte for the emigrant trade. That made me enough money to build a trading store, a dry goods store, a post office and an Overland stage station. Those were good times. Then, one day as I'm stacking shelves in the store, in walks the prettiest woman I'd ever seen, and she trades the fancy dress she's wearing for an Arapaho one of hide."

Katie chuckled. "I remember the look on your face when I asked you to accompany me to Fort Laramie where they were holding Black Moon in a cell."

"I knew that day there was nothing you could ask that I wouldn't do to help you," Gillette said.

She slipped her hand in his and gave it a squeeze. "There's one more thing I'd like to ask."

"Don't tell me you need to run off somewhere to find Black Moon when he's right here."

"No, not this time. It's Ned. I've seen the way he looks at Rattling Blanket and the way she's been looking back."

"Yeah, I noticed that, too. But if you're asking me to somehow match them two up, that ain't for me to decide."

"Of course not," Katie said. "I know from experience that a marriage based on anything but love isn't always best." She was thinking of Fire Cloud, Black Moon's older brother, the man she had married out of obligation to Turning Hawk for taking her in after Blue Water. Her face relaxed into a secret smile. "It's clear those two dote on each other."

Gillette let out a hearty laugh. "The last time you played matchmaker it was to turn that Cheyenne girl's head away from Black Moon."

"Pine Leaf, yes. You have to admit she and Red Thunder made a good match. But it's not just companionship Ned needs. He needs a purpose, something he can do with his life. I was thinking that you might need someone to help build that new trading store you were talking about. You said yourself that the emigrant travel will only grow heavier, and once the store is built you would probably need someone to help run it."

He gave her sly look. "I might."

"Don't be fooled by him only having one arm. I've been watching him these past months and you'd be amazed at what he can do."

"All right," he said. "I'll take him on."

"He's a good, honest, hard-working man," Katie went on. "You wouldn't be sorry, and—" She stopped in mid-sentence as his words sank in. "You will?"

"Why not? If he's everything you say he is, I'd be happy to take him along, and honored to have him marry my wife's sister. If she'll have him, that is. I ain't gonna force no man on her."

Katie flashed a smile. "If I'm any judge of a woman's feelings, she'll have him."

CHAPTER 36
MY OWN

The wedding of Ned and Rattling Blanket took place in the Moon when the Berries Were Good. It was customary for the man's family to make a feast, but Ned had no family among the Oglala, so Katie and Black Moon and Claw and Running-water Woman gave the feast. As a holy man, Claw stood before the couple and pronounced simply, "He wanted the girl, so they have given her to him." And on a bright, sunshiny day in the month of June it was done.

When the feasting was over and the guests had all gone, Black Moon announced, "The young men are growing restless. I will take them on a raid."

Several days later Black Moon sat astride his bay gelding at the head of the war party. Reaching down, he ran his hand over Katie's cheek. If anything happened to him, he would remember the softness of her skin. Katie watched him go, her eyes fixed on his back, and kept her fears to herself.

Early the next morning, Pretty Owl and Rattling Blanket dismantled their lodge and packed up all their belongings.

Katie stood beside Ned, watching as Gillette lifted his children onto the wagon. When the trader climbed aboard, she looked up at him and said, "Goodbye, my friend. I cannot thank you enough for all you have done for me." There was so much more she wanted to say, but she feared her tears would get in the way.

"You take care of yourself, little lady," the old trader called down to her before cracking the whip and setting his wagon in motion.

Saying farewell to Ned proved to be more difficult.

"I was hoping to say goodbye to Black Moon," he said.

"I suspect saying goodbye to you was harder than he wanted us to know. That is why he is not here. It is not in his nature to show weakness."

She turned to him suddenly and hugged him long and hard and placed a lingering kiss upon his cheek. "We've been through a lot together, you and me," she whispered into his ear.

"Katie, I—"

She pressed a finger to his lips and gave a knowing shake of her head. "You are a good man, Ned Jeppsen. A better man with one arm than some are with two. I hope you live a long and happy life, dear friend."

Ned nodded toward the rolling wagon. "He asked me to help him build his trading store and then to stay on to help run it. He's getting on in years, so I figured, why not?"

He would never know the hand she had in determining his future, Katie thought, smiling secretly to herself. She waited with a quiet lump in her throat as he slipped his foot into the stirrup, mounted, and urged his Minnesota mount into a gallop to catch up with the others. The clunk of the rolling wagon and the jingle of the harness grew dimmer as it disappeared from sight. Her lower lip trembled. She knew she would not see them again.

***

A week passed before the scouts spotted the braves returning through the sun-slant of the late afternoon. Katie ran outside to greet them as they rode in with a thunder of hooves. It was clear by the scalps some of the warriors carried that they had fought their Crow enemies, and had won. Her eyes searched anxiously for one face in particular, unpainted and breathlessly handsome. She watched him throw a leanly muscled leg over his pony's neck, jump down, and lead the pony away.

She was waiting for him when he entered the lodge. As she filled his bowl with meat, she watched from the corners of her eyes as he hung his things of war carefully on the tripod and then stripped out of his clothes. Wearing only a breech clout he leaned back on his latticed chair before the fire.

Katie's heart raced at the sight of those muscled arms and unscarred chest, the taut belly and strong, sinewy thighs. His unbound hair hung long and straight across his shoulders and down his back. She knew every inch of that well-knit, battle-hardened body, and yet each time she gazed upon its near nakedness it was like she was seeing it for the first breathtaking time. She shuddered with yearning for the feel of those long, graceful fingers stroking her flesh. He made love to her the way he lived, with unbridled passion and a fire in his blood. She longed for his possession that invariably released her from the stormy emotions that troubled her. Afterward, she would lie quietly in his arms, sated and content, remembering only the ecstasy they shared.

She knelt before him with the burl bowl. With a practiced hand he caressed her neck and found the silken hollow of her throat. His eyes strayed to the robes. His lovemaking was always strong and powerful in the aftermath of battle. She would have followed him willingly, eagerly, to the robes were it not for the boy who sat in the corner waxing his small bow.

Black Moon buried his hand in her hair and drew her head back for a lingering kiss before offering a reluctant nod and letting her rise.

Later, as Katie worked with an awl and sinew to mend a tear in Black Moon's shirt of tanned deerskin and Black Moon sat smoking his short-stemmed pipe, there came a scratching on the hide door to the lodge. Claw entered carrying a tanned buffalo skin in his arms. Setting it down, he unfurled it to reveal the winter count he'd been keeping since before his sons were born.

As keeper of the winter count, Claw chose a memorable event to represent each year. The very first drawing was of a shooting star whistling across the sky and went as far back as the year the whites recorded as 1821.

Calling Little Storm to his side, he pointed to several of the drawings. "This is the winter when our people captured many ponies from the Shoshoni. This one shows the winter we had to pull our belongings over the ice. And this one," he said, pointing to the drawing of a blood-red cloud in the sky, his voice taking on a melancholy tone, "shows the year your father was born."

Little Storm tugged on Claw's sleeve and pointed to the drawing Claw had made eleven winters ago of two riders astride one pony, the rider in front with long black hair and the one behind with long red hair. "What is that one, *Thunkashila?*"

His grandfather replied, "It was the year your uncle brought your new mother to live among us."

Claw drew the boy's attention to the newest drawing, the paint scarcely dry. It was of a man with one arm wearing a blue soldier's coat and would always be remembered as the year when the one-armed white man had come to live with them.

"He was not such a bad white man," Claw admitted. Nudging the boy off his lap, he said, "Go outside now while there is still light and shoot your arrows at grasshoppers. I want to speak with your uncle."

When he was gone, Claw said wistfully, "He looks more like your brother every day."

"I do not forget the deep river of misunderstanding that existed between us," Black Moon lamented. "I have only to look at my nephew to see the face I miss so much. I would give anything just to hear that gentle voice again. Even if it is speaking for peace," he added with a self-deprecating little laugh.

To hide his anguish over the loss of his first-born son, Claw asked, "How did it go to the west?"

Black Moon's deep voice drifted over the crackle of the flames. "On the way back from Crow country we came across old buffalo bones scattered across a large area, work of the hide hunters. There was nothing to do except turn all the skulls toward the east in a sign of respect, something the hide hunters will never understand." Holding the pipe to his lips, he drew in the sweet-smelling tobacco and let it out through the hard line that formed across his mouth.

"In the time of my grandfather," said Claw, "there was an old buffalo jump just above Buffalo Creek. The hunters would chase the buffalo over the bluff and then butcher them in the gully below. Then, as now, we took everything from the buffalo, the meat for our kettles, the bones for our tools, the hides for our lodges. We gave thanks to the buffalo for helping our people to survive. In my youth the buffalo were so many they shook the land when they ran. Now..." His words trailed off.

"Now the white men take only the hides and leave the rest to rot," Black Moon said, finishing his father's words. "It is just one more reason to drive them out of our country."

"What else did you see?" Claw asked.

"We passed the log walls of the fort on Buffalo Creek. I cannot wait for the Long Knives to leave."

"I heard that Red Cloud sent word to the soldier chief at Fort Laramie that we are waiting for them to leave. He says if they do not leave, we will drive them out."

"Words," Black Moon scoffed. "When have words ever made any difference?"

Grunting his agreement, Claw rolled up the winter count and left.

There was one thing Katie knew that would erase that smoldering look from Black Moon's eyes and chase the bitterness from his heart. Laying the deerskin shirt aside, she got up and added wood to the coals in the fire pit. Then she rummaged through a painted rawhide case and took out a small object and placed it beside him.

Black Moon looked down at the tiny rattle made of deer hide. It looked just like the one he had soaked and filled with sand to dry, and then fitted with a wooden handle filled with pebbles.

"You kept this?" he whispered.

"I could not bear to throw it away."

His voice caught in his throat, caused by the memory. "There should be a little one around to use this."

"There will be."

His quickly put aside his pipe and scrambled to his feet. Standing before her, he took her hands in his. At first, no words came as the realization soaked into his being. "When?" he asked in a husky voice. "During the Winter Moon," she answered, placing his hands gently upon her belly.

He was unable to find the words to match his emotions as his fingers trembled against the slight swell beneath her elk skin dress. When he looked back up at her, the bitterness was gone from his expression and his eyes were tender and bright.

For Black Moon, smoking the short-stemmed pipe was a sign that he had lost a place of high honor, but the highest honor of all was the one that came from being loved by this green-eyed woman. He gathered her to his chest, and brushing a lock of hair from her face, he whispered, "*Mitawa.*"

My Own.

The word wrapped itself around Katie like angel wings. Gazing up into his midnight eyes, her father's words suddenly flooded her mind.

"Katie m'darlin', nothin' stays the same."

McCabe was wrong. For everything she'd been though and all she had lost, one thing remained the same. It was the one constant in her life, the thing that filled her with joy like nothing else could and provided nourishment to her sometimes wounded spirit and hope to her heart. It was the love she had for this dark-eyed Lakota warrior. He was the most precious thing in her whole existence. He was her past, her present, and her future.

Among his own people he was the subject of hero stories. To the whites he was fast becoming a legend as an unrelenting enemy. But legends were like the morning mist off the river that soon dissipates beneath the warmth of the sun. Only she knew him for the man he really was, with faults and flaws and shortcomings, a man who laughed and joked and cried and made love.

"Does this mean you will not go away again?" Black Moon asked. "Have you found your place?"

Katie felt herself flushing with happiness as she gazed up into the handsome face of the man who had left his tracks on her heart.

She knew now that this was where she belonged. Here, the land of her birth, where she gathered plums and buffalo berries in the shallow, wooded ravines and chokecherries in late summer. Where the violet colored blossoms showed the place to find the sweet prairie turnips. Where the wind blew over the tall grass and whispered its gentle song through the cottonwoods. Where the undulating prairie stretched for as far as the eyes could see. Where the land itself had tales to tell. It was here in the Black Hills, the heart of everything that was. Here, in the arms of the man she loved.

Katie drew Black Moon's face to hers and kissed him tenderly on the mouth.

"You are mine. I am yours. This child I carry is ours. I know now where my place is. It is wherever you are."

Smiling, she laid her head against his bare chest and listened to the drumbeat of his heart and breathed in the familiar scent of sage that lingered in his long, dark hair, a great peace invading her soul.

The sun sank low, sending shadows rolling from the hills and into the gullies and meadows. The western sky purpled to the color of a mussel shell.

The restless wind had died, and a gentle wind had guided her home.

Epilogue
Cherish the Land

Powder River Country, late August, 1868

Her name was Makes the Song. She was a happy child with pudgy thighs, a thatch of shiny blue-black hair and eyes as green as tender new grass. On this day in the Moon When the Sun Stands in the Middle, she was bound snugly within the protective folds of the cradleboard her mother had propped against the slender trunk of a cottonwood tree.

At the sight of the man who approached with long, purposeful strides, the child began to giggle. Bending, he reached down and picked up the wooden frame whose hide covering was decorated top to bottom in beadwork.

"She will be the mother of warriors."

Katie looked up from the pot of chokecherries she was stirring over the hot coals and smiled at her husband. "You are not disappointed that she is not a boy who would one day be one of those warriors?"

Nonplussed, Black Moon echoed, "Disappointed? How could I be disappointed when I now have two beautiful women to love? Besides," he added, "Little Storm has seen nine winters and is showing signs of becoming a strong warrior."

"There is plenty of time for him to see warfare."

"I was thinking that the next time we ride against the Crow I will take him with me. He is too young to fight, but he can see to the ponies. Being a warrior teaches a boy to be a man. He learns to act in spite of his fear and how to live his life as an example for everyone to see. He becomes *wica*."

The smile evaporated from Katie's face. Becoming *wica*, a complete man, was not without its dangers. Lakota fighting men were often wounded or killed in battle. Black Moon himself bore a scar from the Wagon Box fight last year where a soldier's bullet has whizzed by and grazed him. But for the distance of a slender hair, he would have been dead.

Eight months after the Battle of the Hundred in the Hand, Black Moon, Red Cloud and Crazy Horse had assembled a force of more than a thousand to drive the Long Knives out of the logging camp they had set up in a meadow west of the fort on Buffalo Creek. The day had been much like this one when the warriors fell upon the wagon box fort with a vengeance. The soldiers had removed the wagon boxes from the wagons and formed them into a defensive corral. The boxes were made of wood hard enough to fend off arrows and bullets, and even though the soldiers numbered only a handful, they were able to hold off the attackers until help arrived. What the warriors could not know was that just a few weeks prior to the fight the garrison had received a shipment of new Springfield rifles that enabled the soldiers to rapidly fire and reload and fend off the attack.

Black Moon had returned from the Wagon Box fight with a bloody gash on his face. The wound had healed, but it left a scar that ran across his left cheek like the track of a wagon wheel.

He had seen the future, and it was shaped by the Army's new firepower. In the council lodge he argued for a change of tactics, and over the objections of Turning Hawk and the other peace talkers, he led a wave of warriors that set fire to the plains around the fort.

Then, as recently as the Moon When the Geese Return, news came that a peace commission had arrived at Fort Laramie to discuss the terms of a new treaty.

Black Moon had refused to go, grumbling, "I have heard too many white promises to believe anything they say."

Word drifted back to the Oglala camp on the Tongue that the commission had ordered the Bozeman Trail to be closed, causing him to scoff, "So, now we can go back to calling it the Powder River Road."

And confirmed that the sacred *paha sapa* were owned by the Lakota, to which Black Moon spat, "We do not own the land. The land owns us."

On this day late in the summer moon, Black Moon placed a kiss upon his daughter's chubby cheek and propped the cradleboard back against the tree.

"I went to see the soldier town on Buffalo Creek," he announced. "I watched from the hills as the cloth that flies on top of the tall pole was taken down and the last wagon left those log walls."

Katie glance up from her work. Fort Phil Kearny, abandoned? For two bloody years Black Moon, Red Cloud and Crazy Horse had fought viciously to stop the invasion of their hunting grounds by prospectors bound for the Montana goldfields. Riders had come to the Oglala camp with news that Little White Chief had been replaced as commander of the garrison. But she never imagined that they would just up and leave, and she could not help but wonder if it was with anger or relief that the troops departed.

That night, while Makes the Song slept and Little Storm sharpened the blade his uncle had given him, Katie nestled against Black Moon's shoulder and confessed, "Sometimes I feel confused."

"You are not thinking of going away?" he said, his body tensing.

"No. Not that kind of confused." She felt his body relax. "It is just that I wonder how this can be a bad time and a good time all at once. Bad because of the soldiers." She paused to draw in a deep breath. "And good because I do not have to see any other place in the world, not even the green hills of Ireland that my father used to talk about, to know that this is the most beautiful place on Earth." She lifted her gaze to his. "And that this is the most beautiful man."

The innate shyness that conflicted with his warlike nature made Black Moon turn his face away.

Katie reached up and turned his face back to hers. With a gentle touch she traced the line of the scar on his left cheek. The remnant of the Wagon Box fight lent a rugged appeal to the raw perfection of his looks.

Her voice took on an incantatory tone. "One fort abandoned does not mean they will not keep coming. It is because we cherish the land that the fort must be destroyed."

He bent his head and nuzzled her temple, his long, black eyelashes brushing downwards as his arm slid around her waist and he kissed her. He held her close, drawing upon her strength.

When the new sun rose over the treetops, Black Moon mounted his bay gelding and rode to the plateau between the two Piney Creeks. With Katie's words racing through his mind, and the steady fire of her belief in him radiating through his entire being, he led his warriors down from the hills toward the abandoned fort.

The logs walls proved to be good kindling, and Fort Phil Kearny was burned to the ground.

http://www.nancymorse.com
Historical and Contemporary Romance
Where Love is Always an Adventure

THE WILD WIND SERIES

WHERE THE WILD WIND BLOWS
BOOK 1

Born and raised in Sioux country, Katie McCabe, daughter of an Indian trader, finds herself alone when her family is killed in battle between the Army and the Indians. Rescued by Black Moon, a fierce Oglala warrior, and brought to live among his people, the love that ignites between these two wild hearts is tested by treachery, abduction, absence, and the tensions between the Sioux and the Army during the tumultuous 1850s. As the Great Plains erupts into war, a headstrong white girl and a proud Lakota warrior fight for their love and the country of their birth.

WINTER WIND
BOOK 2

Struggling to come to terms with a heartbreaking loss, Katie and Black Moon are plunged into a turbulent set of circumstances when the peace of the Powder River country is shattered by a brutal attack on a Cheyenne village. A new threat rises, testing the strength of their love and challenging Black Moon's vow that nothing would ever come between them again. But broken vows, like broken hearts, are as certain as the winter wind.